A FRIEND
IN DEED

GD HARPER

Matador
9 Priory Business Park,
Wistow Road, Kibworth Beauchamp,
Leicestershire. LE8 0RX
Tel: 0116 279 2299
Email: books@troubador.co.uk
Web: www.troubador.co.uk/matador
Twitter: @matadorbooks

ISBN 978 1789016 802

British Library Cataloguing in Publication Data.
A catalogue record for this book is available from the British Library.

Printed and bound in the UK by TJ International, Padstow, Cornwall
Typeset in 11pt Aldine401 BT by Troubador Publishing Ltd, Leicester, UK.

Matador is an imprint of Troubador Publishing Ltd.

London
A few years from now

chapter one

Peter Capaldi was looking down, concentrating. His hands were clasped in front of him, fingers intertwined. The cuffs of his crisp white dress-shirt hung unfolded below his wrists. It looked as if he was at prayer. I scrutinised his face. There was a hint of irritation, a faint echo of the volcanic rages he had made famous as an actor. Whatever thoughts were going through his mind, there was a forcefulness in his demeanour, hinting at the intensity lurking within him.

I scanned the description next to the photo. The photographer was Paul Stuart; never heard of him. Capaldi was born in 1958, which made him a year younger than me. I looked again at the image: salt-and-pepper hair, laughter lines rather than wrinkles. He was in much better shape than I was, high cheekbones still evident, no sign of jowls. Maybe the photo hadn't been taken recently. Okay, 2012 – that wasn't so bad. You can go downhill a lot in just over a decade.

The exhibition was called 'Celebrity'. Photos of famous – or infamous – people. A stroll around the National Portrait Gallery is how I clear my head when I come up to London for work. Like most columnists I write from home, but I do get stir crazy sometimes. So, if I want somewhere less isolated than suburban London I head up to Soho House, getting there early to grab one of the comfy chairs and a table in the corner. I can get lost in my own little world as I type away on either a *Chronicle* article or a piece for one of my blogs. Being a member is a bit of an extravagance, but it helps me project an image of being more successful than I really am these days. And writing to the soundtrack of a buzz of conversation keeps me connected to the human race, taking the sting out of living alone but not intruding on my thoughts.

I hadn't finished with Mr Capaldi. I stepped up closer to admire the way the photographer had lit the shot and stared again at the multi-layered expression on Capaldi's face.

A voice startled me. 'This picture is good, I think. You know this guy?'

From the accent, I knew she would be Russian or the like before I turned to see her. Mid-thirties, if I had to guess. Easily six foot tall and her cheekbones put Capaldi's to shame. I straightened my back to just about match her height.

'Peter Capaldi. Famous actor, been around a long time. Scottish.'

She nodded in acknowledgement.

'Like me,' I added, in case she couldn't tell.

'Very fine photograph. He is movie star?'

'No, not really. TV mainly. Started out in a Scottish movie, *Local Hero*, but he's most famous for playing a foul-mouthed spin doctor on TV. And Doctor Who, obviously.'

Her bemused smile told me she wouldn't know a dalek from a pepper pot.

'*Doctor Who*. Science fiction TV series that started in the 1960s. A time lord who travels in a spaceship that looks like a police phone box. Bigger on the inside … Never mind, it's a long story.'

'Very interesting. Thanks for information.'

She wandered off, and I stepped away to look at the next photograph. Bill Nighy gave me a patronising sneer.

'I know, I know,' I muttered.

I finished my tour of the contemporary gallery and headed up the stairs, walking straight past the early Tudors to get to Elizabethan England. I especially liked the paintings of the courtiers. They looked like a bunch of overdressed psychopaths, their raw cunning, intellect and fearsome belligerence staring out at me from across the centuries. Sir Henry Lee especially. Not someone who looked like he was in touch with his feminine side.

I got to the end of the gallery and was pleased to see the portrait of Richard Foxe on display in the little alcove to the right of the stairs. A sixteenth-century churchman who was one of Henry VIII's advisers, he looked like a nice bloke, which might be why his position in the gallery was not as secure as some of his more nefarious neighbours. 'A man of wisdom, knowledge, learning and truth', he was described as. Something to aspire to, which is why I chose him as my blogger name. He'd been in the basement the last time I visited, making way for an exhibition of Tudor financiers, and I was pleased to see him back.

'Well done, old chap,' I said.

'You talk to paintings?'

I turned to see the Russian gazelle standing next to me. A flush crept across my cheeks.

'Not normally, no. But this one is special to me.'

She nodded like this was the most reasonable explanation in the world. 'So, is he another time lord who has mouth like toilet?' She delivered the words carefully, as if she was playing a game in which the most important part was to keep from laughing.

'Not quite. A Tudor bishop who was at the court of Henry VIII.' I decided it was time to regain some dignity. 'Do you know much about Henry VIII?'

'Guy with six wives? A little.'

'He's back through here. Let me show you.'

We walked back to the Tudor Gallery and stood in front of the Holbein study. Henry VIII in his aggressive, defiant, manspreading stance, complete with thrusting codpiece and phallic dagger hanging from his belt. A study of testosterone in ink and watercolour. Subtle, it wasn't.

'Start of the greatest period in English history. Henry didn't know it, but after all his efforts to produce a son and heir, it was his daughter who surpassed him as a monarch. Look, here she is on her coronation day.'

We paused in front of the *Accession* portrait, Elizabeth looking demure and serene as she posed with crown, orb and sceptre, a simple row of pearls around her neck. Dressed in deep yellow silk to emulate wealth, swathes of ermine to symbolise her purity.

'Such a beautiful dress she's wearing.' The gazelle went up close to the painting. 'But she looks so young.'

'Twenty-five. Looks younger. The royal coffers emptied after Henry's excesses, two of her half-siblings gaining the throne before the crown passes to her. Heads getting chopped off left, right and centre, and this lot waiting to pounce.' I gestured to the dandified Dick Dastardlys filling the walls around her. 'She looks pretty chilled in this painting, but she must have been scared out of her wits.'

'And she survived?'

'More than survived. Here she is at the end of her reign.' I brought her to the Ditchley portrait, painted thirty-four years later. Elizabeth, haughty, self-assured, standing on a globe, her feet planted on the south of England. 'She understood the PR value of a good image, like her father. Literally standing on top of the world. And no more yellow silk to make out she had a bit of dosh. There are more jewels and pearls on this dress than you can shake a stick at.'

By now we'd wandered back to the Richard Foxe painting. It reminded me I needed to get back to Soho House to meet my six o'clock deadline.

'Well, I must be going. Nice to meet you ... Sorry, I don't know your name?' I looked straight at her for the first time.

'Tanya. And you?'

'Duncan.'

'Well, Duncan, that was an interesting tour.' She pronounced the first syllable of my name with a double 'O'. 'Do you work here?'

'No, I'm a journalist. And a blogger. Used to be a novelist, but not anymore.'

'Novelist? What do you write? I think historical fiction.'

'No, maybe I should. I set my books in the 1970s.'

'Ah, so they *are* historical fiction.' I took the barb like a man and smiled magnanimously.

There was an awkward silence. 'I really must be going,' I said eventually. 'Look, I do have to go.' I was repeating myself for some reason. 'But I've enjoyed meeting you. Would you like to meet here again when we've both got more time? Later this week, perhaps?'

Her reaction would be telling. When I reached fifty, I found out it didn't even occur to women in their twenties that I was a sexual being. Moot point, of course; Patti was still alive then and dalliances weren't my thing. Having reached my sixties, the no-fly zone had extended to women in their thirties. A lot of blokes would find this devastating, go into denial and become an embarrassment to all concerned. For me it was liberating, a chance to make new friendships unencumbered by sexual tension, to enjoy again the wasted days of youth. I'd always had mainly female friends; I found their conversation more interesting. Now they were getting younger. Some young women got it; some didn't. Now I'd find out what camp Tanya was in.

The question didn't faze her in the slightest. 'Sure, why not? Maybe Friday, but a little later. Will be busy in afternoon. When does this place close?'

'At nine, I think, on a Friday.'

That was a little more awkward. The gallery, on Friday's late-night opening, was a classic first-date venue in London, as I'd found out when I reluctantly dragged myself back onto the dating scene a couple of years before. Free to get in, quiet enough to have a conversation, and there were always the paintings to talk about if it turned out to be a disaster. I wasn't quite sure it was the vibe I was looking for.

'Okay. Six-thirty then, this same spot? I let you escape me.' A quick touch on my arm and she was gone.

I walked briskly back to Soho House. It was late, and I needed to finish writing my blog. We hadn't exchanged phone numbers, but that was no bad thing. It would be easier for either of us to back out. If we did meet on Friday, it would mean we both wanted to.

Inside, the atmosphere was changing. The daytime entrepreneur crowd was segueing into the more boisterous after-work scene, the background buzz of conversation becoming a bit more raucous. I slipped in some earphones, listened to some endlessly self-replicating Brian Eno music, and settled down to bash out the post.

I post to my blogs under two identities – Richard Foxe for the political commentary and Mark Jackson, my old author name, for the more humorous, lifestyle stuff. The Mark Jackson one is for fun; it's Richard Foxe who pays the bills, as I've built a decent niche as an irreverent, but hopefully insightful, commentator on any political scandals on the go. But I need to keep feeding the machine, and that means coming up with interesting content and getting it out quickly.

I finished just in time to get over to Clapham Halls for the start of the 'Politics, Prose and More' evening at which I had been asked to speak. All a bit last minute: one of the speakers had pulled out the day before and I got an email asking me to step in. Jumped at the chance, to be honest. I don't often get to do things like this, being more usually seen as someone on the way out rather than on the way in. I somewhat shamelessly demanded a fee, but I have to count the pennies these days. They must have been desperate – they said yes, told me not to breathe a word to the others. All felt a bit tacky, but needs must.

A new political party, Act Now!, had recently shocked pollsters and pundits alike by winning the general election, a mere three years after the party had been created. Politics had never been more messy and unpredictable and, whatever you thought of their philosophy, Act Now! was manna from heaven for political commentators like myself.

Ever since they came to prominence, politics had become trendy. All over the country, people were flocking to hear discussion, debate and commentary on their plans to break up vested interests and establishment cliques and to question the value of the organisations that underpinned the political system. They were part of a sea change in politics that had started ten years ago. The Brexit vote had been first, then Trump in America.

To the horror of the establishment, a new type of politics was becoming triumphant. In almost every Western democracy, iconoclastic individuals, mavericks who had always prided themselves on being outsiders who took no part in mainstream politics, had started to form the same political party, same name, same philosophies, in almost every major Western democracy. Act Now! had enjoyed unprecedented success in nearly every election they had taken part in. Idealistic young people and older, disaffected, alienated working-class voters had formed an unlikely alliance to bring down the establishment in a way that hadn't been seen since the 1960s. Back then it had been idealistic, naive and shambolic. The leaders of the counter-culture revolutionaries of today were organised, efficient, and ruthless in their pursuit of power.

There were four of us on the panel. The local Act Now! MP would be defending her party's achievements in already breaking up three government organisations and pulling us out of the G7; a brave member from one of the establishment parties would be trying to convey the danger of throwing the baby out with the bathwater. Some novelist was coming along to plug her new political thriller, and then there was me. I suppose I was the 'More', there to make acerbic comments on whatever the other three said, and indulge in a few shameless plugs for my Richard Foxe blog.

There was a good crowd when I turned up, a hundred, maybe a hundred and fifty in the audience. It went pretty well. The politicians delivered their practised lines; Act Now! telling us multinational organisations exist only to protect privilege and the status quo, that experts are always wrong, and that the secret to good decision-making is decentralisation. The establishment guy went on about the folly of protectionism and the risk to world peace from the destruction of united Western governments. The novelist's book was a satire on the chaos of inexperienced politicians running the country, a few of the more outrageous plotlines bearing an uncanny similarity to real-life events. I did feel a pang of envy when she read out a couple of excerpts from the book, the chuckles and murmurs of appreciation from the audience reinforcing what a good read it was.

For me, such days have passed. I was engulfed in a

11

scandal back in 1995, when it was discovered that a novel I'd written fourteen years earlier had resulted in an innocent man being sent to prison – not that anyone could ever truly describe Michael Mitchell as innocent. I tried to keep going as a novelist, but every new book floundered as my demons came back to haunt me. I've tried three times, and three times I've hit a brick wall. Blogging and newspaper columns seem to be my limit now. I can still come up with a half-decent turn of phrase and bash out a couple of thousand words before panic sinks in.

The liveliest part of the evening was when someone brought up the latest political scandal. Over thirty politicians had been found to have signed up to a sugar-daddy website, propositioning young women thirty, forty years younger than them for sex in return for a monthly allowance. The klutzes that had been shopped had created anonymous profiles, but that hadn't stopped someone hacking into the site and coming up with the politicians' identities. Denials, resignations and humiliations were taking place right across the political spectrum; only Act Now! was in the clear. Scandals, fake news and personal vendettas were dominating the political scene like never before. I was beginning to realise that if I wanted to maintain any sort of profile as a political commentator, I would have to get my hands dirty and start doing some muck-raking of my own.

That's where Nigel came in.

chapter two

Nigel had latched on to me when I'd run an AI seminar a few months before. Artificial intelligence was the holy grail of computer programming and a lot of the big technology companies liked to use writers to teach programmers how to code computers' responses to sound more human, teach them how to develop character and personality. Nigel was big into conspiracy theories, and when he found out I had a political column in the *Chronicle*, he offered to help me with his hacking skills to uncover scandals rather than just report on them. I'd set him a challenge to get him to go away – asked him to find out more about a rumour that Saudi Arabia was to be chosen over the French to build our new nuclear power stations. Bugger me if he didn't send me a ton of data a few days later showing that plans for Saudi Arabia to do just that were more advanced than was being admitted.

It had caused a bit of a stir when the *Chronicle* had run the story although, frustratingly, it did more to help Act Now!'s credibility than anything else. All the fault of the last government, they claimed. Now they were in power, a new broom was in Whitehall, sweeping away all the backroom deals that undermined Britain's independence. But whatever the outcome, it had been the highest-profile piece I had written for months. Nigel had passed the audition to prove that he could be very useful in helping me become a better investigative journalist.

He might have the technical expertise to uncover political secrets, but Nigel's interpersonal skills left a lot to be desired. I had emailed him to arrange to meet at a pub just off Clapham Common which I used for discreet assignations, but that was a non-starter. He didn't like new places, he told me, and no, he couldn't suggest another meeting place. The only reason he had ventured out to my talk was that the company he was freelancing with to write AI coding had insisted he attend if he wanted another contract.

He said he'd prefer to email, video call at a push, but I wanted at least one meeting to be face-to-face. If I was going to trust my investigative journalist credentials to whatever he found out, I had to get to know him better first. It transpired he didn't go out much, lived his life online, did all his work from home. After a few increasingly fraught emails, we finally settled on me going around to his flat to have our chat. It wasn't something either of us felt comfortable about.

It was a long Tube ride up to north London and it was after ten when I arrived. I rang the bell and Nigel almost immediately opened the door, greeting me with a nervous grin, no handshake. I spotted a few tufts of facial hair that he had missed while shaving and a couple of cuts where he'd gone in too deep. I tried not to stare. He was a computer geek straight out of central casting. They say people are the same emotional age all their life. Although Nigel was in his late twenties, he was always going to be a fifteen-year-old boy in emotional and physical development. He had both acne and the beginnings of a bald patch as his two ages fought each other for supremacy. There's a type of salamander called an axolotl that retains some of its physical tadpole features even when it becomes an adult, like furry gills instead of lungs. That was Nigel. He was an axolotl.

I had wanted to find out if he was as unhappy as I was that our story had ended up helping Act Now!. He had said he wasn't doing it for the glory, and he didn't want to change the world. It was the challenge of the hack that interested him, being the one to solve the riddle the forums were talking about – not the actual content or the repercussions.

He showed me into his living room, the space dominated by servers, CPUs and goodness knows what other IT equipment assembled in racks all along the longest wall. Not a single painting on the other walls, no ornaments or decorations. A desk with a laptop and three monitors full of coding took up most of the side wall. In the middle of the room was a treadmill, presumably the only way he got exercise. I looked around for somewhere to sit. There was only a single chair, the one by the desk.

Nigel sat down on it, swivelled into the room and leaned forward, clasping his hands together. It was only when he looked up that he seemed to become aware of me, standing in the doorway. I could almost see the lightbulb go on in his head.

'Ah.' He looked around the room, almost in panic. Then he stood up and went into the kitchen, returned with a hard, wooden chair and plonked it next to him. He slumped back into his chair, folded up his legs and cradled his knees against his chest.

I moved the chair a few inches away and sat down.

Nigel winced and jumped up. 'It has to be where I put it. That's where it always goes when it comes in here.'

I moved it back to where it had been and looked at him for confirmation I'd positioned it correctly. He retreated to his chair again, like a dog returning to its favourite basket.

I decided to dispense with the small talk.

'So, Nigel, all that stuff about the Saudis. I won't ask how you got hold of it, but as you saw, it's had a big impact.'

'Easy-peasy,' he replied, giving a machine-gun laugh. 'He-he-he-he. Lemon-squeezy.' Then that laugh again. I took it as a sign that he was starting to relax. He gave a quick polish to his Buddy Holly glasses, one arm wound with sellotape.

'Want to know where I found it? Department of Energy website.'

I had assumed, with all the gear in the room, that Nigel had built some ingenious program that had outfoxed firewalls, encryption software and whatever other security devices the best brains in Whitehall used to keep our nation's secrets safe from prying eyes, and I was a tad disappointed to find out the truth. It turned out that everything in my exclusive scoop had been already posted online. Part of the mandatory reporting protocols that the last government had introduced a few years back, to head off accusations from the nascent Act Now! that Whitehall was too secretive and corrupt. The initiative turned out to be self-defeating, which was probably the intention. Rather than bring transparency and accountability to government departments, the savvy mandarins running the civil service published a tsunami of turgid, prosaic documentation that caused anyone brave enough to try to plough through it to lose the will to live.

But it turned out that ploughing through hundreds, if not thousands, of disclosure pages on the Department of Energy website was precisely what Nigel had done. Remembering everything, but only truly understanding a tiny part of what he read. What he was looking for, he told me, were inconsistencies, where one report said one thing and another said something else. Where there were inconsistencies, you could find lies. And when you found lies, you found what someone was trying to hide.

Nigel tried to make it sound straightforward, but I knew there was more to it than that. It was like everything was a giant memory game, where you had to spot which object had been moved. Nigel could detect the variations between what he read in two paragraphs hundreds of pages apart, and seemed to have no problem ploughing through swathes of bureaucratic tedium. It also helped that he had no life outside of his computer.

'So, want to do it again?' I kept the enquiry casual, to make it sound like coming up with world exclusives was a humdrum event in my daily life. 'There's lots of stuff about Act Now! I wouldn't mind getting to the bottom of.'

'Yes. I knew that's what you wanted.' Nigel looked at me as if I was mad. 'Otherwise, you wouldn't be here. But now you know I can do it, you need to pay me next time.'

He gave me a grin which was an attempt to make his demand look friendly, but ended up looking more like a cross between Fagin and Dr Evil.

'My hardware needs updating. Everyone keeps saying you can make money selling secrets. That's right, isn't it?'

'Well, sort of,' I replied. I shifted on the uncomfortable kitchen chair, trying desperately not to move it again. 'I get paid a monthly retainer for my articles, and I'd be happy to split that with you for leads, when whatever you find forms the basis of the story. But it has to be verifiable, and you can't do anything illegal. Just so we're clear about that.'

Nigel's face lit up. 'So, I do get paid? You share your retainer with me for stories we work together on. You promise?'

I promised. And if I was smart, it wouldn't end up costing me anything. I could use the fact that I'd broken a major story to demand more status at the *Chronicle*. More cash for the weekly column, the chance to write an article once a month for the weekend magazine, and yes, a budget to cover the costs of investigative reporting. I told him that he'd proven himself, that he'd get well looked after on future stories, and we left it at that. Nothing specific, nothing formal. I said I'd get him a list of topics I'd like him to look into by the end of next week.

I got back to my flat in Croydon about eleven and knocked off a Mark Jackson piece about how best to explain *Doctor Who* and other national treasures to non-Brits. Didn't mention Tanya.

An email from Bobbie popped into my inbox, suggesting a video chat next week. My oldest and dearest friend, she became a pal at primary school. Always just friends, never dated. After the furore of the Michael Mitchell scandal, we didn't talk for almost ten years. The bitter recriminations had soured the closeness between us and when we did try to pick up the pieces and stay in touch, there was always an undercurrent, festering away in the background. She was the one who took most of the flak and she blamed me. She was probably right. Things are better nowadays, we talk more and more often, and we're slowly rekindling the old magic. I fired off a reply confirming a time next Saturday. I thought suddenly of the seventies, hanging out at her Glasgow flat, having to suffer her dreadful cooking. It made me smile.

Good times. Before our lives changed forever.

chapter three

On Wednesday, I was summoned up to London for a *Chronicle* columnists' meeting. It was rare for us to get together and I renewed old acquaintances as we gathered in the meeting room, waiting for Sam, the editor, to turn up. I suspected these hotshot young writers regarded me as a museum piece, an old hippy who used to put flowers in soldiers' rifles and lead chants to attract visiting aliens during the summer of love. It must have come as a disappointment when they found out that I wasn't at Woodstock and hadn't spent my time indulging in free-love orgies involving fur coats and Mars bars.

Sam arrived ten minutes late with some guy in a suit who I didn't recognise, and he gestured for all of us to sit around the table. The two of them sat together, Sam looking uncharacteristically nervous. I started to feel the same.

'Thanks for coming in, everyone, and at such short notice.' Sam smiled, as though to suggest we'd had a choice. 'Look, I won't beat about the bush. This is Jason Stewart, from ARI, the holding company. They're having to restructure some corporate debt in the US, and need to reduce operating costs worldwide. We're going to take a lot more syndicated features from now on, and that means less need to generate our own content.'

A rumble passed around the table. We all realised what was coming next.

'It's not as bad as it sounds,' Sam went on, speaking a little too quickly. 'No one's being fired, no one's getting their word rate reduced. The plan is to restrict our featured columnists to four, one for each of our content priorities – arts, politics, business and sport. They're going to be Zac, Bryony, Sophie and Mia.' I glanced at Bryony, a humourless blonde in her mid-twenties, the one who had just gobbled up my job. She was studiously avoiding making eye contact with anyone in the room.

Sam cleared his throat before continuing. 'We're going to big-up our featured columnists with the readers, build their profile, give each of them a clear brand identity. Everyone else continues to work on a freelance basis. You can pitch an idea, take up an assignment that we post, or submit a piece just like before. Same word rate, but on an ad hoc basis rather than a retainer. And from now on, you get a by-line, but no photo, so we don't clutter out our featured columnists. Any questions?'

A resigned silence filled the room. The savvier of us had known something like this was coming. Print media was a dinosaur in the digital age, and with so much free content out there it was becoming more and more difficult to earn a crust as a journalist.

As the elder statesman of the group, it fell to me to ask the first question.

'So … what, Sam – if you're not one of the chosen few and the paper will be running syndicated pieces from outside, how many crumbs are there going to be for the rest of us to pick up?'

Sam was already raising his hand defensively.

'Let me put it another way,' I went on. 'I'm writing four thousand words a week for the paper now. What can I expect in the future?'

'That all depends, Duncan. It's in your hands. If you've got something good, we'll run it.' He lowered his eyes as he spoke.

I knew what that meant. Sam wasn't going to say it, but my weekly column was history. The four anointed high profile columnists would keep up the pretence that the *Chronicle* was still committed to having superstar writers on its staff. It would take something special to get the bean-counters to sanction commissioning anything that paid my word rate when articles could be bought more cheaply from someone jobbing on the internet. Fifty percent of my income came from my work as a journalist, and it looked like it had walked out the door. I thought back to Nigel, and my promise to get him on the payroll now that I'd expanded my power and influence after the nuclear energy exposé. Embarrassing.

No one else spoke.

'Well, if that's all, I'll follow up with everyone individually by email,' said Sam, eyeing the door. The unnervingly silent Jason shot him a look and began gathering up his papers. Sam took the hint. 'That is, unless any of you want to have a chat while you're here,' he said. 'Door's always open.'

Everyone shuffled off. Whatever Jason was doing there, he hadn't said a word. I presumed that he'd turned up to make sure poor Sam didn't say something that would have a bunch of lawsuits flying his way. I made a point of going up to congratulate Bryony; none of the other survivors got the same courtesy from anyone else. As I left, I noticed Sam alone and rather despondent-looking in his office. No one had taken him up on his offer.

I stuck my head around the door. 'That went well,' I said.

Sam managed a half-smile. 'Thanks, Duncan. I've been up half the night, dreading this. Didn't help that Agent X made me come in early and go through the dos and don'ts one last time.' A quick nod towards Jason, who was on the phone in the next office, door closed. 'Thanks for being gentle with me, mate. I tried to swing it so that it'd be you doing the political column after that great Saudi Arabia scoop, but Bryony ticks all the boxes as far as the owners are concerned. Ah well. You've got your blog; you'll be all right.'

'We'll see. I was about to come to you with my plan to be the next Woodward and Bernstein, but it looks like that's not going to happen. Don't worry; I'm not going to make waves. I've seen the way the circulation numbers have been going, so this didn't come as a surprise. Are you going to be okay?'

'For the moment. But seriously, Duncan, if you want to get something in the paper, do more of that investigative stuff. I keep being told we need something to differentiate ourselves from the rest, and a juicy exclusive on a political scandal is what we're looking for. I can't believe there will be a shortage of material with everything Act Now! is doing. Bring me another scoop, give me first refusal, and I'll make sure we take care of you.'

I went home to collect my thoughts. Sam was right: coming up with a scoop was the only way to survive. It would be a tricky conversation with Nigel, going back on my promise to get him on the payroll and trying to sell him on taking his chances with me as a freelancer. Tricky, but not impossible.

I fired off an email, saying we had to meet up. The subject line was 'Developments' – I wanted to keep him interested, but also didn't want to get his hopes up too much. A reply came back straight away, telling me he was locked in a marathon *Dungeons and Dragons* session and would be free on Monday. I suggested meeting in his flat again and this time he readily agreed. I took that as a good sign, but I was putting my future in the hands of someone who played computer games non-stop for four days. I tried not to think about it.

I looked around. At least the flat was bought and paid for, snapped up when the royalties were still flooding in. But with not much in the bank and a pittance of a pension, the plan had been to keep writing until I was in my dotage. Now this. It would have to be either find something to fill the hole or sell up and move back to Scotland, my life journey going full circle. There was increasingly a ring of inevitability about just that.

* * *

On Friday, I headed off to the National Portrait Gallery to see if the mysterious Tanya was going to show. I arrived five minutes early. She was already there, dressed in a pair of old jeans and an oversized jumper that the wool had

24

balled up on, but still bloody gorgeous. She put her hand on my shoulder and mimed an embrace, stood back and gave me a grin.

'So, professor. Are you going to make tour?'

I hesitated. 'A lot of rooms get closed off after six. Let's head up to the Victorian galleries. There's usually some jazz being played there on a Friday night.'

We walked along a corridor between disapproving-looking Victorian gentlemen with impressive facial hair, following the sound of a piano to a gallery room where a crowd had gathered to listen to a jazz combo playing under a large portrait of the death of Pitt the Younger. I looked around. Love was in the air. Sensitive young men and assertive young women, all conceivable gender combinations, holding hands or with arms around waists, listening to the music.

'On second thoughts, let's go somewhere else. Have you ever eaten here? There's a good restaurant on the top floor.' That was more of a commitment, but I'd panicked.

She looked around, and that made her say yes. Lesser of two evils.

'*Da,*' she said. 'Is good food?'

'Excellent. And a great view over Trafalgar Square. Wait till you see it.'

We walked up the stairs and I prayed the restaurant would have a table. Luckily there had been a cancellation and one was free, with a decent view over the skyline too. We sat down to order, and Tanya took in the floor-to-ceiling window stretching the length of the restaurant. She whispered something that sounded like 'O-ho …'.

'You don't like it?'

She laughed. 'No, no, it's what we say in Ukraine. Here you would say, "Wow!"'

'Ukraine? That was my next question. I know nothing about you, Tanya. What are you doing here in London?'

'I was simple country girl in Ukraine, helping my father grow his potatoes. I know, sounds like cliché! Then this woman came to our town, says she is scout for modelling agency, looking for girls. My mother say her girls would have do more than modelling, but mother was wrong. They pick me, bring me to London, I make portfolio then start working. Been lucky, always had good photographers. So now no more growing potatoes.'

'Sounds very glamorous. And you live here in London?'

'*Da*. But I not model anymore. Too long in my teeth, too many younger girls. I stop modelling at twenty-six. For last ten years I work for your government. British Council. They want Russian-speaking person to organise charity events in Ukraine and Russia, to impress with your British culture. When Saatchi Gallery, Tate Britain, these places, when they send paintings to Moscow and Kiev, I handle reception, make sure top people visit. National Portrait Gallery is organising show of Great Britons of Twentieth Century, so I was here for meeting when you saw me.'

The waitress came over to take our order. We agreed to skip a starter. Tanya was probably thinking the same as me: easier to make an early exit. But we didn't need to worry. I could see why she had got her job as she chatted away like the seasoned networker she undoubtedly was.

'And you, Duncan? You said you are writer? Famous one?'

I decided it was better not to talk about the *Chronicle* job cuts.

'No, not really. I'm more a blogger these days. I write under my author name, Mark Jackson, mainly about the trials and tribulations of working surrounded by people less than half my age.' I smiled at her. 'I do some consultancy for social media sites, and when I go into meetings, I'm usually forty years older than anyone else in the room. The oldies who read my blog seem to get a kick out of enjoying my occasional discomfort.'

'Like taking Ukrainian girl to dating room and feeling like old pervert?'

I laughed. 'You spotted that, did you? Yes, things like that. But you'll be pleased to hear that if I do go out dating, it's usually with someone more my age.'

The conversation settled into deeper topics. I told her about Patti dying of breast cancer, that my love life these days consisted of occasional hook-ups with some women friends who also felt too set in their ways to go out and find another partner at their time in life. I told her about my Mark Jackson books, and my writer's block, but I didn't tell her why. Also, I kept quiet about my Richard Foxe political site. I work hard at keeping the two identities separate; even my Mark Jackson Wikipedia page doesn't refer to it, and so I never let on unless I have to.

Tanya, on the other hand, didn't seem to believe in keeping secrets.

'So, I've told you about my love life, what there is of it,' I said after the waiter had cleared our plates. 'What about you? Anyone?'

'Plenty and none,' she replied. 'British Council seems

to be dating agency between nice posh girls from your Home Counties who work there, and civil servants and bankers who give us sponsorship. I stick out, like my thumb is sore.'

She gave me a grin, and her voice dropped to a conspiratorial whisper. 'Anyway, I prefer bad boys. Plenty of them around in my modelling days. Working in Whitehall, not so many. In London, I am single. Nice girl, no scandal. In Moscow, Kiev, Minsk, I always have company. Oligarchs. Dodgy politicians. Some guys maybe gangsters. You shocked?'

I laughed. 'As long as you promise they're not going to misunderstand us having dinner together, no, I'm not shocked. But isn't that a dangerous lifestyle? I had a friend who got mixed up with a crime lord once, and it all ended in tears.'

Tanya looked impressed. 'Ah, so you are not so white? Who is friend who was with gangster?'

'Maybe another time. It's a long story.' I was annoyed at my momentary indiscretion. I'd blurted out a reference to skeletons that I wanted to keep firmly locked in their closet.

Luckily, she didn't seem that interested in pursuing the story. Instead, I listened to tales about a life of fast cars, private jets and luxury yachts. When Tanya went out to party, she did it in style.

We were among the last to leave as the restaurant closed around nine, along with the gallery. Despite the financial worries of losing my newspaper column, I gallantly offered to pick up the tab as it had been my call to turn our meeting into dinner, but Tanya insisted on going halves. I didn't protest too much. As we got our coats and headed for the lift, she said we'd meet again, and that it wasn't a hollow promise.

Always nice when you make a new friend.

★ ★ ★

From new to old. I settled down for my video call with Bobbie the next day.

Bobbie had given up acting after the Michael Mitchell scandal broke, split up with her husband shortly after and then moved to the isolated community of Scoraig in the Scottish Highlands, where Rita, a friend from London, had gone to live. There's no road to Scoraig; it's either an eight-mile walk from the road end or a boat trip across a sea loch to reach the straggled ribbon of crofts along the side of Loch Broom. That made it difficult to keep in touch. We had been able to chat and message, but it was only the previous year that Scoraig had got fast enough broadband for video. Some of the community had resisted it, said it defeated the point of moving there, but it finally happened. Still no plans for a road; that's the one thing I think they'll never change.

I poured myself a large Merlot and waited for her to appear.

The cheery sonic logo announced her arrival and a few seconds later she appeared on my computer screen. Streaks of grey shining through her curly brown hair, the story of her life etched on her face. Crow's feet around her eyes telling of times of laughter, times of love; the lines on her forehead reminders of darker moments.

I saw Davie lurking in the background. It hadn't taken long for the only single crofter in the community to latch on to Bobbie when she'd arrived. Him, I liked. Solid, practical, reliable; he'd helped Bobbie become more grounded than she's ever been in her life. Not sure if he felt the same about me – he's never been entirely comfortable with the two of us being so close. But he's smart enough not to make an issue of it.

'Hello, Bobbie. How the devil are you?'

There was a slight echo on the line. I could see Bobbie adjusting her microphone.

'Excellent. Davie's going out to check on the lambs. Say hi to Duncan, Davie.'

Davie appeared behind her. Said a gruff hello, but his eyes were smiling.

'A man of few words,' Bobbie said after he had left, and she laughed. 'So, come on, tell me your news.'

'You first. How's the photography business?'

'Great since I got the new website. Now the world can buy prints of the Scoraig landscape in its ever-changing glory!'

'Well, I love mine, and lots of people comment. You have a great eye, always did.'

'Thanks, Duncan. So what about you? Still the fearless reporter holding our dodgy politicians to account?'

'Until this week. There was a big cost-cutting meeting the other day. I was summoned to the office, along with all the other hacks. There's only going to be four in-house *Chronicle* columnists going forward. They've thrown the rest of us to the wolves. A vague promise that we'll be considered for an article, but only if we come up with something groundbreaking.'

Bobbie's mood darkened in an instant. 'Duncan, that's awful. Did you see it coming? And why didn't they keep you on? Your writing's the best the paper's got.'

'The paper wants new, fresh faces. That's not been me for a long time.'

'That sucks. Can't you sue them or something? Age discrimination? Redundancy at the very least?'

'No such luck. I'm freelance, don't forget. My employment rights amount to zero. Not to worry though, I have a Plan B. Remember that investigative piece I did, about the Saudis taking over our nuclear industry? That was with the help of a guy who dug up all the info. Nigel – bit of a geek. We've talked about partnering up to do more of the same. If I could get a couple of articles like that a year and sell them to the highest bidder, I'm pretty sure I'd come out ahead financially.'

I was trying to convince myself as much as Bobbie.

'Sounds cool. Why not start with Act Now! and what the hell they're up to? Be careful, though. They don't play by the rules. I don't think they'll take kindly to people poking around in their dirty laundry.'

'Tell me about it. I was on a panel with one of them the other day and I'm sure there was a whiff of brimstone every time he spoke. Got to be something about them worth knowing.'

Bobbie wanted to know more about what and who I'd be investigating, and I was making it up as I went along. Didn't mind, though. New dreams began to take flight in my imagination. The more we talked, the more it seemed Nigel really was the answer.

'The plan is that I tell him what to look for. He finds the dirt and I write up the story. Then we share the fee. A partnership, sort of.'

'So, he's a hacker? Isn't that unethical? Not to say illegal?'

'I tell him what I want to find out and insist he's not to do anything dodgy. After that, it's up to him.'

I could hear the false bravado in my voice. Bobbie was right: I was heading into dangerous waters. 'To tell you the truth, I'm conflicted about this guy. I mean, he's an adult, he can make his own decisions. He certainly knows his stuff about computers. He works from home, freelancing for an AI software company, one of the best. But when he operates in the real world, he can be … well, a bit obsessive. He plays computer games non-stop, and he hardly ever leaves his flat. He's fixated on always having the best and most up-to-date equipment and software all the time – told me he changes components and microprocessors and such every three months. That's an expensive compulsion, which is why he's looking for ways to make extra money. You're right; he might take more risks than he should. I need to keep an eye on him.'

'You be careful,' Bobbie said, her voice dropping to a whisper. She looked around as if she expected some Act Now! heavies to burst into her croft at any second. 'The pair of you sound like a dangerous combination. You're not the most practical of individuals. If you're telling me you're the sensible one in the relationship, that's a scary thought.'

'I'll admit, it's a bit of a last-ditch effort to hang in there. And I don't know yet whether the fact that he was first to find out about Saudi Arabia was just good luck. He certainly went looking at the right time. I'm sure the big guys have hordes of researchers, sifting through that stuff all the time. But if you don't take a risk, sometimes you risk even more. I'm a grown-up now, Bobbie. I've even got my senior railcard to prove it. Trust me on this.'

'Trust me, I'm a journalist?' She laughed. 'If you say so. Okay, I'll stop nagging. Last time we spoke you were licking your wounds over your latest break-up. Anyone else come along?'

'Not really. I like my own space these days; not sure if I've got the flexibility to change enough to let someone else join me. Being on my own feels good.'

'Well, if you're happy that's the main thing. Keep in contact with the human race. That's something I've learned living in the back of beyond – it's all too easy to become a hermit.'

I went to take a sip of my Merlot, ended up gulping down half the glass.

'I'm glad you think that. Met someone new the other day. Young Ukrainian lass, reminds me a lot of you, back in the day. Bumped into her at an art gallery and we met for dinner yesterday.'

'Young Ukrainian lass? Dinner? Let me guess – student just arrived in London, looking for someone to help her get a visa.' There was a twinkle in her eyes.

'She works for the British Council if you must know. Helping promote our culture to the Ruskies.'

'Duncan, Duncan, these friends of yours seem to get

younger every year.' Bobbie rolled her eyes and grinned condescendingly. 'Are you sure she's not taking advantage of you?'

I gave an exaggerated pout. 'I don't think so. I like her. And I think she likes me. Don't think she's got any hidden agenda. And the more young people I know, the better I can understand how Act Now! seem to appeal to their generation. Their latest idea is that we do away with government policy-making altogether. Can you believe that? Trust the instincts of the people rather than the experts, decide everything by plebiscite. All the government has to do is make sure the sums add up and join all the dots.'

'It's a brave new world and no mistake. Glad I'm well away from it up here. As long as Davie keeps the croft self-sufficient and people still want to buy my photographs, we can leave the rest of you to worry about where all this is leading to.'

We chatted for another twenty minutes, and after the call I felt inspired enough by Bobbie's good-natured teasing to fire off a quick blog post about my second meeting with Tanya, exaggerating for comic effect my discomfort at leading her into a room of courting couples. It worked well, and I was gratified to see it sparked a debate in the comments, some people congratulating me on my good fortune, and others tut-tutting and calling me a dirty old man. None were really mean-spirited, and more than a few made me chuckle, so I thought I came out of it well.

I drifted off to sleep with Bobbie's warnings about working with Nigel swimming round in my head, and wondering whether it would be more sensible to stick to what I know, writing political commentary, rather than venturing into pastures new.

You can't, I decided, start the next chapter of your life if you keep rereading the last one. But I would have to be careful.

chapter four

My phone beeped at eight the next morning.

So now I am world famous for picking up guys in art galleries? x
Shit. I should have told Tanya what I was posting. But I
was sure I hadn't implied that she had been flirtatious. I
logged on, full of trepidation, and reread the post. It was
all Bobbie's fault: she had planted the seed of my musings.
I looked again at Tanya's message. There was an 'x' – at
least that was something. But no smiley face. Where were
emojis when you needed them?

Should I WhatsApp a reply or call?

Definitely call. If I talked to her, at least I would have
a chance to apologise and explain. Messaging would be
feeble.

I messaged.

*Sorry. No offence intended. It was meant to be funny. Am I
forgiven?*

I added a praying hands emoji. Didn't risk an 'x'.

Nothing.

I checked my phone; the little tick showed she had
read the message almost immediately. A follow-up before
she replied would be pathetic. I got back to writing my
Richard Foxe post – a critique of Act Now!'s populist
policies. A discussion on inviting economic catastrophe

versus respecting the will of the people; a lot less contentious than trying to read between the lines of a message about an encounter in an art gallery.

Three hours later, I finally got a reply.

You are forgiven.

There was an angel halo. Safe to call, I decided.

'Hi, Tanya. You've read my blog.'

'*Da.* I liked. And now I know Doctor Who.'

I looked heavenward in relief. 'It was very rude of me not to tell you I was posting about our meeting. Glad you took it the right way.'

'No problem. Maybe it was me being rude; I googled you. So, we are even-steven, okay? That is right phrase, isn't it?'

'Yes, even-steven. Or is it even-stevens? You probably know better than me. So now you've read what I said about you, do you still want to meet again?'

'Of course. Maybe in a few days, now is very busy. When is good for you?'

We arranged to meet at a nice little fish restaurant where Soho meets Holborn. You see fewer tourists there and less of the theatre crowd, and it's cheap by London standards. I was seeing Nigel at five, so seven-thirty was a safe bet for Tanya. I couldn't see any meeting with Nigel taking long.

I sent Nigel a message, checking if we were still okay to meet. He replied straight away saying he didn't understand the question. I messaged back to say I was making sure nothing had changed or he hadn't forgotten.

Nothing has changed. I never forget. Don't ask me unnecessary questions.

I arrived at his flat ten minutes early, but decided to wait until precisely the time we'd arranged. I was beginning to realise that Nigel liked things to be as he expected them. That was going to make this conversation a challenge.

At five, he opened the door, stood to one side and stared at the floor as I entered.

'Should I go through to the living room?' I asked.

'Yes. And then you should tell me about developments.'

Nigel had already positioned the kitchen chair in the same place as before. I sat down as he took his seat opposite me.

As usual, no small talk.

'You might read about some changes at the *Chronicle* which are going to be announced tomorrow,' I said, trying to sound as positive as possible. 'They're cutting back the number of journalists on retainer to four, and I'm not one of them. From now on, I have to pitch any story I want to write to the editor, and he'll decide if he wants to run with it, and if so, how much he'll pay for it.'

Nigel started doodling on a pad of paper. I waited for him to say something, but as every second passed, he dug his pen deeper and deeper.

'But not to worry. I've worked out a deal that I think you're going to like,' I said, flashing a cheery smile that went unnoticed. 'The restructuring is actually good news. If we're going to do this right, I need to focus. Rather than spend some of my time writing a weekly column and monthly articles on other stuff, all I'm going to work on from now on are our investigative projects. I'll sell them as finished pieces to the *Chronicle* and we'll split the fee fifty-

fifty as agreed. If the story's as good as the last one, four stories a year will pay more than we'd make on retainer, and if they don't want the story, we'll take it elsewhere. What do you think?'

Nigel started swinging in his chair. Finally, he spoke.

'You need to keep working at the *Chronicle*. You need to tell them to keep paying your retainer. Then you can be sure you get paid. You promised me I'd get paid. How can you promise me, if you don't work there anymore?'

'I already worked freelance. It's like with your contracting work. But instead of being paid the same every month, now I get paid when they take an article. I promised you'd get paid if they took an article, so for you, nothing's changed.'

'No, no, no.' As Nigel became more agitated, the chair swinging got more frantic. 'You promised I'd get paid, because you get paid. Because you work there. Now you don't work there and only get paid if they want to pay you. So, I only get paid if they want to. That's not what you promised. I want what you promised.'

The swinging was starting to unnerve me.

'Look, Nigel, calm down. I can't stop things from changing. But our deal stays the same. When we get a story published, we split the fee. That's what I promised.'

'You promised me I'd get paid. You promised me I'd get paid.'

He was starting to annoy me. 'Nigel, you will get fucking paid, all right? When we have a story. Now stop swinging in that chair.'

'Promise me. Promise me I'll get paid. Just like if you were still at the *Chronicle*. Promise me.'

I took a deep breath. 'Look, my retainer was for was sixty grand a year, and for that I did a short weekly column and a major article once a month. Forget about the weekly column for a minute, and let's say that half the articles would be based on stuff you gave me. We'd be splitting thirty grand fifty-fifty on these six articles. Let's agree that if you get me data on six projects, I pay you your share, fifteen grand, even if the *Chronicle* doesn't publish them. If they pay more than thirty grand, I keep the extra. That way we both get what we want.'

Nigel stopped rocking his chair and looked confused. 'So you are promising I get paid?'

'Yes, I am promising you get paid.'

'Okay.' It was like a switch had been flicked in his brain; suddenly he was calm again. 'But if you break your promise, I'll be annoyed again. I don't like being annoyed.'

'You don't have to be annoyed, Nigel. You won't be annoyed because I promise you'll be paid. And I don't break my promises.'

'You almost did.'

'We misunderstood each other. I'll make sure I'm clearer next time we talk.' My anger had dissipated now, and I was feeling a little sorry for him. I started to say each sentence slowly, pausing between them. 'Now we've straightened everything out, I need to go. I'll call you next week with what I need you to work on, and you can get started. Is that okay?'

'That's okay. Goodbye.'

Nigel turned around and started typing. I presumed I had been dismissed.

I stepped out onto the street and closed the door

behind me. I took a few deep breaths to calm down and reflected on what had just happened. Nigel was seriously bizarre, that much was certain, and I'd agreed to give him fifteen grand I didn't have. I hesitated for a second, wondering if I should pull the plug on the whole thing, go back and tell him it's over and then run like hell. Sod it. I didn't have a Plan C. If working with someone who was a bit weird was what it took to keep going as a journalist, then so be it.

★ ★ ★

The fish restaurant was busier than usual, and I was glad I'd booked a table. I knocked back a glass of the house white before Tanya arrived, helping to settle my nerves after the Nigel contretemps. Tanya spotted me from the host station and greeted me with a cheery wave.

The banter picked up where we had left off – some light-hearted exchanges re-established the mood. But if she'd googled my author name, she would know all about 1995. No avoiding it anymore.

'So, you checked out Mark Jackson? Then I guess you found out why I don't write novels now.'

I could feel my skin prickle. I hoped I wasn't flushed.

Tanya looked bemused. 'I saw your last book was published in 1995, the same time as that court case. Is that what you mean?'

I gave the faintest of nods. My links to Michael Mitchell are permanently embedded in who I am, thanks to Wikipedia and a few real-crime websites. But I'm lucky. The internet wasn't around much in 1995, otherwise typing my name would launch page after page of the recriminations and controversy that raged about one of the highest-profile miscarriages of justice in the late twentieth century, swamping everything else I'd done in my life. It still meant people found out, like Tanya, and I'd have to spend the rest of my life justifying what I wrote and what I said. But that's a small price compared to what Michael Mitchell went through. Fifteen years for a crime he didn't commit.

'Yes.' I launched into my confession. 'Michael Mitchell was a Glasgow gangster in the 1970s, big into money laundering and loan sharking. He was the boyfriend of my best friend at the time, Bobbie, and he ruined her life. Used her to blackmail a police officer and when that police officer turned up dead, she fled to London and tried to start a new life. I'd just had my first book published, based on a true story. I was struggling to think of an idea for my second novel, and so I loosely based the plot on what happened to her.'

Tanya gave me a look of barely concealed astonishment.

'I know, I know,' I stammered. 'But this was two years after it all happened. That seems like a long time when you're in your twenties. And it was only the germ of the idea for the story, the plot itself was completely different. I went ahead and wrote it, stupidly thinking there would be no repercussions. And there were.'

'What happened?' Tanya pushed her plate to one side.

'A journalist started sniffing around, tracked Bobbie down and she freaked out. She finally went to the police, which she probably should have done in the first place. Mitchell and his accomplice were arrested, given life imprisonment for the murder of the cop. My book became a bestseller because of all the publicity.'

'And it turned out he didn't do it? That's what it said on the internet.'

'Right. Ten years later they found that another gangster killed the policeman. He was trying to set up Mitchell for the murder. This guy also ended up dead, and the rumour was that Mitchell killed him in self-defence, but nothing was ever proven. There was a retrial and Mitchell was acquitted.'

'And you blame yourself. Why?'

There was the slightest beginning of a tear forming in my eye, so I spoke quickly to chase it away.

'Because it was my stupid book that caused it all. That's what led to Bobbie going to the police and testifying against him. But we were both convinced he was guilty. There didn't seem to be the shadow of a doubt. That guy was evil, Tanya. Believe me.'

'I believe you. But Mitchell got what he had coming to him, no? He was a gangster, you tell me.' She ran her fingers through her hair, like my angst was being transmitted to her. 'Doesn't that mean he should go to jail?'

I had my emotions back under control now.

'It was never proven he murdered the other gangster; he was never even charged with it. Mitchell was certainly a crook, but he was in jail for fifteen years. That's a lot more than he would have got for money laundering.'

I dropped my voice to a whisper, as if even after all these years, my words might have repercussions. 'The authorities were under a lot of pressure, having a cop killing unsolved. When Bobbie came forward, they saw they had a case against Mitchell and arrested him, kept quiet about the other evidence so they could get a conviction. When he was finally acquitted and walked out of court a free man, the recriminations started.'

'Against you?'

'And Bobbie. She was an actress then and had starred in a movie adaptation of my book.' Tanya's wavering smile couldn't hide her incredulity. 'I know. We were both pilloried for being responsible for sending an innocent man to prison and shamelessly benefitting from it.'

'Why? He was hardly baby sleeping in the wood. In my country, the police arrest who they want first, find the evidence second. Sometimes justice needs a little help.'

'That's not how we do things here, Tanya. Or so I thought. The cover-up came to light during a public enquiry into another miscarriage of justice case in the early 1990s. Bobbie took it worse than me, gave up acting, got divorced. We took out our anguish on each other, both said things we shouldn't have and didn't speak for years. I discovered, when I tried to start writing, I'd lost all my confidence and couldn't write with any commitment. I packed it all in, did lecturing and ran training courses for a while and finally got into journalism and blogging for a living a few years ago.'

'I not understand,' Tanya said. 'Bad man gets what he deserves. Maybe not best way, but you say, "That guy was evil, Tanya. Believe me." I believe you. You are hero, not villain.'

'That's not how the world saw it. And it's not how I see it myself. Bobbie and I both gave evidence at the trial; like it or not, we were both part of the plot to get someone – anyone – arrested for a cop killing. I would have said anything to put Mitchell behind bars. I didn't tell any lies, but I still feel as if I was part of the whole shitty witch hunt.'

'Then you are stupid Scottish guy, and your Bobbie friend is not much smarter. You tell me this story, I'm proud of you, not ashamed. If man does bad things, he deserve bad things happening to him. This was long time ago. There is old Russian proverb, "Don't wake up trouble, let it sleep quietly." You need to let it sleep.'

'I've tried. I kept telling myself I had done nothing wrong, but every time I see Mitchell on TV the past comes back to haunt me. He became a human rights campaigner on his release, specialising in criminal injustice. A bit of a celebrity, ironically enough. I've never written another book since. Now I'm—'

I could feel a bone stuck in my throat, and tried hard not to choke. I looked down at the grilled brill on my plate. The rib bones were shaped like talons, almost a centimetre long. Vicious-looking things.

I popped a piece of bread in my mouth to try to dislodge it, sipped a glass of water. Nothing.

'I think I've swallowed a bone.'

Tanya gave me a worried frown.

'Excuse me a minute,' I croaked. Without waiting for a response, I picked up the rest of the bread and headed for the loo.

I tried everything; no use. Spat out some saliva, full of blood. Nothing else for it – if it wasn't going to move, I had to go to A & E. Bloody embarrassing.

I went back to the table to explain my predicament. I suggested finishing our meal, see if the bone would come loose, but Tanya was having none of it. 'People die from choking on fish bones,' she said. 'Go to hospital.'

We paid the bill and went outside to hail a taxi.

'I'll say my goodbyes now,' I said. I was starting to be able to talk normally, but I could still feel the bone lodged in my throat. 'Sorry to finish dinner so abruptly. I'll tell you the rest of the story next time.' I leaned forward to kiss her on the cheek.

'I'm coming to hospital with you. Check you're okay.' As Tanya spoke a taxi appeared and she hailed it. 'To the nearest hospital, please,' she said to the driver.

'That'll be Charing Cross, love. Jump in.'

I hesitated. 'You really don't need to come,' I said. 'I'll be there for hours; there's nothing for you to do. Thanks very much, but I'll be fine.'

She jumped into the taxi. '*Da*, you will be fine. But you will need company while you wait, and I want to make sure you okay. Come on.'

I relented and climbed in. The taxi dropped us at the hospital and I got myself checked in. When the triage nurse came through from the back and I explained what had happened, she said they'd get to me in an hour or so and told me to take a seat. I had to assume that if I ended up writhing on the floor and gasping for breath, that time frame would be brought forward. Back in the waiting area, Tanya had nabbed two of the few comfy seats.

'Well done getting these,' I said, every word causing the bone in my throat to vibrate, reminding me of its existence.

'I win race to get them. I tell losers other seat needed for my poor sick grandfather.' She winked. 'So, *dedushka*, what can I do to cheer you up? Is bone still painful?'

'Only when I talk. Sorry.'

Realising I wasn't up for conversation, Tanya played with her mobile phone and then burst out laughing.

'It say here choking on fish bone is number three in list of dumbest ways to die,' she told me. 'You want to know number one?'

I gave a weak nod.

'Strangled by pet python. Good news, Duncan. There are even more stupid people than you.'

It was three hours before I saw a doctor, and it took him two minutes to get some long tweezers and extract the bone. He offered it to me as a souvenir, but I declined. Sheepishly, I returned to where Tanya was waiting.

'All done, we can go now,' I said. 'Well, you can't say I don't know how to show a girl a good time. Thanks for waiting with me. You were right; it did help a lot you being here. Sorry I wasn't much of a conversationalist.'

She shrugged as if spending three hours in an uncomfortable waiting room was no big deal. But my brush with the Grim Reaper had given me a new perspective on things. Tanya was right. Maybe it was time to stop waking up my past. Let it sleep soundly.

chapter five

My plan was floundering.

Nigel had come up with a load of stuff on Act Now!'s fracking ban, purporting to show that they'd wilfully ignored scientific data saying there were no safety issues when they pushed ahead with a total ban in England and Wales. But I'd struggled to turn it into much of a scoop. What Nigel had uncovered was massively technical, and difficult to make much sense of. In the end, all I could do to squeeze a story out of it was to extract a few quotes that did seem to imply that the experts thought the government was acting irresponsibly in making the decision for populist reasons. But hardly anyone cared, and those that did mainly agreed with Act Now! that the experts shouldn't be trusted. The *Chronicle* bought the story for the equivalent of my monthly retainer and I still had to pay Nigel. No one else wanted to cough up any syndication fees. I started looking at house prices in Scotland.

The only positive thing was that after the meltdown when I told Nigel that things had changed at the *Chronicle*, I had worked out how best to interact with him. I'd already seen how stressed he got with an unexpected turn of events, and I saw the same reaction when things were physically changed from how they had been before. I made sure I started off by saying the same things to him every time we met, and even wore the same clothes if I was organised enough, so that he stayed calm and was not distracted by anything other than what was important to talk about. He took in every last detail of the things that were around him, and I could imagine his mind being bombarded with stimuli, all fighting to overwhelm him, all being lodged in his brain, never to be forgotten. He took everything literally, and at face value, and so we developed a code where, if I only promised to do something, it meant I would try but might not succeed. If I solemnly promised, it meant it would definitely happen. I might promise him that I'd try to get a story published, but I could *solemnly* promise I'd pay his retainer every month.

I also had to force myself to endure endless discussions, or rather monologues, about conspiracy theories. Who killed JFK? Were the moon landings faked? Did an alien spacecraft land at Roswell? You name it, Nigel was into all of them. Intrigues and collusion were his daily obsession, and almost every meeting with him got to a point where, when my eyes started to glaze over, I would have to politely but firmly tell him this was all very interesting, but we had to get back to talking about what pays the bills.

Other than that, however, he was able to function well. Socially inept, but I soon learned to understand that as eccentricity, not malice. And forget any attempt at sarcasm or irony. But as long as I was careful with my words, gave him time to assimilate what I was saying, he could be an invaluable asset in the new role I was trying to carve out for myself. Point him in the right direction and he delivered. The only problem was, I didn't know which direction that was.

★ ★ ★

If I wanted a conversation with a normal human being, there was always Tanya. We were seeing each other every other week and I started to get to know more about her past, as she opened my eyes to the realities of growing up in eastern Ukraine, living out her teenage years against a backcloth of hostilities between Russia and Ukraine.

'When I was young girl, I was super-excited that Ukraine decide to look west for our future, not to stay country cousin of Russia,' she told me one evening. 'We enter Eurovision Song Contest for first time, then win it the following year. I remember thinking we were now most super-trendy country in Europe.' She laughed. 'Russia tell us to start behaving, or they switch off gas pipeline to Kiev, but we not care. Too busy dancing in the street singing Ruslana's song, thinking one day we join the West.'

Her face darkened. 'But no way was Russia going to risk Ukraine going over to NATO while there was big naval base in Crimea. Then people in Crimea suddenly decide they want to hide under Mother Russia's apron again, Russian troops are sent in and in five minutes they are having referendum there to say goodbye to Ukraine, become patriotic Russians instead.'

She shook her head, her lips pressed into a fine line. 'So, bam! Vote is taken, people there say yes to deal, Kremlin goes "Thank you very much", and before Western governments wake up to what goes on, we lose our historic Crimea.'

As she spoke, there was real passion in her voice, with a cynical edge I had never heard from her before.

'I remember that,' I replied. 'The first time a country had forcibly taken back territory in Europe since the end of the Second World War. Without a shot being fired. New way to invade, I guess.'

'Oh, there were shots fired.' Tanya gave a bitter laugh. 'My younger brother, Taras, was living in Donetsk at the time, biggest city in eastern Ukraine. All of a sudden there were thugs on the street, fighting to have even more of Ukraine back in Russia. Moscow denied being involved, but the guns and bombs they were using were all Russian. And one of these bombs killed Taras.'

I was shocked. 'Your brother was killed in Ukraine's civil war? I had no idea.'

'Of course not. How could you?' Her tone was snappy and she attempted a smile to soften the impact. 'Oh sorry, Duncan. I am being shitty bitch. But I not often talk about it. Taras and Donetsk are part of Ukraine's dirty little secret that everyone wants to ignore. But I not forget.'

I dropped the subject. I should have asked more, but I couldn't help but compare Tanya's openness with the fact that I still hadn't told her about my political blog and the new investigative reporting I was getting into. She knew nothing about my Richard Foxe alter ego; I was sticking to my rule to tell no one, no matter how close. Bobbie knew, but that was only because I had told her when it was starting up a few years ago.

Then Tanya said something to me. Something I had to act on, something that would be a betrayal of the very trust that bound our friendship together.

It started innocently enough. We had been due to meet up at the weekend, but she called to ask if it was okay to cancel. She had an old boyfriend coming to the UK, and he'd invited her to Northumbria for the weekend. I said fine, and instead we met for a drink before she left, at a subterranean wine bar near the Thames Embankment.

'It's very understanding of you to let me cancel,' she told me after we'd squeezed into a table in the stygian gloom. 'I promise I make it up to you; I will invite you to my flat and cook you best-ever *spaghetti a vongole*.'

'Not a problem. Who is this guy? I don't think you've mentioned him before?'

'Anton Shub. Have you heard of him?'

'No. Should I have?'

'Big oligarch playboy in charge of Axos Technology. His father bought the government operation that ran Chernobyl reactor after the accident. When everything in old Soviet Union was being privatised. Paid almost no money for it, then used their scientists and technology to build nuclear reactors all over Africa and Central Asia. Now the father has retired, Anton is new big boss. Half his time he is high-powered businessman, half his time he is party animal.'

She shot me a grin to show she approved more of the latter.

'He came to my openings in Kiev, always good to me. We dated a few times, nothing serious, but now with Ukrainian crisis we don't do shows in Kiev anymore, so I not seen him for a while. Now he come to visit Northumbria, wants me to spend weekend with him. Says if things go well, he might be spending lot of time in England and maybe we should be couple again. So, I said, why not?'

It was good that the few candles lighting up the darkness in the wine bar were not able to show the expression on my face. When I'd done my investigative blog about Saudi Arabia building more nuclear reactors in Britain, the angle had been that we should be worried about foreign governments being responsible for our energy requirements. I had speculated that with Act Now! in charge, there might be a move to bring the nuclear expansion programme back under British control. That would certainly fit with their protectionist and isolationist tendencies. Now the Russians seemed to be involved. It didn't make any sense.

All of a sudden I had something for Nigel to investigate. I contacted him as soon as I'd said goodbye to Tanya. It was late, but we arranged to talk. If there was a story around Shub's visit to England, I had to make sure I got to it before anyone else.

I Skyped him as soon as I got back to my flat.

'I've got a young Ukrainian friend who dates dodgy Russian oligarchs,' I told him.

Nigel stared at me blankly, then burst into that annoying laugh of his. 'He-he-he-he. Is she pretty?'

'She is, actually, but that's beside the point. She has an old boyfriend called Anton Shub, who is in charge of a company called Axos Technology. They build nuclear reactors based on the same technology that was used in Chernobyl. He's coming to Britain for a meeting next week to explore doing business here. I want you to find out who Axos Technology are, and what they are up to. Whether they're about to take over from the Saudis.'

To my surprise, I could see Nigel starting to rock in his chair. I thought he was having a panic attack, but it turned out he was getting excited. His voice quickened.

'I know all about Chernobyl. It wasn't an accident, have I told you that? Everyone was told it was a nuclear power station, but it was making weapons-grade plutonium for a secret missile base next door, disguised as a goods factory. Less than a thousand miles from Germany.' Nigel was speaking louder and louder as his excitement built. 'When the CIA found out, they ordered a crack team of US Navy Seals to break into the plant and sabotage it, but they did too much damage and exposed the reactor core, causing it to go into meltdown.' Nigel jiggled about on his chair so much that he knocked his webcam over. All I could see was the edge of a keyboard and a pile of papers.

'Really?' I replied. 'That's all very interesting, Nigel, but let's discuss this another day. And can you fix your webcam, please?'

The image on my screen jumped about as Nigel righted the camera.

'But I haven't told you the really good bit yet,' his disembodied voice continued. 'It could have been worse. There was an eyewitness at the scene who saw a ball of fire in the sky, six or eight metres in diameter, and two rays of crimson light came out of the ball and fired on the reactor, stopping it from melting all the way to the earth's core. Then the ball sped off; it was tracked by air traffic at Kiev-Zhulhany Airport, until it disappeared.

The camera was upright again, pointing to his excited face.

I said, 'Aliens came down from outer space and averted nuclear disaster? That was lucky they were passing.'

'Yes, very lucky. So, this is what you want me to investigate?'

'No. Listen carefully, Nigel. I want you to find out what Axos Technology are doing in Britain. I don't want you investigating what happened at Chernobyl with US Navy Seals or anything to do with aliens. And you need to show me proof of everything, no theories. Solemn promise, okay?'

Nigel looked like a balloon slowly deflating. 'All right. Solemn promise.'

'Thanks, Nigel. When you've finished, we can talk some more about Chernobyl, if I've got time. That's a promise, but not a solemn one. And please, be discreet when you're investigating. I need to be careful about my friend. She doesn't know anything about my Richard Foxe blog, and I don't want to tell her. She told me something not realising the implications. It could be nothing, or it could be very interesting, and we need to find out what's going on without anyone suspecting her. I don't want to get her into any trouble.'

'There's a lot of chatter about Russian dirty tricks at the moment,' Nigel said. 'Let me see what I can find out.'

'But no one is to know about Anton Shub. That's really important, Nigel. I don't want anyone to pick up on any chat room gossip about who he is or what he's getting up to. Whatever story comes out of this, it's not going to mention my friend.'

Saying these words out loud made me stop and think about what I was doing. I had stumbled over this story because of what Tanya had told me. As a friend. Someone she thought made his living writing amusing blog posts. She had no idea who I really was, that her indiscretion could lead to all sort of problems for Shub, even for her.

I ended the call with Nigel and sank into a state of sullen self-absorption. I had to be sure the story could never be traced back to Tanya. But I had already stupidly blurted out to Nigel where the story had come from. He spent all his free time hanging out in dark corners of the web, creating theories and trading secrets about anyone and anything. I could see him being tempted to divulge more than he should about what he was investigating. No matter what I said to him, I was kidding myself that I could completely control the story.

In the end, I agreed on a compromise with myself. Wait to see what Nigel comes up with. If nothing, the problem solves itself. If it's a scandal, then decide whether to tell Tanya or carry on deceiving her.

I hadn't decided which of the two options I was hoping for when Nigel messaged me two days later telling me he had come up with something. I found myself wishing that he hadn't. We arranged to meet face-to-face; this was too big a deal to do over the phone. When I arrived at his flat, I sat myself down on my usual chair. Unease crept through my bones. I found myself hoping that I was about to listen to a load of make-believe, to Nigel spinning out his wildest fantasies.

Nigel was looking pleased with himself.

'Shub's company, Axos Technology, had been applying for operating licences in the UK, Germany and Portugal, the three countries where Act Now! is the party in power. The UK licence was waved through a couple of weeks ago without any fanfare, only the statutory announcement buried in the Department of Energy's website. But I found it. He-he-he-he.'

'Can you show me?' I still hadn't got it out of my head that I'd be hearing something about ET landing in northern England.

'Here.' He opened up a bookmark to a page on the Department of Energy website. I looked over Nigel's shoulder, careful not to touch him, which he always detested. I peered at the screen. The announcement looked genuine enough.

'What do you think is going on?'

'Boring. Some business deal. I wanted to tell you what the chat rooms were saying about Axos, but I made you a solemn promise only to tell you about things which have proof. This is all I've got. They're expanding out from the countries who don't care that much about safety as long as the reactors are cheap enough, and coming into western Europe. They're going to get the contract for supplying Britain's long-term nuclear energy needs instead of Saudi Arabia.'

'All without a word of public debate.' I gave a low whistle of surprise. 'Nigel, this story is going to be shocking. A big thing about Act Now!'s appeal is that they mean different things to different people. To idealistic kids, they present a challenge to the status quo, a questioning of society's sacred cows. To the disenchanted and dispossessed, they provide an opportunity to rage against wealth and privilege. And for right-wing Little Englanders, they are the people who will take back our sovereignty from European bureaucrats and American multinationals, no Johnny Foreigners meddling in our affairs. That last lot are going to be furious about this, and the idealistic kids are going to be up in arms that we're building any new nuclear power stations at all. You've done a great job.'

'I know,' replied Nigel. 'It was very tricky to find this. It's been kept well hidden.'

I began saying my thoughts aloud as the implications sank in. 'The party of protectionism and nationalism, the one that wants to rip up our global free-trade agreements, has been secretly planning to hand over our nuclear future to the Russians. And not only that, but to the company that built Chernobyl.'

'No, the people who built Chernobyl were the Soviet government. Then it was all sold to Axos. You made me make a solemn promise to tell you the truth.'

I laughed. 'I know I did, Nigel. But it's how some people will see the truth. It's called perception.'

This was huge. It challenged everything Act Now! stood for. And I had stumbled across it all because Tanya had told me she was off for a shagfest with an old boyfriend.

That's where the guilt came in.

It was an important story, and I knew I should publish it. People had a right to know. I was an investigative journalist now, and investigative journalists shouldn't have any scruples in breaking a story. Tanya certainly didn't seem to have been told Shub's visit was supposed to be hush-

hush. From what I could find out, Anton Shub didn't seem to be the most disciplined of international businessmen. If he was stupid enough to meet up with an old girlfriend on a clandestine trip to England, he deserved all he got.

So, I wrote the story. Axos Technology, the company that built its nuclear expertise on the work of the scientists and the technology responsible for the Chernobyl disaster, was in secret talks with the British government to construct the next generation of Britain's nuclear reactors. I had double-checked and triple-checked everything that Nigel came up with. He would not exaggerate deliberately, but I had to make sure that not a single word of fantasy had crept into what he had told me. As I went through all the sources of his data, I became more and more amazed by his ability to hold so much information in his head, to be able to spot the links and disparities between two pieces of information that, on the surface, seemed miles apart. Whatever his problems as a human being, he was a phenomenon as an investigator.

All that checking meant it was two weeks before I wrote up the story, which had the extra bonus that it didn't look like it was linked to Tanya and what Shub told her during his visit. I told myself that that justified writing the story without Tanya's knowledge. But in truth, I just wanted the whole shitty business to be over so that I could put it behind me and never think of it again.

The *Chronicle* offered to match their payment for the fracking scoop, but I decided to dig my heels in. I didn't know if I'd ever get a story this big again, and I wanted to use it as a bargaining tool to redefine my relationship with the paper. In the end, I negotiated a fee equal to six months of my old retainer, and when the story was syndicated in France, Germany and Italy, I was able to pay off Nigel's year one advance and still come out ahead in terms of income. For the first time, my plan to survive as a journalist looked like it could work.

The Department of Energy issued a flat 'No comment', but there was enough media noise to mean that wasn't going to hold for long. When they changed their stance to say they wouldn't provide a running commentary on commercially sensitive negotiations, it was clear they'd been rumbled. There was a flurry of follow-up stories and Anton Shub's photo was in all the papers. It didn't help that he had a surname reminiscent of a Bond villain and an appearance that, shall we say, didn't immediately convey honesty and integrity.

Then the next political story came along: Act Now!'s decision to hold a referendum to abolish all government quangos in three years, unless a quango was able to justify itself to the electorate and secure a majority in an online vote to save itself from the chop. '*Only pay for the experts you believe in*' ran the slogan. All hell was breaking loose over the idea, but the establishment was finding it impossible to counter the populist appeal of letting people vote on just about anything.

In all the furore, Anton Shub and Axos Technology being let in the back door to run our nuclear industry were blown off the front page. But it didn't matter; I reckoned the story had run its course anyway. I sent Nigel off to go digging on the quango abolition, to see if there was anything dodgy about it.

After our last success, he couldn't wait to get started.

chapter six

I deliberately avoided meeting with Tanya while the Shub story was in the news. She didn't call, and I wasn't going to mention it first. But there was little point in putting off meeting up again forever. I texted to take her up on her offer of *spaghetti a vongole* and headed off to her flat a few days later. A basement in Battersea, tucked away in a back street. I arrived and texted her to tell her I was standing outside. Doorbells seem to be a thing of the past with young people.

She greeted me warmly. That was a relief. But her flat was a surprise – sterile, lacking in personality, nothing that reflected the vivaciousness of her character. She showed me into the small kitchen and poured me a glass of wine from a half-finished bottle she produced from the fridge.

'*Nostrovia,*' she said. 'Welcome to humble abode.'

'*Slange var.*'

We clinked our glasses.

'So, how was Northumbria?' I asked. I tried to make it sound like small talk. 'I've never been.'

'Windy,' Tanya replied, as she threw the clams into the frying pan with garlic and ginger. She popped on the lid. 'Strange place to run a training course. That's what Anton said he was doing there when he invited me up.

But I found out later he was there for secret deal with government. It was in newspapers; did you see it? Anton called me asking if I'd spoken to newspapers about his visit. When I said no, he told me to tell him if anyone made snooping around me.'

'That was him?' I tried my best to look shocked. 'I knew the name sounded familiar. It all sounded a bit dodgy. I thought Saudi Arabia and the French were building the new nuclear power stations.'

'When we were in Northumbria he told me all is to change. He drank too much champagne the first night, was boasting that Russian government is owed big favours from Act Now!, Russians do lot of dirty tricks to help Act Now! win election. Russia is to be Britain's special partner, do lots of deals together. Back in Moscow, all oligarchs are rubbing hands and buying new Ferraris.' She peered into the frying pan. 'Dinner's ready. Let's eat.'

I needed to sit down anyway. Back in 2016, there had been rumours about the Russians being involved in the Brexit vote. Then they said the same thing about the US presidential election. Things had gone quiet since, but if what Tanya was saying was true, the Russians were now even more heavily involved than anyone thought, colluding with Act Now! to get them into power and being rewarded with a big nuclear power station contract. And who knows what else.

I decided to change the subject. Taking advantage of Tanya once for a story might be understandable; exploiting her friendship a second time would be unforgivable. I moved the conversation on to safer topics and enjoyed the rest of the evening.

The next day, I couldn't help myself – I decided to indulge in a little brainstorming about how Act Now! and the Russians could be in cahoots with each other, to see how much of what the party was doing could favour Russia. It turned out not to be a difficult exercise. Looking at Act Now!'s political agenda through the prism of acting in Russia's interests revealed that just about every major policy initiative they had underway would be good news for Russia.

I went through their manifesto. Abolish trade agreements, NATO, the World Trade Organisation, the G7. Support Act Now! in other countries to break up the EU. All things that would strengthen Russia's position on the world stage.

The list went on. Pull out of the Paris Accord on climate change; great for an economy like Russia's, based on oil. And when vast swathes of your country are Siberian tundra, global warming might not be a bad thing.

Abolish fracking: good for the barrel price of oil.

Tighten regulation and control of UK businesses, especially in the financial services sector: good news for a country whose businesses are not subject to the same restrictions.

Reduce the power of parliament and have more decisions made locally or through plebiscites: more opportunities to manipulate and hoodwink people into making decisions that could undermine Britain's economic and political power.

If I was feeling paranoid, I could imagine two-thirds of the manifesto had been written in the Kremlin to turn Britain into a country that was doing everything it could to be brought under Russian control and everything possible to boost Russia's status as a global superpower. With Act Now! lauding the fact that their core manifesto was the same in every country in which they operated, soon all of western Europe would be pressing the self-destruct button and handing power over to the Russians.

And now, evidence of preferential treatment to Russian companies when awarding government contracts. I'd written a provocative story linking Axos Technology's seemingly effortless ability to steal a nuclear construction project from under the noses of Saudi Arabia and the French. But to go further than that with this information was pure speculation. The only piece of hard evidence I had, if you could call it that, was a couple of throwaway comments made by a Russian playboy when he was alone in a bedroom with his lover. It wasn't exactly Pulitzer Prize material.

I wasn't quite prepared to have myself labelled as a wild-eyed conspiracy nut just yet, so I decided to have a chat with Nigel about my theories, to see if there was any technical basis to how the Russians could be operating. The thought filled me with dread. Usually, I had to fight off his attempts to tell me about his wildest fantasies. Now I was going to invite him to open the floodgates.

I went to see him and outlined my theory that Act Now! was a puppet of the Russians, acting under their control. He gobbled it up, nodding furiously.

'I can see how Russia would love to have Act Now! in power,' I told him when I'd finished. 'What I don't get is how they could undermine the existing political parties from Moscow. Surely you can't hack into the computers of major political parties willy-nilly? And if you could, wouldn't you get found out and wouldn't there be an almighty ruckus?' I shook my head. 'It all seems too far-fetched.'

'Hacking's easy-peasy,' Nigel replied. 'People who are hacked don't talk about it, because if they did it would make them look stupid. Looking stupid is bad. Ian looks stupid and he doesn't like people telling him.'

I resisted the temptation to ask who Ian was.

Nigel was getting animated now. 'If you want proof, look at how many news stories are based on what they call leaks. They're not leaks; they're hacks. Saying they're leaks is telling lies, and that's bad too. I never tell lies. If I tell a lie, it means I have to think about something that didn't happen. And then I have to think about all the other things that didn't happen. And then I can't stop. There are too many things that don't happen; I can't think of them all, it makes my brain explode. I only think about things that do happen.'

Animated was starting to move towards agitated.

'I know you don't tell lies. That's very good. Don't think about news stories telling lies. Tell me about people stealing data.'

'When people steal data, they don't keep quiet about it. They steal it to tell the truth about things all over the internet. It's bad to steal, but good to tell the truth. They cancel each other out, so that sort of stealing isn't bad. It's not like stealing from a shop. That's bad.'

'That's very true, Nigel. But how do you know it's Russian intelligence helping people steal data? Couldn't it be a bunch of geeks with a lot of time on their hands, enjoying making mischief? There's a lot of people who like to find things out for fun.'

'Yes. It's fun seeing what you can find out. But the Russia hacking is different. They're not doing it for fun. They always do it the same way; the fun is doing it the way that you invent. And what they do costs a lot of money. They track down software flaws that nobody knows about and use them to breach firewalls. And as soon as anyone finds out what's going on, they're off to find another one.'

'But how do you know it's the Russians? Couldn't it be our political parties doing it to each other?'

'No.' I'd never seen Nigel so sure of himself. 'What happens when the hackers breach security is that they plant malware on people's computers, which lets other super-smarts get access to juicy, juicy files. When they go snooping around looking in files, they're professionals; they know what they're looking for. The fun of hacking is that you get to look for cool things to find out and then have a good time telling everyone. The Russians don't do that.'

Nigel leaned towards me, staring at the floor again, his voice now a whisper. 'And you know what else? The operating system used to develop the malware uses Cyrillic, and the hackers work in the GMT-3 time zone, Moscow time.

'And all this is known? How come it's not front page news?'

'Some of the guys in the chat room have told the newspapers, but they just get laughed at. "Circumstantial evidence" they get told. That means it's not real evidence, like finding a gun with fingerprints on it.'

'I suppose the Russians simply deny that they're involved, and there's nothing definitive that can prove otherwise ...' I was surprised to find that everything Nigel was saying was making sense and there was not an alien or a Loch Ness monster in sight. 'And there's also the realpolitik dimension. One government trying to find out another government's secrets. It's the second oldest profession. They spy on us, we spy on them. And we all know we're doing it to each other; that's why you have MI5, CIA and Russia's FSB and SVR. Especially the SVR.'

'Yes!' said Nigel, banging his fist on the table. 'What's different now is that it's being used in a new sort of way. It's called hybrid intelligence.'

'And that is ...'

'Super sneaky. The hackers can get into anything, the folders on your computer, your emails, search history, everything. And there's no point in deleting stuff; they can set up a secret cache on your computer where anything deleted is copied to and then they check that as well. Very funny. You delete something naughty, and that makes sure it gets spotted. He-he-he-he.'

He stopped laughing. 'Then the games begin. Boring information turns into rumours of rivalries and arguments; spicy stuff people want to stay hidden ends up on the front page. And there's always the chance of coming across something shady or embarrassing that a naughty politician thought was safely deleted or hidden away on their personal computer.'

'For fuck's sake, Nigel, why haven't you told me this before? I had you running around getting reports on shale oil extraction for a fracking story that nobody wanted to read, and you were sitting on all of this stuff. This is dynamite.'

Nigel looked alarmed. 'Dynamite is bad. Blows things up. Like Wile E. Coyote does to Road Runner.'

'I didn't mean real dynamite. It's a metaphor … Never mind. And how exactly do they get this malware onto people's computers? Surely there must be airtight security on any computer used by someone who has access to such sensitive information?'

'No, they are very clever. Even cleverer than Ian, and he's very clever, even though he looks stupid. They set up a domain name which is almost identical to a name someone would regularly use, but with a very small typo. When you and I make a typo, it's a mistake, but this is a typo that's done on purpose. Which means it's not really a typo. But I don't know what to call it if it's not a typo. Can I call it an anti-typo, like the antimatter in *Star Trek*?'

'That's good. Call it an anti-typo. What do they do with the anti-typo?'

'They design a website that is identical to the public site but which installs malware on any computer that visits it. It only needs one silly person in a political organisation to be tricked into clicking on the link to visit the bogus site for the malware to be installed on the other side of a firewall. Then the first thing it does is delete all trace of how it got there and the history showing what bogus site it came from. Then, every time the silly person's infected computer emails someone or visits internal web pages, the malware gets spread. That's why you should never click on a link someone sends you. You know that, don't you?'

'I do. And that's how they find out what's on people's computers?'

'And tell lies.' Nigel looked disgusted. 'The same designers who copy public websites can also copy internal documents and email. Even if they don't find anything damaging, they plant a nasty sentence into something nice and smart someone wrote to make them look bad or stupid. Then they overwrite the original and leak the nasty new one. And that's bad leaking. Because it's even worse than telling lies. It's pretending that other people are telling lies, even when they didn't. It's telling lies twice.'

I went home that night with my head spinning. Yes, Nigel was right, these stories weren't new; I'd heard about these rumours before. But now I had something more. Rather than Act Now! being the innocent recipients of all this Russian largesse to get them elected, what I was finding out was that they were in cahoots with the Russians, receiving support in return for putting forward a manifesto that had practically been written by the Kremlin. And Act Now! was repaying the favour by lining the pockets of favoured Russian oligarchs and the Russian exchequer with lucrative business deals.

It was this last bit that made my story unique, and it was also the part that I had the most qualms about publishing. I couldn't use Anton Shub's stupidity as the reason to publish this latest part of the story, and yet again, the only reason I'd started looking at all this was another throwaway comment from Tanya.

I agonised overnight about what to do next. I realised I could only do the story if I told Tanya everything, and she said it was okay to go ahead. But if she didn't, would I really walk away? I'd like to think so, that I wasn't the sort of person who could exploit someone like that. I thought back to my light-hearted piece about our first meeting. How ironic that I worried then whether I had taken advantage of her. Something so trivial. Now this.

I needed to talk it through with someone. I called Bobbie that evening. I explained the background to the story and was about to ask how best to tell Tanya what I'd been getting up to. But I never got that far.

'You never bloody learn, do you, Duncan?' she yelled at me from my computer screen. 'You might see yourself as the saviour of Western civilisation, but think about that poor girl for a moment. Do you want to do to her what you did to me? Either your story will be ignored as the ramblings of a nutcase, or it will be taken seriously, in which case your friend will be crucified by people trying to discredit her and hounded by others trying to find out more. Don't even think about it.'

'The chances are no one will ever trace the story to her. And I'd tell her everything before I did anything. Give her the right to say no.'

'You did that to me with your Michael Mitchell book and look what happened. I can't believe you're even considering going down that road again.'

She was right. I knew it even before I spoke to her. I just needed to hear the words.

'Then I won't do it. In fact, I should probably tell Tanya I was responsible for the Axos Technology story. I learned a long time ago it's not always good to keep secrets from people.'

Bobbie's tone softened. 'Look, I'm sorry. You get caught up in your stories, Duncan, expand them a little, it's part of your charm. But you need to be careful about what you write these days. This isn't the 1970s; you can't just disappear if you want to escape from something. Nobody can hide for long these days.'

I thought back to the horrors of that time. Bobbie fleeing for her life down to London, abandoning everything she knew, all her dreams. The constant fear that her past would catch up on her. Me being threatened, then beaten up, for refusing to tell Michael Mitchell how he could find her. As always, she was right.

Bobbie hadn't finished. 'Think carefully before you tell Tanya that you've already posted something based on information she's given you,' she said. 'She might react badly, and it sounds like you've got away with it. You've got a good friendship there. You shouldn't put it in jeopardy.'

I said I'd think about it, but I'd already decided that Tanya had a right to know. She'd twice given me ideas for stories and, given the company she kept, she'd probably say something equally newsworthy again. She needed to know that I wrote about politics. She needed to know I was Richard Foxe. I sat down to email my confession, and tried to justify myself to her by saying I kept my political identity completely secret. I said I didn't want there to be any more secrets between us, no compromising situations involving what she said to me.

As I typed the word 'secrets', I suddenly froze. What the bloody hell did I think I was doing? I'd just spent a couple of hours listening to Nigel telling me that Act Now! was hacking into all and sundry and here I was, the journalist who'd just exposed their subterfuge, composing an email that couldn't incriminate Tanya more if it tried.

I backspaced through the text until everything was gone; I didn't know if that was better than just deleting the draft, but best be on the safe side. I realised I couldn't risk the phone either. I had to tell her in person.

I decided to turn up unannounced, and headed off to Tanya's flat. Tomorrow, I'd buy a second mobile, pay-as-you-go, for any vaguely sensitive calls, and a second tablet as well. I would set up new email and video calling accounts, and use them only for those occasions. I arrived at her flat and banged on the door. Nothing. I walked back up the steps from the basement and stood in the street, trying to work out what to do next. There was a post office on the corner, and I went in and bought paper, envelopes and a pen and sat down outside Tanya's flat and wrote out again what I had typed up earlier. As I sealed the envelope, I looked up and down the street one last time, hoping to catch a glimpse of Tanya arriving. I waited another five minutes, then posted the envelope through her letterbox.

No going back now.

I was preparing dinner when the doorbell rang. I opened the door and there was Tanya, her face grim, tense. I'd never seen her like that. I blurted out her name and then regained my composure.

'Do you want to come in?' I asked, my stomach churning. She didn't speak, simply nodded. We headed into the living room.

'Can I get you something? Coffee? Wine?' Banal, but I needed to say something – anything – to ease the tension.

'*Nyet*. You shock me, Duncan. You take what I say

about Anton, and you write scandal story? That is very bad thing to do.'

'I know, I'm sorry. But I didn't mention what he said to you or give any clue that you were involved. His visit to the UK wasn't a secret. If he told you, he probably told others. It's important people know what's going on, but I shouldn't have done this without you knowing who I really am. That's why I wanted to tell you all about Richard Foxe. I was tempted to write another story, so you had to know. Who knows what you might tell me in the future? I couldn't promise myself I'd never be tempted to use something you told me, so I had to make sure you knew all about me.'

There was a long silence. Tanya looked around the room, like she was struggling to speak. When, finally, she did say something, her voice was quiet, with the faint hint of reproach.

'You should have told me sooner, Duncan. But I can see that revealing Richard Foxe is a big decision for you. I'm happy you decide to tell me.' She walked slowly to the window and looked out onto the street. Without turning, she said, 'Tell me more about this big story you write. I like Russians, but not Russian government. You remember my brother.'

'Yes, of course,' I said. 'Dreadful.'

'It was the Russians behind these riots. Ukrainian government starts looking to the West and Russians go crazy, destabilise everything, get Crimea people to become part of Russia, so they keep big naval base. If they are playing the same game in the UK, then you need to tell. Somebody else should not lose brother.'

I felt my mouth opening in astonishment. I hadn't even considered the possibility that she might agree for me to write the story without the need to be convinced. I told her all that I had found out, how everything Act Now! seemed to be doing could be seen to be in Russia's interests. How Russia seemed to be behind a massive, well-funded, sophisticated hacking operation that was talked about in the dark recesses of internet chat rooms. And how, in return, Russia was being given big favours. Tanya sat listening until I came to the new information, the piece that only I knew, the evidence for which had come from one of the very oligarchs who was a front man for the Russian payback. At that point, I could see fear and anxiety grip her like a vice.

'I gave you missing piece of jigsaw,' she said, her voice a mixture of dread and wonderment.

'Exactly. It's a first, tiny bit of proof that all of this conjecture is not pure paranoia. But even if I don't reveal why Anton Shub's company is getting a government contract, you are too close to the story. And if the press find out who I am, and that I know you, it would put you in a dangerous position. I don't know why I even thought about writing this story. The more I think about it, the more I know I could never publish it.'

She gave me a surprised look, like a child catching an older person in a foolish statement. 'But if you think it's true you must publish it. What are the Russians going to do, give me sushi full of polonium? I don't think so.' Her face lit up with the fire of conviction. 'These bastards in the Kremlin killed my brother. If they are trying to do to Britain even a little bit of what they did in Ukraine, they should be stopped. If you think your story is true, tell it.'

I pressed my hand against my chest; fingers splayed out. 'Let's both think about this for the next couple of days,' I said in a weakened voice. 'My blog is pretty high profile at the moment, after the first story I wrote about Shub. This story would be bound to get noticed. I'm not even sure it's not libel the way it's written at the moment. I've been in the eye of a media storm once in my life already; I'm not sure I can do it again. I never expected you to say all this. Let me think about it.'

The next day I set up the new accounts and I reached Bobbie that evening. I chose the username 'Duncansnewphone' so she'd know it was me. I told her about my new security measures and gave her an update.

'Things have taken an unexpected turn,' I said. 'I told Tanya about Richard Foxe and the article I was thinking of writing. She didn't mince her words about what she thought. Now I really am in a dilemma about what to do next.'

'Some things are more important than writing a story, Duncan. If she's told you not to publish the story, then you should respect that. I wish I'd been less supportive of you writing my story all those years ago.'

'That's just it. Tanya didn't object; she insisted I went ahead. Her brother died in a riot a few years ago in Ukraine and Tanya blames the Russians. She sees my story as revenge for her brother.'

Bobbie gave a slow shake of the head. 'She has no idea what she's getting herself into, Duncan. You need to tell her. This could ruin her life.'

'I did – and the conversation turned surreal. She tried to convince me to write the story and it was me doing all the arguing against. If I'm honest with myself, telling Tanya wasn't just about me doing the right thing for a friend. Deep down I was having cold feet about going ahead and needed an excuse to pull the plug.'

Bobbie laughed. 'God, Duncan, you do get yourself into a pickle, don't you? You plunge headlong into being an intrepid reporter, stopping at nothing to get your story. Then as soon as you do come up with the goods, you get the heebie-jeebies about going ahead. I'm pleased you're scared. It shows you've finally got some common sense in your old age. It's only complete idiots that aren't afraid of anything.'

'So I'm not a complete idiot, then? I suppose that's something.' I paused to think for a second. 'You're right, I shouldn't rush into this. I'll take Tanya through what happened to you again, use it as an example of what the consequences of something like this can be. If she's still okay with it, I'll show it to the *Chronicle*. They've got lawyers and editors who can tell me whether it's even something I'd be allowed to publish. That is, if you're okay with it. Don't want any publicity about me to reverberate back to you again.'

'Oh, I'll be all right,' Bobbie said, with a quick laugh. 'If anyone does show up in Scoraig, Davie and a couple of the lads here will make sure they're soon on their way. We had a journalist turn up last year on the anniversary of Michael's acquittal, wanting to do a "Where are they now?" story. Let's just say they didn't stay long. If you want to run the story, I won't stand in your way.'

I lay in bed that night wondering what sort of monster I had created. I'd make absolutely sure that Tanya knew every single ramification of what being involved in a story like this could potentially do to her. I wanted her to be the one to say no.

But the trouble was, she didn't. Taking Tanya through the repercussions one more time only strengthened her resolve to see the story come out.

FAVOURITISM CLAIMS OVER RUSSIAN NUCLEAR CONTRACT, screamed the headline in the *Chronicle*. Tanya was referred to as 'a source close to Axos CEO, Anton Shub'.

This time it wouldn't get pushed off the front page by the next news story to come along. Act Now! and Russia was shaping up to be the political scandal of the year, and I was going to try to make sure I was right in the middle of it.

chapter seven

I stared at the photographs Nigel was showing me. The same person, Zelig-like, showing up in every shot. An anonymous, middle-aged man with a pencil moustache, looking like a grey accountant, the sort of person you'd forget five minutes after meeting him. But you wouldn't forget the others. A picture of him in the background of a news photo of the Russian president meeting IT technocrats in the noughties; pictures of him with a British businessman, a French newsreader and a German environmentalist, all taken about ten or fifteen years ago. All three of them, the current leaders of Act Now! in their respective countries. Two of them had already won an election and formed a government.

Nigel was spinning in his chair with barely contained glee.

'Who is he?' I asked.

'Pavel Mikin. He was a professor of neuropolitics at Moscow State University when he came to the attention of the Russian government. He has a moustache. I don't like people with moustaches.'

'And apart from his moustache, do you know anything else about him?'

'Oh, yes, everything. He was a teacher. I don't like

teachers either, apart from Mrs McGregor. But Mikin wasn't like a normal teacher, who tells you to be quiet all the time or you don't get to go on field trips. He wrote stories that were published in technical journals, just like you and your newspaper stories that get published in newspapers.'

'And what were his stories about?' Slowly, slowly, one step at a time, I told myself.

'Dunno. They're in Russian. But there were other stories written about him at the beginning of the century, and they were in English. About how he was saying that in the new millennium, more and more people in the West would be living in filter bubbles where they used social media to live in a community that reinforced and radicalised their beliefs.' Nigel had slipped into the trance-like voice he used when he was reciting something by heart. 'A community that made no distinction between who you knew online and who you knew in real life.'

He paused for a second, stuck his lips out in a pout. 'That's silly, isn't it? You're standing there breathing oxygen and turning it into carbon dioxide, and Ian is on my computer. I can tell the difference between you. You haven't got wires coming out of you, and you're not powered by electricity. And you're not just breathing oxygen and breathing out carbon dioxide. You're breathing in 78% nitrogen and 21% oxygen and breathing out 6% water vapour, 74% nitrogen, 15% oxygen, 4% carbon dioxide and 1% argon. Plus some small quantities of other gases, but I guess you don't want to know about them.'

'That's right. That's because they're irrelevant, which means they're not important to what we're talking about.

What Professor Mikin means is that you think of both … Ian? and me as people you know, even though you've never seen Ian in person.' I paused to let Nigel take in this information. Particularly the meaning of the word 'irrelevant'. 'What else did the stories say?'

'That Professor Mikin had said the political establishment had failed to notice this, and he predicted that it would mean that "certain groups would reject the messages of mainstream media in favour of their own, self-generated opinion formers". That's what they said in the article. Not sure what it means, though.'

'It's why so many countries have got the governments they have now. A massive rejection of the status quo. People putting two fingers up to the great and the good when they tried to tell them what was best.'

'You shouldn't put two fingers up. That's rude.'

'That's right.' I laughed. 'Very rude. That's why we got the Brexit vote, Trump, Five Star in Italy. Lots of rude things happened a few years later.'

Nigel didn't get the joke. 'Professor Mikin published one final article, calling social media "the soft underbelly of democracy in the west". Yuck. It was in Russian, but I got the gist of it from Translate. He said that if the Kremlin recruited an army of what he called anthropological technologists, Russia could use them to influence Western elections, divide and destabilise the West. That was around the time that first photo was taken. Do you think that's important?'

'Yes, Nigel, it's important. Where did you get these photos?'

Nigel frowned. 'That's another thing that's not right.

80

They should have been easy to find, what with face recognition software and the metadata. But they were hidden away. You'd never find them using a search engine or trawling for keywords. You've got to get into deleted caches, use searchbots, all that sort of stuff. Tricky.'

'So, these photos have been airbrushed out of the web's history? Interesting. And how exactly did you … Oh, don't bother to explain. A Russian academic comes up with a theory as to how to overthrow the West, disappears for ten years and then pops up again as a powerbroker for the future leaders of Western governments? That's a hell of a story.'

'Oh good. I knew Mikin was a nasty man when I saw his moustache. But you shouldn't say hell.'

'You know, all this is starting to make sense.' I was speed talking now; I couldn't help myself. 'There was a scandal back in 2017 when Russia was accused of meddling in Western elections. There were inquiries into Trump's connection with Russia and the social media campaigns supporting Brexit. "Seeking to weaponise information", it was called. That was small beer in comparison to this; ten, twenty thousand tweets, a couple of hundred grand spent planting fake news, and real amateur-hour stuff like paying for ad campaigns in roubles, stupid incriminating mistakes like that.' I was talking as much to clarify my thoughts as to explain to Nigel. 'What if 2017 was a test programme, to see if Mikin's ideas could pay off? Then after the Brexit and Trump votes went the Kremlin's way, he got the green light to scale everything up, make the whole thing much more sophisticated? It all went underground, and the result is Act Now!.'

And Tanya's ex-lover was one of the beneficiaries, I realised. I had a flash of panic, like when you're swimming in the sea and you find your feet don't touch the ground. My imagination was running away with me, surely. This was too ridiculous to be believable. I was spending too much time in Nigel's company. I needed to drag myself back to reality.

'Nigel, we have to take a deep breath here. This Mikin guy does seem to raise a lot of questions. But we can't go from him having his photograph taken with our future prime minister to accusing the PM of being a Russian spy. That's being ridiculous.'

Nigel jutted out his chin. 'But it all makes sense. You said yourself that everything Act Now! does seems to be for Russia's benefit.' His eyes were blinking rapidly, his movements becoming jerky. 'You're annoyed that I found this out rather than your Russian girlfriend. If you don't want the story, I'll find someone else who does.'

His sudden change of mood was unsettling.

'She's not my girlfriend. And she's Ukrainian, not Russian.'

Nigel snorted. 'Same difference.'

'No, it's not the same. Tanya accidentally discovered something she shouldn't have, and I took advantage of that. I need to start acting more responsibly if we're going to keep going with this story. That means not accusing the people running the country of being in the pockets of the Russians until we've got more proof than what could be a perfectly innocent photograph.' I was getting worked up too, and forced myself to calm down. 'Because otherwise, people would say we were telling lies. And we don't want to be liars, do we? To be sure we're not liars, we need proof.'

'Proof? Like Sherlock Holmes?'

'Exactly. Sherlock Holmes always had his proof before he accused anyone. We need to be like Sherlock Holmes and Dr Watson.'

Nigel obviously liked this analogy as he calmed down just as suddenly as he'd got animated. 'More proof? Like what?'

'I don't know. Something else. We could put the photographs out there and ask Act Now! for an explanation, but likely as not they'd brush it off as a coincidence. Let's hold our fire on this for the moment. These photos are more than a decade old, and no one else has ever found them. They can stay hidden for a few weeks more.'

But I didn't want to leave it too long. Sooner or later Nigel would blurt out what he'd found in one of his chat rooms or sidle up to another journalist who wouldn't have the same scruples. I was aching to talk to someone about it: Tanya, Bobbie, maybe even Sam at the *Chronicle*. But that was a cop-out. No one else should be involved. This was a dilemma I had to resolve myself.

Then I made the mistake of appearing on *News Today*. A flagship current affairs programme, they wanted to do an in-depth discussion about the issues my article on Russian favouritism had raised. They agreed they would interview an Act Now! spokesman and me together, and I was guaranteed anonymity, sitting in a separate darkened studio. As long as I stuck to the facts, I reasoned, I wouldn't come to any harm.

I couldn't have been more wrong. The Act Now! guy was Damian Zane, a real political Rottweiler, and he went on the offensive from the word go. After an avuncular introduction from the show's presenter, Fiona Wallace, he was asked for his reaction to my story.

'Well, Fiona, I see you've persuaded "Richard Foxe" to come out of the shadows.' He said my name with dripping disdain and almost theatrical exaggeration. He looked at my darkened profile on the TV screen in the studio. 'To an extent at least. I think your viewers should know he's skulking in the next studio, too afraid to come in here and discuss this with me face-to-face. That's right, isn't it?'

Fiona baulked a little. 'Mr Foxe agreed to come on this programme if we respected his anonymity. That's why we have this set-up, which you knew about and agreed to in advance.'

I went to speak, but Zane got in first. 'I'm not sure why he should be afforded such a privilege, particularly as he believes in revealing everyone else's secrets. So, let me tell your viewers who Richard Foxe really is. Duncan Jones, better known as Mark Jackson. A failed novelist. If the name sounds familiar it's not because of his books, I can assure you. They're poorly written trash. It's because he was at the centre of a scandal a few years ago. An innocent man was put in jail for a crime he didn't commit, because Duncan Jones told the police a pack of lies.' Zane jabbed his finger towards my profile on the screen. 'He's a man who was recently fired as a columnist by his newspaper and is so desperate to earn some money that he'll write anything to get paid; the more outlandish, the better. That's who you've got on this programme attacking the credibility of the government. An unemployed fantasist whose stories have been proven in court to be a pack of lies.'

I sunk back in my seat, stunned at my naivety. I hadn't thought through that Act Now! would come prepared to destroy me, not the story. Through the roar of blood rushing through my head, I could hear the interviewer's question.

'Richard Foxe, care to comment?'

I hesitated for a second, debating whether to deny everything, but that would make it worse.

'Yes, I wrote novels under the name Mark Jackson. And one of them was indirectly linked to a miscarriage of justice in the 1990s. I wrote it as a work of fiction, based on events that happened to a friend of mine. It spurred the police on to launch an investigation that we now know was both misguided and corrupt. But that investigation was nothing to do with me. I did nothing unethical or illegal, and neither did my friend. And we were completely exonerated at the enquiry that was held afterwards.' I straightened up, tried to regain my composure. 'I think we should focus on what we're here to discuss. Why has Act Now! awarded a nuclear power contract to a company whose technology is based on that used at Chernobyl, and why are they so secretive about it?'

I tried to turn the tables, but the damage was done. Anton Shub had denied ever telling anyone that Act Now! owed Russia any favours. Without bringing Tanya into the story, all I could argue was that the number of dirty tricks played on Act Now!'s opponents at the last election, and the party's seemingly inexplicable about-turn on being opposed to foreign involvement in building power stations in the UK, must somehow be linked. It was all speculation and any chance of support from the presenter had evaporated after Zane had revealed my less than illustrious past.

Zane stonewalled every question, lacing his replies with taunts for me to come out from hiding and join them in the studio. The slot lasted six minutes. A total car crash, and when the interview came to an end Zane was given the final word.

'Nothing this known liar has said today or in his newspaper story is backed up by a single shred of proof. Unless he comes up with something more substantial, he should keep quiet and crawl back into the shadows where he obviously feels most comfortable.'

I tried not to wince.

'And there we must leave it,' said Wallace. Her tone betrayed the fact that keeping quiet about my past until it was revealed on air still rankled. 'Maybe we've heard the last of the story, maybe not.'

It was obvious which she believed.

I met up with Nigel the next morning.

'So now do you think I was right to go easy on the Pavel Mikin photos? I take it you saw me on *News Today* last night.'

'That man was rude to you, calling you names. Rude and childish. It was bad children at school that used to call me names. Mrs McGregor used to tell me that sticks and stones will break my bones, but names will never hurt me. She told me not to worry, they weren't real. Like you didn't have real dynamite with you on Tuesday, 27th October so you couldn't blow me up like Wile E. Coyote tried to do to Road Runner.'

I smiled. 'Mrs McGregor was right, Nigel. Names are just names. It was my own silly fault agreeing to the interview. I couldn't believe they found out my real name.'

'I found out about your Mark Jackson and Duncan Jones names after the first time I met you. Easy-peasy.'

'What? You knew about my past?'

'Lemon-squeezy.'

'Why didn't you say anything?'

Nigel shrugged. 'You didn't ask me if I knew your other names.'

'I don't ask you a lot of things. Sometimes you shouldn't wait to be asked. If you find something important, you should tell me. Sherlock Holmes didn't wait to be asked.'

'Well, if you want to know something important, you have the most rubbish security on your computer. I could see anything I want on it. Except that's being bad as well. It's called being a Peeping Tom. We had a talk at school about Peeping Toms once, after some boys got into trouble. I don't want to be a Peeping Tom, but I bet Act Now! is not so well-behaved.'

I felt my skin tingle. 'Really? Show me.'

Nigel brought up the contents of my hard drive on his computer in five minutes, my bank account in ten.

I was slack-jawed in amazement.

'But I've got anti-virus, anti-hacking, firewall, you name it,' I said. 'I panicked about sending a compromising email the other day, but told myself later I was being paranoid. Is it really that easy to get around them? That's shocking.'

'You need end-to-end encryption, using open source systems that don't share your secret key; and off-the-record messaging software that you can overlay onto the rubbish security that comes with most video conferencing software.' Nigel opened a few more programs. 'It doesn't even look like you're doing two-step verification and you haven't encrypted your hard drive. And your passwords are rubbish. If Act Now! hasn't already hacked into your computer, they will do soon.'

'Shit. All that stuff you've just said I should do. Can you put it on my computer and show me how to use it?'

'Easy-peasy, lemon-squeezy. And you'll want to run Tor on your computer – that's an open source program that shuffles your data through a network of volunteer servers. Will make you almost impossible to trace. Bring me your computer and I'll make you super-safe. He-he-he-he.'

I tried to think what could already have been found out. I'd never typed anywhere that Tanya was the source of my Anton Shub story, and the only video conversation I had had about it with Bobbie was when I set up that second account after my panic attack about security. Sounded like a second account would make me safe for one or two calls, but unless I did all the stuff Nigel was suggesting, even that would be compromised in time. I'd had a lucky escape. I promised Nigel I'd bring my computer over straight away.

I got ready to leave. 'One thing's for sure, I'm not going to respond to that shellacking I got today by throwing more petrol on the fire. Zane challenged me to come back with proof. If I do ever call his bluff, it's going to have to be bomb proof.'

Nigel looked startled, and I promised myself I'd start keeping my metaphors under control. 'What I mean, Nigel, is I need more evidence before I say any more.'

'Oh, I've got you that,' Nigel replied. 'You should have asked me. Look at this.'

I couldn't believe what I was seeing. A bunch of long-deleted tweets from Mikin to our new prime minister, well before Act Now! was set up, congratulating him on business deals, wishing him happy birthday, even congratulating him on his engagement to be married. I took off my coat and sat down again.

'This proves that the photograph was not a one-off.' Nigel giggled. 'Mikin and the PM have been friendly for years. You go back through the PM's tweets and you find these have all been deleted. But they can't destroy the ones that were retweeted; they're indestructible. I did a search of all of the tweets of all of the prime minister's followers and I found these on the Twitter feeds of his followers from years ago. The prime minister and Mikin knew each other; these tweets prove it. And once Act Now! got started, someone tried to erase this history. They did a good job, but not good enough to stop the amazing Nigel.'

Nigel stood up and struck his best superhero pose.

'And this is inconvertible? Nobody can claim we've invented it, made it up?'

'Yep. I've laid a breadcrumb trail from the PM's personal Twitter feed from back then to every one of these personal messages from Mikin.' He paused, and puffed out his chest in pride. 'I was waiting till you asked me if

I'd found anything else out, but now you've said to me I should tell you without waiting. If you'd only said that earlier, then you could have gone "ha-ha, gotcha" to that nasty man when he was rude to you.' Nigel sat down, hooked his thumbs into his belt hooks, gave a satisfied grin and gently swayed in his seat.

I tried to conceal my exasperation.

'Well, I've learned a lot this morning, Nigel. And I think you have too. No more waiting to be asked in future. If you've got something important, you tell me straight away. Solemn promise?'

★ ★ ★

Once Nigel had fixed my computer, I started writing up what I had just found out. I was still feeling bruised by my appearance on *News Today* and kept the tone of the article as even and professional as possible. All I was proving was that the prime minister had a personal relationship with a senior Russian academic and political adviser going back many years, which he had attempted to deny and hide any traces of. Whether the relationship was more than a personal friendship, whether it had any political ramifications, I left for others to speculate. Sam was delighted when I gave the story to the *Chronicle*. After the *News Today* debacle it was obvious that he thought me damaged goods, and that the paper would be tainted by association. Now Damian Zane's taunt could be thrown back at him. He'd asked for evidence and now he'd got it.

Act Now! responded with an outright dismissal,

claiming that the prime minister had always been a popular guy and avid Twitter user, and couldn't be expected to remember every tweet that he'd ever responded to. The deletions from his feed were put down to an over-zealous junior aide deciding to tidy up his Twitter history a few years ago. Some people believed Act Now!'s version of events; for others I was the hero of the hour.

All this publicity meant that traffic to the Richard Foxe blog site had gone through the roof and I decided it was only fair that Nigel shared in the increase in site revenue. It wasn't part of the original deal, but he deserved it. I told him when I next visited his flat. I took along a poster of Benedict Cumberbatch and Martin Freeman as Sherlock Holmes and Dr Watson, as a thank-you for getting me out of the mess of the *News Today* programme and for making my computer safe. Nigel had told me he had watched every episode of the TV series over and over again. Holmes, a detective with remarkable powers of observation and memory and an ability to concentrate, someone who could link things in quite unique ways but was incapable of relating to people – he and Nigel, I couldn't help thinking, had much in common. I told Nigel I'd be his Dr Watson, and for the first time I thought I saw genuine emotion in his eyes as he looked at the poster and shot a quick glance at me.

'I'll put it up for you,' I told him. I surveyed the walls of his flat, every one of them painted white and completely bare. 'That is, if I can find somewhere to hang it.'

Nigel looked confused. 'You can hang it anywhere; there's nothing on any of the walls.' Then his face lit up with a grin. 'Oh. That was a joke, right? There's lots of space to hang it up, and you pretend there's not so that you can be funny? He-he-he-he.'

It was the first time I didn't find his laugh annoying.

chapter eight

I went back to my flat that evening and decided I couldn't put off clearing out the emails from my blogger inbox any longer. I had a 'Message Richard Foxe' button on the site which I was thinking of switching off, as it was getting flooded with trolls, crackpots and fantasists. Comments ranging from claims that I should rot in hell for what I was writing, through to hailing me as the saviour of humanity. Then there were the ones that claimed that what I was uncovering was a plot by alien lizard kings to colonise the planet. I always prided myself in responding to the messages I received, which had been very manageable when I used to get half a dozen messages a week, but now they were in the hundreds. I struggled to read through them all, never mind reply.

That's how I saw the message from Dmitry Vlasov. He ran a blog from Moscow in Russian and English, criticising the current regime. Didn't have much of a profile in the UK. I had only come across him by accident when I'd researched previous Richard Foxe stories a year or so ago. We'd never been in touch, so I was intrigued to see what he wanted to talk to me about.

The message was from yesterday.

You're onto the truth. You need to tell more. Can we talk?

Terse and intriguing. I looked at the email address and went to Dmitry's website to check it was from him. They matched.

I emailed straight back, sending it through the Tor node that Nigel had told me to use only for extra-sensitive communications.

When? How?

I could be terse too.

I almost missed his email the next day; it was from a different email address.

Dmitry here again. Hope you get this, I've no doubt my emails are being monitored, so I'm using another computer to reach you. Can we talk? Maybe eight o'clock this evening, your time?

It was a buzz, the thought of a clandestine chat with someone who really was caught up in political subterfuge. For all my success, I felt a bit of an imposter, someone who had inadvertently stumbled onto something rather than a real investigator.

Eight o'clock precisely, the call alert came up on my computer. As I pressed Accept I was feeling more than a little nervous. A blotchy-faced guy appeared on the screen, not even the faintest smile of a greeting.

'Dmitry, good to meet you. How are things in Moscow?' I winced at my banal intro.

'Good. We have first winter snow, like the make-up on an old whore. Hides the mess, make everything beautiful. But when it melts, Moscow will be ugly again.'

Best to ignore, I decided. 'So, Dmitry, it's an honour and surprise to hear from you. I first heard of you when you wrote about Litvinenko and I've been following your human rights articles.'

'Yes, I know. You are on my mailing list; I checked when I saw your story. I thought, this is a man who wants to talk about what Russian government is doing and is good at looking under the stones. Finally, someone talks about Mikin. If you want to know more, I can help you.'

'In what way?' I asked, keeping my voice as level as possible.

'Mikin is head of Kremlin's asymmetric warfare. He set up Act Now! and he's been feeding it money, power and influence ever since. Once he identified who should lead the party in every country, he made sure these people became very rich with dark money he found for them.' Dmitry's voice was devoid of any emotion.

His lip curled as he continued to talk. 'Mikin set up troll factories and botnets to turn people in the West against each other, to divide and destabilise. All the fake news that explodes like a dirty bomb across the internet, it's not from bored teenagers in Moldova trying to earn pocket money from clickbait. It is systemic. It is cognitive. It is the diplomacy of the future, and it is Russia's revenge for losing the Cold War. This time they don't use weapons, they use technology, to change the minds of your people so they vote the way Moscow wants. And it is working.'

I sucked in a quick breath. 'Wow, that is a hell of a claim, Dmitry. Have you got anything to back it up?' I leaned forward to peer at him on the screen, trying to see if I could tell from his face whether these were the ramblings of a lunatic.

He fixed me with a stare, as if he knew exactly what I was doing.

'You need to see for yourself. I have story here, but if I put on my blog, no one in the West listens. You listen, maybe a few hundred more around the world. Then next day my server get DDOSA, Distributed Denial of Service Attack, and my voice goes silent. I see it happen. Then there will be a knock on door. I get told problem with my taxes, now my life is trying to stay out of jail. I need someone in the West to say what I know, someone who has ears for what is happening. You start reading me many years ago, when Richard Foxe first appeared, but never get in touch. That makes me decide you are not someone who could be trap for me. I think if I show you the story, you tell it well.'

I leant back in my chair. It was a lot to take in, and if it weren't for the fact that I knew him to be a serious writer, I would have dismissed him as merely another attention seeker. People don't email you out of the blue and promise to hand over the scandal of the century. I was sceptical, but I also wanted to know more.

'You say you have the story? Then I promise I'll go through everything you send me very, very carefully. If it stacks up, then yes, I'd be interested in telling it. What can you send me?'

I could see Dmitry shaking his head, a wry smile on his face. 'No, Mr Foxe, this is too big a story for an email attachment. You want the story, then you come to Moscow. I show you places, take you to meet people. I hand you my files in person, no computer trail. You make it your story, not mine. The mysterious Richard Foxe. Safer for me that way.'

This was getting all too James Bond for my liking. I needed time to think.

'You … want me to come to Moscow? Can you not send me some initial stuff and then we can decide what to do next?'

There was a flash of anger in Dmitry's eyes. 'You sit there in London, nice and safe. I offer to give you a big story and to become more famous. I don't ask for money; I give you the story because Russia will only ever be free when the West knows the truth about us. And it too much trouble for you to come to Moscow to collect your prize? I find someone else.' He leaned forward to terminate the call.

'No wait, I didn't say I wasn't coming. I wanted to think through the logistics, that's all. If I come over, I want to be prepared. Can you give me twenty-four hours? We can talk tomorrow. I really appreciate what you're offering me, Dmitry; I want to make the most of it.'

'Okay, twenty-four hours. We talk same time tomorrow.'

'Eight o'clock tomorrow. I appreciate this, Dmitry, I won't let you down.'

Dmitry ended the call without replying.

I was way out of my depth and had no one to talk to. Sam at the *Chronicle* was an obvious choice, but the story would have more impact on TV. That meant *News Today*. They'd been pretty tough on me after the interview because I'd kept them in the dark about my previous life as an author, but the editor, Alex Richards, had checked me out. We had had a brief email correspondence and she saw that I had been telling the truth about my involvement in the Michael Mitchell scandal.

I emailed Alex. I said we had to talk urgently, and that I had a deadline for the next evening that I needed to discuss with her. Then, exhausted by the evening's events, I had a large scotch to settle my nerves and went for a good night's kip.

There was an email from Alex in my inbox when I woke, giving me her mobile number and asking me to call before her editorial meeting at ten. I was straight on the phone, trying to sound calm and professional. I took her through what Dmitry had said to me the day before. Made sure I didn't give her an inkling of who he was, referring to him as my 'Moscow contact'.

'And this guy is for real?' she asked when I'd finished. 'You can vouch for him?'

'I've never met him,' I replied. 'But he was one of the first bloggers I followed when I set up my own blog eight years ago. He seems like the real thing, genuinely wants to see change in Russia. Bit of a thorn in the side of the Russian government, but maybe too far down the food chain for them to do anything too heavy. And it looks like he wants to keep it that way. I guess that's why he contacted me.'

'I'm going into a meeting now. I'll discuss what you've told me with my senior staff, only in very broad terms, and I'll get back to you with a response early afternoon. Can you wait that long?'

I spent the next few hours frittering the morning away. I couldn't concentrate. I thought about calling Bobbie to talk about it, even Tanya, but decided against it. The fewer people that knew, the better.

Alex called around two.

'Okay, we're interested. Tell your source that you'll meet him in Moscow. We'll pay for the trip, and we'll send Simon Green along with you – our reporter who did the follow-up on your story. Once we see what this guy's got to offer, we'll take it from there.'

I knew when I was being railroaded. Simon Green was their star reporter, but rather too full of himself for my liking.

'That's not how I want to play it, Alex. This is my source, and it stays like that. If you're interested in the story, I'm happy to work with you as I develop it. But if I go to Moscow, I go alone.'

I waited for her reaction. If it had got *News Today* that interested, I was going to Moscow with or without their help.

I heard a sigh at the other end of the phone.

'I thought you might say that. You should say yes, Richard. This is serious stuff. Simon is an experienced hand at sensitive investigative political reporting. You need someone like him to make sure you don't miss the story, or even worse, get taken for a ride.'

'I appreciate that, Alex, but I don't want anyone else involved, at least not yet.'

'OK, if that's how you want it. In that case, we can't pay you any expenses and there's no fee unless we like what you bring back and agree to run with the story. Your choice.'

'It's the way I want to do it, Alex.'

'Come into the office before you go. Let's run through a few things we'd be looking for. And I'll give you some gear to take out with you. A simple broadcast-quality camera, for example, in case you can do an interview or something while you're out there. And a digital sound recorder. No point in going all the way out there and not being prepared.'

It was overwhelming, but I suppose she was only being practical. If this story was as big as it promised to be, I'd be stupid to miss any opportunities. I said yes, and that I'd call back once I talked to Dmitry.

I had to pinch myself. I would be getting on a plane to Moscow, armed with a TV station's audio and video recording devices, and I hardly knew what to expect. Where were these places Dmitry was going to take me to? Who were the people we were going to see? I was headed for secret meetings with a Russian dissident. Three months ago, I would never have believed it.

chapter nine

I was woken by the phone ringing in the bedroom of the Hilton Leningradsyaka. I blinked at the unfamiliar surroundings and reached out a hand to pick it up.

'Good morning, Meester Jones, this is Dasha on reception. Your eight o'clock wake-up call.'

A spike of adrenaline eliminated the three-hour time difference. I was about to meet my Russian informer. It had taken three days to get my visa. So far, all my expectations about Moscow had been confirmed: the long snaking queue to get through immigration; the haranguing by dodgy taxi drivers the minute I entered the airport terminal; the sense of relief when I saw a driver, courtesy of *News Today*, holding a card with my name. Last night, as I headed into the city, there was already deep snow in the birch forests lining the long straight road from the airport, making me wonder what the depths of winter would be like.

I had had my first glimpse of the outer suburbs as the evening light was failing. Tower block after tower block of grim-looking apartments – the dream and then the betrayal of the Communist utopia. Then into the city centre, the old buildings painted in pastel blues and yellows, the wealth of the inhabitants increasing with every kilometre.

The city roads got wider and wider, first four lanes, then six, finally eight. Billboards lined the route like a jostling crowd, every one of them a paean to conspicuous consumption, imploring me to buy the fastest cars, the latest mobile phone, the most expensive perfume. A brief respite as we circled the Kremlin, the rust-red walls of the former fortress giving me goosebumps as it brought back memories of my Cold War childhood. Finally, we arrived at the hotel, my breath sucked out of me by freezing air as I stepped out of the car. A gruff *'Proshchay!'* from the driver and he was off.

That was last night. Now I looked around, trying to get my bearings in the dawn light. The Hilton had been converted from one of Stalin's 'Seven Sisters' skyscrapers built in the 1930s, the others dotted randomly around the city, looking like Gothic spaceships dropped in from another planet. I wandered over to the window and looked down to the streets below, the traffic on the arterial roads spreading out in all directions from the hotel. I stared for a few seconds, trying to work out the way I had come in, watching the traffic edge through the massive intersection. It was strangely calming, like watching fish in an aquarium. I smiled to myself as I thought how it wouldn't be the same for the poor souls below, stuck in a traffic jam that seemed to go on forever until it faded into the distance through a diesel haze.

I showered and dressed, grabbed my rucksack and headed down to the restaurant. Dmitry had said he'd join me at nine. He arrived five minutes early, giving me the most perfunctory greeting, and we ordered breakfast. He was shorter than I had imagined, with a huge beer belly and a haircut that would have been fashionable on a Soviet engineer in the 1970s. He looked around the room with a mixture of irritation and suspicion.

'Lot of people,' he said to me. 'But should be okay. Did you choose the table?'

'No, the waitress did,' I replied. I presumed I had failed the first test of spy school.

'Let's move somewhere else. Just to be on safe side.'

We switched tables, much to the bemusement of our waitress, and Dmitry started talking, his voice deep and clipped. His breath reeked of tobacco and there was a faint undertone of last night's drinking.

'I tell you my story. I grew up member of Nashi, the Russian youth movement. Full of idealistic, patriotic young people. We'd go to summer camp and sit around the campfire every night, talking about how we were going to do good and rid Mother Russia of the evils within.'

'Bit like a political version of our boy scouts?' I ventured, trying to lighten the mood.

'Yes, at the beginning.' Dmitry spoke every word in a deep monotone. 'We did work in orphanages and old people's homes, helped restore churches and war memorials. Until political crisis and everything changed. We were told to break up fascist demonstrations, use violence if necessary. To prevent enemies of the state from overthrowing the constitution, they told us. Then enemies of the state became anyone who criticised what the state was doing.' Dmitry stared down at his hands. 'I joined as an idealist and ended up becoming part of a paramilitary force, a weapon of Kremlin, intimidating, bullying and harassing anyone our leaders told us to.'

'Scary.' I felt I should say something more, but didn't want to interrupt his flow.

'Scary?' He looked at me, his face a mixture of condescension and contempt. 'More than scary. I quit. Got on with my life. I was IT guy, so set up a digital advertising agency. Sexy new business, helping Western companies sell to our young Russians. But I never forgot how our country's rulers betrayed the Nashi ideals.' He pinched the bridge of his nose, eyes closed, then shrugged. 'I sold my business a few years ago, to the highest bidder. Made a lot of money, many Western advertising agencies wanted a piece of Russian pie, buying Russian company is the best way to get started. Now for three years, I run my blog, Storozhevaya Sobaka, making the West aware of how Russia is going to use technology to finally win the Cold War. But nobody listens.'

'I listen. I've been following you since you started.'

'Yes, I know. And I also look at your Richard Foxe blog. And when you run the story about Pavel Mikin, I say, here is the man who can be my voice to West.'

The restaurant was emptying now, the business clientele heading off for their meetings. Two burly men in ill-fitting suits came and sat down at the table next to us, despite almost two-thirds of the tables being free. I shot Dmitry a glance and gestured to the lobby. He nodded, I gulped down a last mouthful of scrambled egg, picked up my coffee and left.

We sat down at a corner table. I looked over at the restaurant. The two men were tucking into their breakfasts, oblivious to us moving away. I felt ridiculous at my paranoia.

'So, what do you want to tell me?' I asked.

'I know the power of technology from my digital advertising days. With power comes responsibility to use it right. But what we are doing in Russia is evil. We come up with fake news, use troll factories and botnets to spread it across the media. We game the algorithms to make sure fake stories get to the people who will be influenced by them.' Dmitry muttered a few words in Russian under his breath. 'Every story is one more nudge to make people think the way we want them to think. We do tactical stuff as well, running DDOSAs during elections. I told you about them when we talked. Distributed Denial of Service Attacks, when you suddenly find yourself locked out of the internet. Used to bring down the opposition's internet campaigns at crucial times during elections. Now Russia has set up political parties in the West, making sure they have unlimited money. And unlimited access to their opponents' secrets.'

'There's only circumstantial evidence. Everything is being denied. But if you can show me Russia is doing all this, that it is making Act Now! even stronger, then it helps me build my case.'

Dmitry smiled. 'That is why I invite you here. What I show you today will be enough to make people take notice, start to ask questions. That is, my friend, if you do your job right.'

I took a sip of my coffee. I wasn't sure if that was a dig or not, so I decided to ignore it.

'What do you want to show me?'

'This time in Moscow, I show you two things. How Russian government finds out political secrets that will

105

help Act Now! – and how they run propaganda campaign in your media.'

Now it was my turn to keep emotions in check. I didn't want to look too eager. Dmitry brought out a lever arch file and placed it on the table. 'This is the file I told you about.'

I picked it up, holding it at arm's length like it was going to bite. 'What is it?'

'It is printout of code for pages of a website. A website that exactly mimics the official site of Act Now!'s main opposition. It is the same in every detail, except for a few pages that contain links to Trojan viruses. If they want access to someone's computer, that person gets an email that looks like it is from someone they know, with a message containing a link to a page on the political website that they might be interested in.'

'I know about these,' I replied. 'Except the email is fake, and when they go to the page and click on the article, it puts a virus into their computer which allows the Russian IT specialists to take control, look into any file they want to. And once the virus is in the computer, it embeds itself in any email attachment the infected computer sends out so they can take over all the recipients' computers too. Then after twenty-four hours, the virus self-destructs, wipes itself clean, leaving no trace. The hackers have had that time to look for any incriminating or sensitive files and the people targeted will never know.' I tried to sound like an expert on what Nigel had told me just a few days ago.

Dmitry looked impressed. 'It is good to see I am not dealing with an amateur.'

I sneaked a quick look at the file, like a poker player checking the final card he'd been dealt.

'Looks very technical. But the contents could easily be fabricated. How do you know someone didn't just type this up and give it to you?'

'Because one of the programmers, he took a big personal risk to give it to me. And he knows a back-door code – a username and password – that would let your IT experts into the site to see it is a real site, that this file is no fake. I send you the code when you are back in UK. And my guy, he then closes the door behind you, so no one will know you've been inside. Do you have on your team IT guy and someone who reads Russian?'

I wasn't sure how big an operation Dmitry thought I had behind me. I had Nigel, and presumed he was up to this. Someone who understood Russian would be easy to find in London. I said yes with my fingers crossed. If all else failed, I could let *News Today* in on it and lose my exclusivity. But I couldn't miss the opportunity.

'Good. You get things set up to go in around three in the morning Moscow time when you are ready. They can have half an hour before they have to log out and my guy covers their traces. Should give enough time for screenshots and checking. Let me know the time when you get back to London.'

'Can I talk to your guy? I need to know he's genuine. If we're going to have people believe us, I need proof this is not something he's made up.'

Dmitry pulled the folder from me. 'You think I bring you to Moscow to play fucking games? When you see this website, you will see that only Russian government could do something this big. This not a little hacker in a bedroom. This is serious. I thought you a serious man. Maybe I was wrong.' His eyes had lost the rheumy glaze they had when he arrived. Now they were cold and hard.

'No, I believe you. I want to make sure others do too.' My voice croaked from the stress. I took a sip of water. 'I trust you, Dmitry.'

He relaxed his grip on the folder and put it down on the table between us with a sarcastic smile.

'"*Doveryai, no proverai.*" "Trust, but verify." Old Russian proverb Reagan used with Gorbachev. Don't worry, my friend. By the end of your visit, you will have all the proof you need. For that, we go for a little journey. Have you ever been to a troll factory?'

'N-no, not recently, no.'

'Then I take you to one on outskirts of Moscow. Two hours from here, maybe longer if traffic is bad. I show you the outside of building, explain how it works. Then we meet someone who works inside the troll factory. They tell you their story, but they are not as idealistic as me. They want *vzytka*, a little money for their help. That is Russian way.'

I hesitated over whether to bring up my suspicions again. 'How much are they talking about? I need to know a little bit more before I agree.'

'Fifty thousand roubles. Guy we meet, he worked in troll factory. He needs a new job, and he needs money. He says he tells you story for money. Me, I think he is crazy. But if he wants to do this, then he does this. I show you outside of the factory, see what you think. Then if you want to meet, I call him. He lives nearby.'

Fifty thousand roubles was around six hundred pounds, I calculated. The trip had already cost me two grand. This could be a shake-down, but it would be worth the gamble.

'What does a troll factory look like?'

'Troll factory is where trolls work, setting up false email accounts, flooding the fake news with likes, upvotes and shares. And Sergey, the one you meet, he knows Russian trolls in England, the ones who write the news. You can make visit to them when you go home.'

'There are Russian troll factories in Britain? Wouldn't we have noticed?'

'Not a big building like I show you. You think Russian geeks can write posts that sound like English English? They find some native English speakers in your country, looking for some money, give them story idea. Then they write the post in – what do they call it? – millennial vernacular.' Dmitry smiled again, as if to congratulate himself on his English. 'Then, when the news is dropped into filter bubble, it sounds like everyone else in the bubble. There are lots of people working at fake news for Russia in your country. Sergey knows only their emails and usernames. But some not too smart, use work emails or emails with their own website address. So easy to find them and ask them their story.'

'This is what I came for. Shall we go? How do we get there?'

'My car is outside.'

If I thought the traffic was terrible coming from the airport the night before, the trip out to the troll factory was even worse. Dmitry's black Range Rover was like a tank, ploughing through a seemingly interminable traffic jam. It should have made the journey less of an ordeal, but once out of the hotel, Dmitry lit his first cigarette, opening the driver window a centimetre as his concession to my comfort. He chain-smoked all the way to our destination. By the time we arrived I was nauseous, my head spinning with the smoke. I stepped out of the car into the fresh air, resisting the urge to retch after my two-hour ordeal.

We stood across from a dreary-looking factory.

'Used to make carpets,' Dmitry explained. 'Now inside it is full of desks and computers. Two hundred people work there, maybe more. All young people. We wait so you can see.'

Dmitry went back to his car and got inside. I walked round to the passenger door and opened it to talk to him. 'I'll stay outside if you don't mind. The cigarette smoke's making me feel a bit sick.'

Dmitry shrugged, the thought that he might be considerate and abstain for a little while apparently not occurring to him. I stood out on the street, hands in pockets and collar turned up to keep out the cold. After ten minutes, I knocked on the window. Dmitry lowered it, letting some of the blue fug escape.

'What exactly are we waiting for?' I asked.

'That,' he said, pointing up the road. 'People coming to work. They will need to show security pass to get through the turnstile, have their bags checked before they go inside. Too big security for a normal factory.'

I watched as two spotty youths with pudding-bowl haircuts walked down the street and up to the factory. I surreptitiously videoed their arrival and captured five other geeky-looking guys leaving. I slipped my camera back in my rucksack and waited for more to happen. After five minutes, my feet were going numb with the cold. I'd had enough.

'This isn't achieving much, Dmitry. If all we're going to do is stand here watching people going in and out of a factory gate, I don't think that proves anything about what is going on in there. Let's go and meet the guy who wants to talk to me. Oh, and would you mind not smoking till we get there? I really am feeling unwell.'

Dmitry ignored my tetchiness as he took out his phone and made a call.

'Okay, it is ten minutes away,' he said once he hung up. 'You have money?'

I nodded. I'd taken the extra I needed from the hotel ATM before we'd left. I could see now why Dmitry drove a four-wheel drive car. The potholes on the road were the size of craters. The vehicle lurched from side to side, competing with the cigarette smoke to see what would make me throw up first.

After closer to twenty minutes than ten, we pulled up outside a grim, grey tower block, like the ones I'd seen on my drive in from the airport. Graffiti everywhere, rubbish blowing about in the street.

'We go here,' said Dmitry, fishing in the back of his car for a yellow crook lock. He secured the steering wheel and got out of the car. 'Rough neighbourhood,' he said, somewhat unnecessarily.

I was desperate for fresh air, but the smell of decaying rubbish was not much of an improvement. We stepped inside the hallway, the smell of dank cabbage clinging to me like a rash. If anything, the amount of graffiti had increased. We waited as the lift wheezed and rattled its way down to us. It arrived and the doors started to open, greeting us with the stench of urine. The doors stopped halfway and closed again. On the second attempt, the doors fully opened.

'Can we not walk?" I asked.

'Thirteenth floor. Don't worry; you'll be safe. Good solid Russian engineering.'

I presumed he was being ironic.

Dmitry pressed the lift button, which was encrusted with God knows what. Every button had a scorched halo charred into the metal around it, giving some indication of the state of the wiring beneath. I literally and figuratively held my breath until I stepped out onto the thirteenth floor, one long gloomy corridor with two rows of identical doors facing each other, each one only ten metres from the next. A mass of humanity crammed into a proletarian dumping ground, living a drab and cheerless existence. We stopped at the third door down. Dmitry knocked, and I forced myself to look positive.

The door opened and a beanpole of a man greeted us. '*Dobra den*. You must be Richard. I am Sergey. Come inside.'

His apartment was in marked contrast to the dreariness outside. Surprisingly tasteful, colour-coordinated furnishings, art house movie posters on the wall. I perched myself on the edge of a chair; Dmitry sat across from me. Sergey wandered over to a kitchenette in the corner of the room.

'Coffee? *Chai*?'

We both declined.

He returned with some tea he had made for himself from a small samovar sitting on his work surface.

'So, Dmitry tells me you are famous English journalist.' He stared at me, like he was looking at a specimen under a microscope.

'Scottish, actually. I want to know all about what goes on in the old carpet factory on Vladirskaya Street. Dmitry told me you used to work there.'

'And did he tell you something else?'

I looked blank for a second, then remembered the wad of cash in the hotel envelope.

'Ah, yes, he did. Here you are, fifty thousand roubles. It's all there.'

Sergey took the cash, slipped it in a drawer without counting it and sat down on the third chair in the room. He ran a jerky hand through his hair.

'So, what exactly do you want to know?'

'Just a moment,' I replied. I took the video camera out of my rucksack. 'If you don't mind, I'd like to record this in case I forget something.'

Sergey shot a glance at Dmitry and then at me.

'No camera,' he said. 'Not part of the deal.'

News Today had told me how to deal with this. 'Let me put it on a tripod on the shelf behind you. It will point at me, only show the back of your head. That way you won't be recognised.'

'No, I'm sorry. Much too dangerous.'

'If I ever need to use this footage, I'll make sure that an actor voices the words you say and we pixelate any features that could identify you. You can trust me on that.'

'They could identify the room we are in. Or you could forget your promise when you are back in London. I am taking big risk.'

'I completely understand,' I said. 'In your position, I would be just as careful. If we take down the posters on the wall behind me it will be a blank wall, nothing to identify where we are. And you don't have to worry about me forgetting to protect you. I promise I will. Not only because I owe it to you personally, but also to protect my sources. If people who talked to me got into trouble, I wouldn't be able to do my job. I wouldn't ask you to do anything I considered risky.'

I could hardly believe I was saying this. I had no idea whether this would lead to Sergey being found out or not, and I was talking like an old hand, a world-weary, hard-bitten journalist bloodied by experience, rather than the complete neophyte I actually was.

'Only if I get to see the video at the end, make sure of that,' he said eventually.

I tried to hide my astonishment that my duplicity had worked. I placed the camera and sat down on the chair, from where I could see the red light of the camera over Sergey's shoulder.

'Have a quick look through the viewfinder to make sure you're happy with what I'm showing,' I said.

He looked through the lens and moved the camera an inch or two.

'Is that okay?' he asked.

'Of course,' I said, without checking. I just wanted this to be over. I settled down to start the interview. 'So, tell me a little about yourself.'

'I studied journalism in the city of Perm, came to Moscow two years ago, looking for a job. After a month of doors slammed in my face, I got a phone call asking me to come for interview. Very strange call, not from head-hunters, and not for any job I had applied for. Went along to Vladirskaya Street, waited in reception area inside. Cameras everywhere on the walls, lots of security men in uniforms. And they looked professional, not like the usual big *okrannik* guy you would see outside offices. My interview was short, all they asked about was my background, who are my parents, brothers, sisters, all the places I lived. A big test of my English language skills. Next day I was told I'd got the job.'

Sergey had become more and more animated as he talked and I noticed he was now blocking the camera from seeing me. I shifted the chair, had a surreptitious glance to check I could see the red light again. I smiled a reassurance. 'And what exactly was your job?'

'I sat in an open-plan room; desks crammed together, you could see everything that everyone else was typing. There were sixty, maybe eighty of us there, all young, early twenties. Our job was to set up email accounts in the West, our location hidden by proxy servers. We were to join social media groups, make comments on news articles, set up blog accounts. Write twenty articles a day; make fifty posts; the same number of likes and shares; all saying positive things about this Act Now! party in UK. There was a central database of stories we were to use, some directions on the opinions we were to express and then we were told to get on with it.'

'Do you know who was behind this? Could it have been your government?'

'I don't see who else it could have been. This was only one part of the operation, and it was huge. The office was separated by partitions. Once you had been there a few months, had some experience, you could go to the second group. There, you had to find people in UK you could groom to help you, use them to find new groups to join, even find some to write this stuff from inside the UK, if the bosses thought they could be trusted.'

I leant back in my seat. 'Couldn't it have been a wealthy benefactor who wanted Act Now! to succeed? Lots of political parties play dirty tricks to win elections.'

'But why have the operation in Russia? The paymaster has to be part of Russian establishment. Maybe some oligarch wanting to have influence, but why go to so much trouble?'

I shrugged. 'People can go to great lengths to get what they want. Was everything you did to support Act Now!?'

'Yes. Every article was sent to supervisors for checking before you posted it. They measured everything, how much you wrote, how many people responded to it. If you fell behind what everyone else was doing, you were fired. And if you turned out to be a superstar you got selected for the *elitnyy klass*, the elite. They were in another part of the building, with even heavier security, their own entrance out to the street. That was where Igor worked.'

'Igor?'

'Igor is my friend. My boyfriend.'

I nodded.

'I can see you are not Russian,' Sergey said, smiling for the first time. 'Russian men are not so relaxed about gay relationships. I met Igor in a bar near here, we find we both worked as part of the operation, but he had moved to the *elitnyy klass*, so I never saw him at work. But he told me what he did there.'

'And that was?'

Dmitry chose this moment to light up a cigarette. I looked sideways at him, careful not to interrupt Sergey's flow. Sergey leaned over and handed him an ashtray.

'The *elitnyy klass* were in big league. There's a parallel operation in St Petersburg. There they build fake websites to get inside computers of Act Now! opponents. Once they do so, Igor and the other *elitnyy klass* get to work.'

'The people in St Petersburg. They build fake websites to get you past firewalls?'

'Yes. Then once someone's computer is hacked the *elitnyy klass* guys go through their files, looking for useful information. But Igor's job was especially creative.' There was a gleam in Sergey's eye for a second. 'Igor's job was to watch and wait, look at all the emails someone was sending and receiving. Practise becoming these people, writing like them, talking about the things they talked about. And once his bosses were satisfied he could pull it off, he would start corresponding as them with other parts of their political organisation, using a false email address that was only slightly different from the real one. Draw people into making incriminating statements, incite them to do something dodgy we could later expose, spread confusion and disinformation. Then delete the false emails that started it all, so that all that was left was the incriminating evidence. You needed to be an artist to pull it off, and Igor was one of the best.'

'Was? Does he not work there anymore?'

Sergey's face had a pinched expression. 'Someone found out about the two of us. I thought where I was working was new Russia, where no one cared whether you were gay or straight. But some things never change. We were a security risk, they told Igor. Kicked him out of *elitnyy klass*, had him back in the main building, writing shitty blog posts all day. Me, they fired the same day they found out. So now I am back to finding a job again. I need the money you gave me. I'm not proud of that, and I'm not proud of being part of that *shrashkina kontora*, that con operation. But I need to eat.'

'I'm sorry,' I said. I meant it. Despite my initial disquiet at Sergey demanding payment, he seemed genuine enough. We talked for another ten minutes while Sergey told me more details of the operation he used to be part of. He could describe everything, and never contradicted himself. Either this was an elaborate hoax that he had pulled off, inventing and then remembering every piece of minutia, or it was real. As best I could tell, he believed what he was saying to me.

Finally, I ran out of questions. I stopped filming and the three of us played back the interview, Sergey chewing on his fingernails as he watched. When it finished, he gave a resigned nod.

I wished him good luck with his job search and got ready to leave. Then, trying hard to sound casual, I said, 'Would you speak to Igor for me? I'd love to hear his description of *elitnyy klass*, now that he doesn't work in that department. I could pay more, maybe even two hundred thousand roubles, for his side of the story.' I was being rash, but if he said yes, I was sure it would be worth it. 'Might give the two of you the money to find a breathing space to try something new.' I felt like shit.

Sergey's gaze ping-ponged between Dmitry and me.

'If he spoke to you,' he said, 'it would be even more dangerous. But I will ask him. He's disgusted by his job, hates them for what they did to us. We both want to start a new life, away from this *shrashkina kontora*. Your money would help. I'll ask him. If he says yes, I'll tell you his price.'

'I go back to London tomorrow evening. Can you find out today and let me know? If he agrees, I can meet him before I go.'

Sergey agreed to try. We said our goodbyes and headed off to the lift. The grimy corridor compounded my feeling of revulsion at what I was doing. Inveigling first Sergey, now Igor, to be so foolhardy as to agree to be interviewed. I promised myself that whatever I did with this information, I'd keep it as discreet as possible.

Dmitry seemed pleased with what Sergey had told me and laughed when I said how uncomfortable I had felt about talking him into doing the interview.

'Old Russian proverb,' he said. '"If you are afraid of wolves, don't go into the forest."' He sounded upbeat, almost chummy, like I'd passed some test. 'Tonight, I was going to show you fun side of Moscow, take you to drink best Siberian vodka. But my little girl is sick, and I need to be home with my wife to look after her. We do it next time. I will tell you when I hear from Sergey. If you meet with him tomorrow, great. If not, I find you someone else to talk to.'

I climbed into Dmitry's car and prepared for my kippering on the gruelling trip back to the hotel. We had just set off when I spotted a red Metro sign at a crossroads.

'If you have to be home, I can take the Metro?'

Dmitry looked over. 'Yes, Strogino station. But tricky for you, I think?'

'I'm sure it will be okay. I saw there was a station close to the hotel. Point me in the right direction and I'll be fine.'

'Okay. You brave. Take this line to Ploshchad Revolyutsii, then change to the red line and get off at Komsomolskaya. Your hotel will be front of you when you exit. Are you sure?'

Dmitry helped me buy a ticket and I set off on my adventure. The escalator took me deep underground, far deeper than in London. I stood on the platform and stared at the map on the wall, the station names in both Latin and Cyrillic alphabet. I could see why it had taken us so long to get here; my hotel was on the other side of Moscow. A rush of air and then, with an ear-splitting roar, the train appeared, row after row of massive rectangular steel carriages. I got on and stood in the carriageway. A pair of sullen babushkas sat on the seats across from me clutching heavy-looking plastic bags. A bored teenager sat next to them, flicking through a tawdry gossip magazine.

The train shot off with tremendous acceleration, almost throwing me off balance. I flung myself onto one of the hard plastic seats – just in time, because suddenly there was an equally tremendous deceleration as we burst into the next station. I peered outside to check the station name, but couldn't see any signs. Then we were off again, the announcement saying something in Russian which I thought included the name of the next station, Molodyozhnaya. Bloody long names. I had to calibrate as we arrived at each station, trying to figure out where I had to change. The train got busier as we headed into the centre of Moscow, the regular passengers seemingly unperturbed by the rollercoaster ride, taking it all in their stride, like old seafarers riding the storms with their sea legs and stoic resignation.

At Ploshchad Revolyutsii there was a massive exodus, and I found myself on the platform waiting for the crowd to clear, looking for the red line signs. Nothing. I headed up the nearest short flight of stairs and into a long corridor. Breathtaking. Red and yellow marble arches resting on low plinths, each faced with a contrasting stone. Every arch flanked by a pair of huge bronze sculptures: soldiers, farmers, industrial workers. I'd heard about these Moscow Metro stations and it was surreal to finally stumble across one of them purely by chance. I dawdled along, only half-looking for my train. There were arches and statues everywhere, fifty or sixty at least, an incongruous backdrop to the swelling crowds hurrying past them without a glance as the early evening rush hour got underway.

Finally, I found what I thought was a sign for the red line, only to end up back on the same platform I had disembarked on ten minutes before. Fewer statues and a few more signs would be helpful. I cursed inwardly and tried again, climbing the stairs, concentrating this time. A two-minute walk and I was at the red line platform as the roar of a train announced its arrival. Then I was on my noisy, rattling way to Komsomolskaya.

Just as Dmitry had promised, the huge Gothic tower of the Hilton loomed ahead of me when I exited the station, like something out of *Ghostbusters*. I walked up to the hotel, ridiculously smug that I'd managed to navigate myself back safely. I decided to head up to my room, write up some notes and wait to find out what the score was going to be about meeting up with Sergey's boyfriend. If it was going ahead, then I'd have to check with Alex at *News Today* that it was okay to be paying whatever he said his price would be. The Metro had helped me put some distance between myself and the tawdriness I had felt earlier when talking to Sergey. Moscow was a tough city, and people here did tougher things than that to survive.

I couldn't find my key card so I went to the desk to get a new one, the receptionist giving me that slightly unsettling lascivious grin that young Russian women have, the one that comes with full eye contact. I showed her my passport and she made me a new card. 'Here you are,' she said, making it sound like she'd be right behind me in five minutes. 'And you have a letter waiting for you.' She handed an envelope to me and flashed that come-hither smile again, like we were sharing some intimate confidence.

That put an abrupt end to my musings. No one in Moscow knew I was here except Dmitry and Sergey, and I had just said goodbye to them. I managed a strangled 'Thank you' as I took the envelope, walked over to a lobby chair, sat down and opened it.

A plane ticket, made out in my real name. Business class on the next flight back to London. I turned the ticket over, then looked inside the envelope. No message, but it could not have been clearer. Someone knew who I really was, knew I was in Moscow and wanted me gone.

I sat there, gasping for air. For a few stupid seconds, I thought it was a prank, maybe a test of some sort by Dmitry. But that didn't make sense. I looked at the ticket again; the flight was in three hours. Being brave enough to ignore the warning didn't enter into my thinking even for a second. I went back to the receptionist, her Slavic charm now irritating rather than endearing.

'There's been a change of plan,' I said. 'I have to return to London. Can I get a taxi to Sheremetyevo airport?'

'Certainly, sir,' she replied. 'Straight away?' Ashen-faced guests being issued with death threats were apparently a regular occurrence.

'Yes, please. My flight is in three hours, will that be okay?' Without waiting for an answer, I added, 'I'm going up to my room to pack. Can you have the car ready to leave when I get back?'

'Yes, of course. You will have to be quick. It will take maybe two hours to get there in traffic.'

I ran off, cursing myself for dawdling in the Metro. What did I think this was, a sightseeing trip? I bundled everything into my rucksack and was about to head back downstairs when I thought of Dmitry and Sergey. If this was happening to me, things could be even worse for them. I looked at my watch to decide whether I had time to call now or do it in the car. One quick call, I promised myself.

I dialled Dmitry's number. He answered and I heard a baby screaming in the background. 'Dmitry, I need to be quick. I'm heading back to London straight away, the next flight home.' He started to speak, but I talked over him. 'No, please don't interrupt. I've got to rush if I'm to make the plane. Someone knows I'm here and has made it clear I'm not welcome. That means they also know about you. And you've got to get in touch with Sergey, warn him, I don't have his number. Can you do that?'

Dmitry started demanding more information but I had to be curt. 'I'll call if I've got time when I get to the airport,' I said, ignoring his questions. 'Look after yourself, Dmitry, and make sure you call Sergey. I've got to go now.' I hung up and switched off my phone.

The receptionists were all serving other guests and I waited to be checked out, shifting from foot to foot. Finally, I was in the car and off to the airport. My driver couldn't speak any English and I kept staring out of the window, looking for landmarks I might recognise from the journey in. I willed the car to get through every light, prayed for every traffic jam to clear. We turned onto a motorway with an airport sign – I could just about decipher 'Sheremetyevo' from the Cyrillic. I looked at my watch. An hour and a half till departure. I might just make it.

I sank back into the seat and started to breathe normally for the first time. My rucksack was lying next to me on the back seat and I decided to organise the contents and get my passport ready, to save time at the airport. I opened up the bag and stared in horror. There, in the zipped compartment of the bag, was the folder that Dmitry had given me at breakfast. In my rush to get off to the airport, I had completely forgotten about it.

I stared at it as like it was an unexploded bomb. What to do? We were tearing along the motorway; there would be nowhere to stop until we got to the airport. Besides, if I chucked it into a rubbish bin I was throwing away my story and any chance of future cooperation from Dmitry. I gingerly opened it, looked at the incomprehensible computer code, a mix of Cyrillic Russian and English computer terms. I hadn't felt so scared since that day I helped Bobbie pack up her flat and escape down to London. Whoever gave me this ticket expected me on that flight and they would surely be waiting for me at the airport to get their hands on anything incriminating I had picked up while in Moscow.

I stepped out of the taxi with twenty minutes to go before the flight closed. I walked up to the BA desk still unsure of what to do.

'Anything to check in?' I heard the guy say, distant in the red mist of panic that was enveloping me. Suddenly, I realised what to do.

'Yes, this bag.' My rucksack was tagged and I watched it move down the conveyor. No one stopped it as it disappeared through the wall and into the baggage area. Unless someone was standing on the other side of the entrance, the only way to get to the bag would be to delay the flight while they searched for it. And if that happened, good luck to them. They could have the contents of the bag without having to confront me. If the rucksack wasn't there when I got back to London, the evidence would be gone. But I had no choice.

I arrived at the gate. Boarding was almost finished. I had a few minutes to call Dmitry back. I switched on my phone, noticed two missed calls from him and two voicemail messages. No time to listen to them. I called Dmitry and he picked up straight away.

'Richard, what's going on?' Dmitry sounded more annoyed than scared. 'You sounded like a madman.'

I told him about the plane ticket and that I was at the gate, ready to board.

'Did you get hold of Sergey?' I asked, full of trepidation.

'Phone switched off, no voicemail. But that is normal for Russians, voicemail expensive. I'll text him now I have the full picture.'

I could sense the resentment in his voice that in my panic it had taken me this long to call him. I flushed with embarrassment at my cowardice as I noticed that the last passenger had boarded. The boarding staff beckoned me to come over. I gestured I'd be one more minute and replied to Dmitry.

'Keep trying. He's in danger. I should never have agreed to this. I've taken advantage of his problems and if anything happens to him I'll never forgive myself.' An image flashed into my mind of Sergey being bundled into the back of a police van, a look of terror on his face. 'And you, Dmitry, what are you going to do?'

He gave a throaty chuckle. 'You are Moscow virgin, my friend. Don't worry; I am not on my way to gulag. That is only for big fish these days. Russian government says everything I say is lies, don't you remember? No one listens to me and they know to keep it that way, it is best to ignore me. If I disappear, my friends make noise.

But little Sergey, yes, for him I worry. I tell you what I find.'

The boarding staff were becoming more and more insistent that I go through, so I said goodbye and got on the plane. Cocooned in the Britishness of the environment and sitting in unaccustomed luxury at the front of the plane felt completely incongruous. I was four rows from the cabin door and I didn't take my eyes off it, waiting for the appearance of the authorities to arrest me, or worse. Then came the captain's announcement that we were delayed thirty minutes because of air traffic delays. My paranoia convinced me they were after my bag and the incriminating evidence inside it.

The plane started taxiing out to the runway, stopping in a holding bay a few minutes later. That was a good sign, I convinced myself. If I was to be bundled off the plane or my rucksack confiscated, they would surely have done that before we left the gate.

I peered over the shoulder of the guy sitting next to me. I saw a yellow flashing light and strained to see what it was. My neighbour was getting irritated with me, but didn't offer to swap seats. Whatever the flashing light was, it disappeared back to the terminal building, then outside was only darkness.

When the plane took off, I almost felt like crying, the release of tension was so great. My eyes never left the flight tracker; I knew roughly where the national boundary was and I wasn't going to fully relax until we had left Russian airspace. Each time the map refreshed there was a shiver of adrenaline that the plane had moved closer to safety. I told myself I was being ridiculous, that turning around a British Airways plane in mid-flight would be an international incident. And I was right. We landed at Heathrow and there was my rucksack on the carousel, nothing touched.

There was a text from Dmitry, telling me there was still no news about Sergey. I texted back saying I'd arrived in the UK and would call tomorrow.

Someone wanted me out of Moscow, and they wanted me scared stiff. They had succeeded on both counts.

chapter ten

I was too scared to go back to my flat that night, so checked into an anonymous motel near the airport. When I woke in the morning, there was still a sickening dread in the pit of my stomach. I had got myself into something that was turning out to be much more serious than I could have ever imagined. Yes, the story I was investigating was a dramatic one. But piecing it together had been like a puzzle, something abstract that didn't have any real-life implications. Now someone had threatened me. Someone who was powerful enough not only to know that I'd gone to Moscow, but also what I was doing there, even what hotel I was staying at. The only people who knew were *News Today*. But why would they compromise a source?

I forced myself to structure my thoughts. There were three things that I had to worry about: the safety of Dmitry and Sergey; whether I could trust *News Today* anymore; and the folder that Dmitry had given me.

There was nothing I could do about the first; I had warned Dmitry and had no way of getting in touch with Sergey directly. As far as the second was concerned, if someone at *News Today* was a mole for Act Now! I needed to be very careful what I told Alex. I couldn't hand over the video of my interview with Sergey. Someone could make a copy and give it to the Russians to identify him from his voice or from something he said that needed to be edited out. And if I handed over the folder, the same could happen; a copy would allow the Russians to take down the site and cover their tracks before the story broke, maybe even identify who it was that had given it to Dmitry. I could tell *News Today* I'd come back empty-handed and publish the story on my blog, but then the story would never have the impact it needed to become a major scandal.

Alex thought I was still in Russia, so I reckoned I had a day's grace before I had to hand over whatever I thought was safe. I had to give her something. If I held back on my story and it appeared elsewhere, she'd never work with me again. But I couldn't take the risk that I might endanger the people who helped me.

I decided. Nigel must know a way to make an audio copy of the video interview and put a voice disguise on it. I'd say that my informant only agreed to audio and had put the voice distortion on it before I left Moscow and kept the original. I'd tell them everything that Dmitry told me, but not hand over the file. *News Today* would still have the story, but not the raw intelligence behind it.

That left working out what was in the folder. Another job for Nigel, but everything was in Russian. I could either find someone to translate it for me or I could go to Tanya. That would be a shitty thing to do; I'd already involved her far more than she deserved. But finding a translator, that was also a risk.

In the end, I decided it needed to be Tanya, at least to get started. I'd ask her to have a quick look, to give me the gist of what it was saying and then help Nigel navigate around the website.

I texted Tanya and asked if I could see her, very important and urgent. Got a reply saying it was a busy day, but we could have a quick meeting at lunchtime. I called Nigel, telling him I was heading out to his flat and what I needed him to do. Before I left, I decided to contact Dmitry and see if there was any news about Sergey. He said he'd call me back from a different phone. I used to think all these precautions were a bit over the top; now I was convinced otherwise.

I accepted a video call from an unknown number, said hi to Dmitry and went over the story of the plane ticket again. I could hear the consternation in his voice and was annoyed with myself for being so wrapped up in concerns for my own safety. I was two thousand miles from whoever was threatening me.

I told him of my suspicions that *News Today* had leaked my investigation to someone in Russia, and that I was going to be very careful what I shared with them. He told me there was still nothing from Sergey and he was starting to get worried.

'So, what do you want to do?' I asked. 'I've still got the document you gave me. No one tried to take it off me at the airport. If you want me to, I'll destroy it and won't print a word about what I found out.'

I willed him to say yes. It would make it a whole lot easier for me to walk away from this if I did it to protect the safety of someone who had trusted and confided in me. But he didn't.

'It couldn't have been the FSB that left you that plane

ticket. They would have been at the airport waiting for you, confiscated the folder, your computer and everything else you had. And if the Russian government didn't want you in Moscow, they would have refused your visa or deported you once you arrived. No, it must have been an individual, most likely an oligarch who didn't want you screwing up some business deal they'd arranged through Act Now!. That does suggest there's a person at your TV station who is in the pocket of someone powerful who wants to scare you off the story. And if they know about you, they know about me. But if they'd wanted me silenced, I wouldn't be talking to you now. I've got nothing to lose. I've had threats hanging over my head for years. If you want to go ahead, go ahead.'

Damn.

'Well, I'm not going to trust *News Today* again until we get to the bottom of the leak. I'll give them enough to run the story, a disguised audio file of my interview with Sergey and everything you told me, but not the folder on the bogus website. That is, if you are okay with that.'

'"He who does not risk will never drink champagne."' Old Russian proverb. I am a known troublemaker here in Moscow. One more piece of bad behaviour will make no difference.'

'Okay then, here's what I'll do. It's going to take a while to fully understand what's in that folder you gave me. We'll go in the back door tonight at midnight UK time, the middle of the night in Moscow. And if we find anything, I'll give the story to my old newspaper. I've known the editor there for years, and if the Russians have got their tentacles into every media outlet in Britain, we may as well give up now. *News Today* will be furious, but I can say that I uncovered it after my Moscow trip, so felt it was a different story, not covered by the scope of our agreement.'

'*Da*. Okay.'

'I'll get the audio file made now. Let me know if you hear anything from Sergey.'

'I am going to drive out to his flat right now to find out what is going on,' replied Dmitry. 'Good luck, Mr Richard Foxe, you have been making people upset with your investigating. I send you text now, with username and password I promised you. This phone number is still secret, I hope.'

There had been two messages on my voicemail from Alex already. I couldn't put off contacting her much longer. I texted her back, saying I needed to clarify something before we talked and then headed off to Nigel's. If I was quick, I could be back in time to meet Tanya for lunch. Then I needed some time to collect my thoughts.

I took Nigel through the events in Moscow. I thought he was going to spin himself dizzy when I explained about the plane ticket and my tension-filled flight back to London. He'd already set things up to do the voice change and I handed him the video file.

'What voice do you want?' he asked. 'I've chosen Cyborg Warrior, but Cave Troll is also pretty cool.'

I looked down the choice of voices on offer. Golem, Zombie Man, Orc, Half-Orc, the list was endless. I was obviously in super-geek paradise. And what on earth was the difference between Orc and Half-Orc?

'None of these look right, Nigel. I need something

that will make people take us seriously. Have you got something more normal?'

'We can do Human Woman if you like. But that's boring.'

'No, it's perfect. Get started.'

Nigel pressed a few keys and began Sergey's aural sex change. When it was done it sounded nothing like him, but not too goofy either.

While the file was ripping, I told him of my plan to bring Tanya along that evening to help translate and navigate the Russian website. Nigel's mood changed from the euphoria of playing secret agent to one of outright hostility.

'I don't like new people. Especially girls. We're Sherlock Holmes and Doctor Watson. They didn't need girls to help them.'

'She's ten years older than you, Nigel, she's not a girl. We need her because she speaks Russian. She's not a detective.'

'I can do Russian. I can use Translate. If she turns up with you, I'll tell her to go away.'

'Nigel, we need to be smart here. We only have a short time inside the website. We can't afford to go back and forth if we come across something that doesn't translate. Sherlock Holmes had Mrs Hudson to help him sometimes. Think of Tanya as Mrs Hudson. Once she's helped us, it will be only Holmes and Watson again.'

At Nigel's insistence, I made this a solemn promise and that satisfied him. Now I had to convince Tanya to help us. If she didn't, I was stuffed.

I met her at a coffee shop in Mayfair, tucked down

one of the side streets in St James's. She greeted me with a relaxed, disarming smile.

'Hey guy, what is big panic?'

'Would you believe me if I told you I've been given the blueprints for a website the Russians built to hack Act Now!'s political opponents? I've been in Moscow the last two days to meet with a guy who said he could help me expose what's going on. I was wondering if you could have a look at the blueprints and tell me roughly what they say.'

Tanya's eyes narrowed. 'You have been to Moscow, Duncan? And you tell me when you come back? That is not behaviour of a friend.'

'It was dangerous, Tanya, that's why I didn't tell you. And it turned out to be even scarier than I thought.'

I told her about the plane ticket. The phone in my pocket started buzzing. A text from Alex. I could guess what it was saying.

'I'll get that later,' I said. 'So, given what I told you, do you want to see what I brought back with me? If you don't want to get involved, I completely understand.'

'You kidding? This is hot stuff. Show me.'

She flicked through the folder, then looked up at me. 'It is coding for website. I not know what it means, you need expert. I can tell them what Russian means, that's all.'

'That's what I thought you'd say. I'm going to see Nigel this evening, the computer guy who helps me with my stories. Could you come along, explain it to him?'

'Sure, I think no problem. He know about me?'

'A little. I should warn you Nigel's a bit odd. Not very

135

good with new people, so you need be very careful around him. Don't move anything in his flat and whatever you do, don't touch him. He hates that.' I stirred my coffee. 'Oh, yes. And you need to call yourself Mrs Hudson. That's the name I gave you. She was Sherlock Holmes's housekeeper. Elderly lady.'

'You're saying he's the one that's odd? You want me to dress up as Mrs Hudson too?' Tanya collapsed into a fit of giggles.

'Very funny. I've learned that any new things he's introduced to have to fit within constructs he's already comfortable with. He thinks of the two of us as Sherlock Holmes and Dr Watson, and so I had to make you another Conan Doyle character. You'll understand when you meet him.'

'This is what the Russians are up against, is it? I bet they would have quaking boots if they knew they were fighting the three of us.' She had a relapse of the giggles. 'Sherlock Holmes, Dr Watson and Mrs Hudson. Off to solve the case of the Russian bear. I love it.'

I laughed with Tanya, played along with the jokes, but my heart wasn't in it. She had to get back to work at the British Council so I headed off and had a print shop make a scan of the brochure, just to be on the safe side. I popped the original into a left luggage locker at Victoria station and steeled myself to head back to my flat. It was anticlimactic. No sign that anyone had broken in and no knock on the door as I waited for my midnight meeting with Nigel. The texts from Alex were getting more and more irate, so I finally sent her one, asking to see her tomorrow morning. The reply was instant, ten o'clock in her offices and also to call her now. I texted back saying sorry, I needed some time before we could talk. One way or another I had to make a decision first thing in the morning as to what to tell her.

I had time to kill, so I sat down at my computer and started to work up the gist of the article, should I ever decide to publish it. Reporter heads off to Moscow to meet with Russian dissident. Dissident gives him blueprint for a website cloning operation at heart of Russia's dirty tricks activity to discredit mainstream political parties in Britain and help Act Now! take power. Visit to troll factory on the outskirts of Moscow. Dossier purports to show existence of secret list of email addresses of people in UK, who unwittingly or otherwise are taking fake news stories dreamt up by Kremlin black ops puppet-masters and writing posts and tweets in different urban argots. These blend with huge number of micro-operations that cumulatively have enough critical mass to sway a general election. Narrowly escaping threat to his life, reporter hightails it back to UK, where with the help of accomplices he translates website blueprints and hacks into cloned website, uncovering further proof of scale and sophistication of operation. Maybe even confronts some of the 'useful idiots' the Kremlin has working for them in UK. Useful idiots break down and confess their part in operation.

I wrote page after page, the words flowing out of me. Powerful stuff. As I reread it, I made a decision. I'd supply *News Today* with the minimum I could get away with to satisfy my obligations to them, and then I'd take the rest of the story to Sam at the *Chronicle* and offer him the exclusive on the next chapter of the story.

Then another text pinged into my phone. From Dmitry, telling me he had been to Sergey's flat and had found him there with his boyfriend, both okay, but that morning Igor had been fired from the troll factory and Sergey's landlord had served him notice to quit the flat. Retribution of sorts, but not as severe as I had feared.

I called Dmitry to get some more details. He told me both men were resigned to having to move on and make changes in their lives. They were going to face the future together and were glad to be leaving their days of working in the troll factory behind them. I thought about them after I hung up. It was going to be tough, two gay guys in Moscow, trying to pick up the pieces of their life and move on with the state against them. I had no illusions about that. I tried to convince myself they'd be happier in the long term, but I still felt revulsion at the part I'd played in bringing their lives down around them.

Just after ten, Tanya and I headed off to meet with Nigel. Two chairs awaited us as we walked into Nigel's living room.

'This is Mrs Hudson I told you about,' I said.

Tanya looked at the Sherlock Holmes poster on the wall and pursed her lips. I shot her a look and she forced herself to keep a straight face.

Nigel ignored Tanya completely and sat down at his computer and brought up the website.

'Wow, this is all fake?'

He double-checked the website URL against the real one. Just two letters were transposed. He switched to the real website and clicked on a few random pages, comparing them with their equivalents on the other.

'They're almost identical. Except where there's a breaking story, the two sites mirror each other completely.'

He scrolled again through the pages of the bogus website, then the genuine one.

'Ah,' he said, looking pleased with himself. 'There it is.' He brought up the same section from both websites on two different screens. 'Look – see this block of text has an extra link in it?' He right-clicked. 'Thought so. That's the link that would install the malware if I'd left-clicked on it. Great. Now I know where to start looking.'

I looked over at Tanya. She was clearly impressed.

'You spotted that after whizzing through all these pages? You have some memory, Nigel.'

Nigel continued to ignore her. 'Okay, let's see what's behind this. I'll switch to a Cyrillic keyboard; then I'm going to need Mrs Hudson's help to type in the password and navigate around it.'

He pulled up a drop-down window and I handed him the username and password that I'd got from Dmitry. He pressed Enter and suddenly we were into a black screen covered in Russian computer code. With that, there was no going back. If someone went looking, they would know there had been a log-in on the site. A little voice in the back of my head was screaming at me to stop. If anyone else had suggested it, I would have.

'Okay,' Nigel said to Tanya. 'Stand behind me.'

I was pleased to see Tanya kept her distance, standing as far back from Nigel as she could while still being able to read the screen.

'You're looking for something like Access Folders,'

Nigel said without turning around. 'Site Architecture, that sort of thing.'

'Site Architecture. There it is.' She leaned over him and pointed to an icon on the screen.

Nigel stared at the floor, forcing himself to tolerate her presence until she moved away. He clicked on the icon. 'Now is there anything that says Show Folders or similar?'

'*Da*, here.'

Yellow folder icons filled the screen.

'Okay, we need to download these. They'll show me how they code the malware. I've written an app to open them and take screenshots automatically and I'm going to an FTP to download these onto my hard drive.'

'FTP?' I felt I had to say something.

'File Transfer Protocol.' Nigel looked stressed. 'Duncan, shut up. Let me work with Mrs Hudson to get this done.' The tension of the moment was keeping Nigel focused; he was displaying none of his usual behavioural peccadillos. He activated the app and the computer screen was a flurry of activity, files opening and screenshots being grabbed at lightning speed, as the same time as copying everything onto a memory stick.

'Okay, let's go back up a level. Is there anything that says Network Tools, System Preferences, something like that?'

'System Preferences. There.' Tanya pointed to an icon. Nigel clicked.

'Users? Or User Groups?'

'That one.'

Nigel clicked again and an address book came up.

'Voila!' he said. 'Everyone who works with the site.' He hit Select All and Copy and a few seconds later they were downloaded. 'Easy-peasy, lemon-squeezy. He-he-he-he.'

'Can we log out now and have a look at what we've got?' I didn't want to be logged into the computer a second longer than we had to.

Nigel shrugged his shoulders and logged out.

'I feel like burglar on the prowl,' said Tanya. 'Very scary. Next time find another Russian translator.'

'And next time they can find another journalist,' I said. 'I'm getting too old for this. That almost gave me a heart attack.'

Nigel seemed less perturbed; he was busy copying all the files onto another memory stick.

'Finished,' he said, as he handed it to me. 'For your meeting tomorrow. From Sherlock Holmes to Dr Watson. Proof.'

'To solve the case of the Russian bear,' Tanya added.

Now that he no longer needed help with translations, Nigel studiously ignored her again.

'Well, we've got this stuff, what do we do with it?' I asked, as much to break the awkward atmosphere as anything else.

'We need to translate these downloads,' said Nigel. 'Somewhere in one of these folders should be the Trojan virus that they used to take over people's computers and search through their hard drives. Find them and work out how sophisticated they are and you've got the story.'

'No problem,' said Tanya. 'When do you want me to start?'

'We decide what to do, not you!' Nigel started rocking in his chair. 'Go away, now, and leave us alone. Tell her to go away, Watson. Go away.'

I moved quickly to defuse the situation. 'I'll take her away, Nigel, no problem. You were super-quick when you were logged into the computer. Well done.'

Nigel stopped rocking but sat staring at a computer screen, his face inches from the monitor. He was obviously not going to say another word till Tanya left.

'Okay, Tanya and I will go now. Talk soon,' I said. 'Solemn promise not to tell anyone about this?'

'Solemn promise. And you make solemn promise not to have her here again.' He continued to stare at the screen.

We walked back to the car.

'I'm sorry Nigel was so rude and ungrateful,' I said. 'I did warn you about him. It's just his way.'

'No problem. Really, Duncan, it's not an issue. I didn't take it personally. What are you going to do now?'

'I've got to hand this over to a news organisation to help me get it translated. I haven't got the resources to do it and even if you wanted to help, we're talking days of translating time.'

'You know I would help if you wanted me to. So, you're going to give it to that TV programme? I suppose that makes sense.'

'No, I suspect they were the source of the leak that meant someone found out I was in Moscow. I'm going back to the *Chronicle*. I know I can trust them, and this is going to be a big story, with all the detail to back it up. Probably better it appears in a newspaper.'

'And you're definitely going to run with it? No second thoughts after what happened to you in Moscow?'

'I was having cold feet until I saw what Nigel uncovered tonight. If I decided to run away from the story now, I'd never forgive myself. I'll sleep on it and make my decision in the morning'. I looked at my watch. 'It's late, I'll drop you home. It's not far out of my way.'

'It's halfway across the city, Duncan,' she replied, but with a grateful smile. 'But yes, it's late. Thank you for being gentleman.'

Our conversation was sporadic on the drive to her flat; I was still decompressing after the tension of the night's events. As I parked outside, she said, 'So, hotshot journalist. What is your decision? Do you publish story or say goodbye?'

'I don't know, Tanya. That's a crap answer, but there are too many factors at play. All I know is that tomorrow I have to decide.'

'Then we need to talk till you decide. Come with me. It will take you an hour to get home, now it very late. We talk, you decide, then you sleep on couch till you meet TV bosses in morning. Okay?'

Truth be told, I needed someone to decide for me. I gave a resigned nod and we headed inside. Her flat was so different in the dark, and Tanya put on only a few lights. We sat across from each other in the living room.

'It comes down to courage,' I admitted. 'In all this excitement, I have a heady urge to keep going, but I was terrified on that taxi ride to Moscow airport. I don't want to have to go through that again.'

'Once things are out in open, you'd be safe. Do you

think anyone would make it more of a story by threatening you again, or worse? Running away might seem safe option, but it means you are always a loose end, waiting to be tidied up.'

I hadn't thought of that. I remained silent for a few minutes.

'You're right, Tanya. I'll keep going. It's my story and I'm going to stick with it.'

She smiled, and there was an unsettling intensity in her eyes. 'My brother would have been proud of you. I am proud of you.' She got up and sat next to me on the sofa. She put her hand on my shoulder and kissed me on the ear.

'I'm … I'm not sure this is a good idea.'

'Terrible idea. Shocking.'

'No, really. It's complicated enough without—'

I never got to finish my sentence. Suddenly we were a tangle of arms, legs, hair, tongues. Before I knew what was happening, I was on my back on the sofa, Tanya towering above me, her arms on my shoulders pinning me down.

'Let me show you just how bad an idea this really is,' she said. She purred into my ear. 'We'll see if you complain in the morning.'

chapter eleven

The first thing I felt as I started to wake up the next morning was the warmth of Tanya's body lying next to me. I turned to look at her. In repose, her expression looked severe, intense; like she had the weight of the world on her shoulders. It was a little unsettling, like I was seeing past a mask she wore for the world. I wondered if that was what she always looked like when she was sleeping, or if, in her dreams, she was already regretting what had happened between us.

I slipped out of bed, gathered up my clothes and crept into the bathroom to get dressed. No doubt we would have to talk, and I wanted to avoid making it too excruciating. Clothes would help. I made the mistake of looking in the mirror, then I sat down on the toilet seat for a moment and ran my fingers through what hair I had left these days. I put on my clothes and, taking a deep breath, walked back to the bedroom.

Tanya was awake. 'Sneaking off after having your wicked way?' She gave a sleepy laugh. 'I thought old guys had manners.'

'I was getting dressed,' I said, the heat rising in my cheeks. 'I'm shocked you thought I was running off.'

'Lighten up, darling,' Tanya laughed. The first time

she had ever called me that. 'It was joke. You remember jokes?'

'Sorry, I'm feeling ... I don't know. Awkward, that's all.'

Tanya pulled the bedclothes round her and sat up. 'About last night? It was just sex, Duncan. People do it all the time. Was it so bad?'

'Of course not. So, you're okay with it? Really okay?'

'I was not virgin, Duncan. I made first move, remember? You found out big news and decided to do right thing. So, I did right thing too. Right for last night. Today you are Duncan again. My Scottish friend who makes me laugh.'

'And makes you coffee.' I smiled with relief and went into the kitchen.

We drank coffee in her living room, sitting across from each other, this time at her dinner table.

I looked at my watch.

'If I'm to bring down the government with an exposé of international intrigue, I'd better be going,' I said. 'I promised the folks at *News Today* I'd be at their offices by ten. Don't want to be late.'

Tanya read me like a book. 'You can escape, don't worry.'

I grabbed my coat, perhaps a little too hastily. 'Well, yes. Thank you.'

Tanya laughed again. 'Duncan, I never seen you like this. Everything is okay. Last night was nice. Very nice, actually. Now go off and write your story and stop worrying about me. I will survive my broken heart.'

Her last sentence was dripping with irony. She gave

a satisfied, catlike stretch and stood up as a signal for me to go.

As I drove to the *News Today* offices, I forced myself to focus on the meeting ahead.

Alex had already assembled her team in the meeting room before I arrived, briefed them on what I'd been up to. I took them all through everything that happened in Moscow, including the menacing plane ticket, which I produced with a flourish. Some of the younger members of her team were open-jawed in fascinated horror, but Alex maintained a professional composure. I went through everything that Dmitry had told me, but omitting any details about the website folder. I played the audiotape, a female Sergey explaining all about the troll factory in a computer-generated American accent. Finally, I sat back in my chair and forced myself to appear proud of what little I'd revealed.

'So, what do you think? Much of a story?'

Alex didn't hide her disappointment. 'Not really. The troll factory interview is all hearsay; your informant couldn't provide any tangible proof of what he says was going on, and the Russians will deny everything. And in any case, you've told us he's not prepared to go on the record and is about to leave Moscow. We have to track down the trolls working in England to hear what they tell us and I'll need your Russian contacts, Sergey and Dmitry, to go on the record. If we can do all that, we might have something.'

'Surely there's enough already to show the Russians are behind Act Now!?' I glanced at the rest of her team to see if they shared her scepticism.

'I don't think so,' Alex replied. 'It could be Act Now! themselves for all we know, doing all this. And we certainly can't go so far as to claim that the Russians are behind the formation of Act Now! all around the world and are now looking for payback. The most we can say is that the Russians might have a vested interest in Act Now! succeeding and are willing to do a few underhand things to help them along. There's no evidence that Act Now! has colluded in these dirty tricks or even knew they were going on, never mind that they are under the control of their Moscow puppet-masters. I'm sorry, Duncan. I know you took some personal risk in getting us this story, but that's how it seems to me.'

'What about Professor Mikin being photographed with every Act Now! leader years before they came to prominence? A Russian academic actively involved in the grooming and promotion of Western leaders? That shows how deeply the Russian government is behind Act Now!.'

'Could be a coincidence. Or a bunch of would-be politicians picking the brains of someone who shared a similar philosophy. No, the most this story is ever going to be is the suggestion of some Russian mischief-making in Western elections. Whether it's the Russian government or someone with the time and money to do it off their own bat, we can't say. It's a story, I suppose. Just about.'

I gave a fake smile. 'The same story that's been running for years. Okay, I'll ask Dmitry if he wants to go on the record, but don't be surprised if he says no. It's one thing sitting here in a cosy office discussing all this; it's another sticking your head above the parapet in a country that doesn't have a particularly forgiving attitude to its dissidents. But I'm only going to ask Dmitry, not the person I interviewed – even if I could get word to him before he and his partner quit Moscow. Dmitry's a grown-up; he knows what he's doing. I might have ruined the life of that young person who gave me the troll factory interview; I don't want to make things any worse.'

'I'm disappointed in your scruples, Duncan. You owe it to us to at least try, if you won't let us contact your source directly.'

I remained tight-lipped.

'Okay, then, if that's how you want to play it. We'll doorstep some of these UK trolls that we can identify from their email address and see what we get from that. You get in touch with Dmitry and write up your blog story, which is of course embargoed until our programme airs. You can coordinate your efforts with Nathan here. He'll be producing the story at this end.' A hipster in a checked shirt nodded. 'And one last thing, Duncan. Don't ever ignore my phone calls and text messages again.'

She looked around the room. 'Okay, you've heard everything, folks.' The news team got up and left.

I went into Alex's office to talk money. I told her that I'd had to pay for the Sergey interview; she wasn't impressed. She offered me a small fee for what I had come up with, only just covering my expenses, and said I had to pay the money I gave Sergey out of my own pocket as it wasn't authorised. She softened the blow by saying there would be something a little more decent if I could interview Dmitry on the record, but if not, there would probably be no story.

Once we'd sorted out the money side of things, I

decided to tell her my suspicions that someone at the TV station had tipped off the Russians that I was in Moscow.

'That's absurd,' she said. 'And a bit of an insult. Do you know how difficult it was for me to convince the station bosses to let someone who's never been in front of a news camera go out to Moscow in our name to investigate a story?' She gave a disgusted snort. 'Especially after Damien Zane ripped you to pieces live on air. And the way you repay my faith in you is to come in here with next to nothing from the trip and accuse me of shopping you to the Russians? If that's the level of your paranoia, Duncan, I'm beginning to have doubts if any of this is true.'

'I'm not accusing you of anything, Alex,' I replied. 'But I told no one else that I was going to Moscow. I'm not saying the leak came from you or the news team, but surely there were lots of ways someone here could have found out what I was up to? Whoever made the travel arrangements, for example.'

'That was Emma. She's a twenty-one-year-old intern who spends most of her time checking regional press for human interest stories. If she was a Russian informer, then she'd be feeding them stories of speaking dogs and long-lost brothers being reunited.'

'Well, someone else. I don't know. But you've got to admit it's a possibility.'

'This channel and *News Today* has done more to cover this story than any other news outlet in the country. If you have such qualms working with us, maybe it's best we part ways after this story.' She folded her arms and glared at me. 'After you talk to your Russian contact to see if he wants to talk to us on the record. That's even more important after this conversation. I need to know he's for real before I run the story. He promised you the moon to get you out to Moscow and all he delivered was somebody who told you they worked in a troll factory and who you paid for their story.'

She gave a heavy sigh. 'I should have insisted on Simon Green going with you; then I'd have more faith in the story. Now if you'll excuse me, I need to explain to my bosses why my decision to send an untried reporter out to Moscow has resulted in a story that's weak at best. Let me know about Dmitry by the end of the day.'

I'd deserved my bollocking. Suitably chastened, I scuttled out of her office.

★ ★ ★

I was astonished when Dmitry agreed to be interviewed.

'If someone at the TV station is secretly part of Russian plan, let's play them at their own game,' he told me. 'I think you're smart to give the website file to someone else. But we need the TV station to run the story. If I do an interview, so what? I am linked to troll factory and stories I have been talking about for years. When the story comes out about website folder, you can say it was from another source, not me. I am in no more deep shit than I have been up to now. Maybe even safer, if I am famous on UK news programme.'

With Dmitry's decision, Alex agreed to run with the story. I wouldn't be allowed to front it – that would be Simon Green, who would do a down-the-line interview with me in my home office, interspersed with the Dmitry and Sergey clips. I worked with Nathan to coordinate my blog going live with the ten-minute report they were planning to run. The *News Today* team got some incriminating stuff from the dozen or so UK trolls they managed to track down, but most of them came across as fantasists or mercenaries, rather than idealistic revolutionaries trying to place Britain under Russian rule.

The story got a categorical denial from Act Now!, with Damien Zane saying I was a fantasist whose claims were becoming more absurd by the day, and it was beneath his dignity to come into the studio and debate with me. I guess that meant I wouldn't be on his Christmas-card list this year.

It felt strange going back into the *Chronicle* offices after my foray into TV land, but Sam welcomed me like a long-lost friend.

'You're like a dog with a bone with this Act Now! story,' he said as he closed the door of his office. 'I thought you'd deserted us when I saw you pop up on that *News Today* report. Where did you find that Dmitry source?'

'He emailed me, after the first couple of stories broke,' I replied. 'Good to know that my reputation stands me in good stead, even in Moscow.'

'And you say there's more? What have you got?'

I produced the website folder and described the session with Nigel hacking in through the back-door portal, making copies and taking screenshots of everything he found.

'It's all in Russian, but what it proves is that the scale and sophistication of what is going on now could only have come from the Kremlin. Nobody else would benefit from the political upheaval this operation has caused as much as the Russian government. Tie that in with the mysterious Professor Mikin being photographed with all the Act Now! leaders before they formed parties in their own countries, and our own PM's peculiarly close relationship with him over the years – which he's tried to cover up – and you've got a pretty strong case to suggest collusion between Act Now! and the Russians to help them win the last election.'

'Let's not get ahead of ourselves. We need this translated. We've got translators on file who could do this. I trust them implicitly. But it's a massive amount to get through. Can you leave the folder with me to get started?'

'If you promise me it stays my story, then yes,' I replied. 'This is a copy. I've got the original safely stashed away somewhere no one can find it. Are you sure you can trust your translators? This is pretty sensitive stuff.'

'We rotate them all the time and make it clear that if there's any breach of security, they're permanently blacklisted.' Sam stared hard at me. 'But why are you giving me this, Duncan? Aren't you working with *News Today* now? If I was Alex Richards, I'd be bloody furious that you took the next part of the story to a rival.'

I feigned nonchalance. 'I gave them the troll factory story as a way of apologising for the Damian Zane interview. The *Chronicle*'s where my heart is, no matter how shittily you've treated me. How's Bryony working out, by the way?'

The question distracted Sam.

'Oh, fine, I guess,' he said, tilting his chin down

and frowning. 'Gets on with job, safe pair of hands, but nothing spectacular. Don't worry, I'll keep her well away from your exclusive.'

Damned with faint praise, I thought. Worth remembering.

We agreed to meet when the translations were completed, and I finally turned my thoughts to my now complicated private life.

I agonised over whether to tell Bobbie about what had happened with Tanya. We had chatted a couple of times to reflect on the maelstrom of activity around the story and she was good at keeping me grounded, both in terms of not becoming too pretentious as a result of all the attention, and also in focusing on the way forward. As we had been doing for each other ever since primary school, I reflected ruefully. We'd never kept secrets from each other. Feeling a little like a naughty schoolboy, I called her up.

'I think you should know I accidentally slept with Tanya when I stayed over at her place – after she helped Nigel translate the Russian websites,' I said. I felt ridiculously embarrassed for some reason.

'Accidentally slept with her? What happened, did you stumble coming out of the shower or something?'

'Very funny. It was after a pretty intense evening, coming on top of being scared out of my wits and not being able to get out of Moscow fast enough. It just sort of happened. She laughed it off the next day, but I'm not sure I can do that so easily.'

'It's called being old, Duncan. When we were younger, we never gave one night stands a second thought. Everything's more complicated now.'

'You're right. Especially for men. If I do venture out on a date these days, I find myself wondering what I'll do if the evening promises to end up in bed. When I was younger, saying no would never have been an option.'

'The only person analysing this and trying to work out what it all means is you,' she replied. 'Stop taking yourself so seriously.'

She was right. I had enough to worry about with what I was going to say in the *Chronicle* follow-up. We left it at that.

Once the coding was translated, I was able to come up with some extra spins on the original story. But over the next few weeks, it started to wind down. According to the opinion polls, people regarded it as a juicy piece of gossip but it did nothing to change their opinion of Act Now! and how they were going to vote in future. My fifteen minutes of fame were over and I was starting to think that all my new-found status could do for me was to help edge Bryony out of the picture and get my old job back at the *Chronicle*. Nigel had managed to find evidence of one major political scandal, but it would be sheer good fortune if he did the same again. Investigative reporting was proving too unpredictable and traumatic. I'd tasted stress and I'd tasted danger, and they were a bit too rich for my blood. A return to humdrum column writing sounded very appealing.

That was, until Professor Pavel Mikin got in touch with me.

chapter twelve

I thought it was a hoax.

Hello Richard Foxe, my name is Professor Pavel Mikin. I think you know of me. Can we talk?

It was sent through the contact email on my website. I almost missed it. The email address was from one of Russia's big internet providers. Easily set up and impossible to trace. I emailed back that I did, indeed, know who Pavel Mikin was and if this was him I needed to confirm his identity.

Please tell me how?

Good question.

I decided on a Skype call, to see if the emailer resembled the photos I had of Mikin. Then, to ask about things that would trip up an imposter, no matter how well prepared. We arranged to talk early the next evening – that would give me time to get ready. It could all be a trap, a ploy by Act Now! to discredit me. But if Mikin wanted to tell me the inside story about Act Now!, the results would be sensational.

I couldn't shake off the feeling that it all sounded too good to be true. The key person behind the Act Now! project suddenly wanted to betray everything that he'd worked for, and had chosen me to help him?

It was incredible beyond belief. I was desperate to talk to someone about it, someone I trusted, who was smarter and more experienced than me in these things, who could listen to what I knew and tell me what to do.

But that someone didn't exist. *News Today*, Alex Richards and her team – they were all tainted by my suspicions about the leak, and in any case relations had been strained since the *Chronicle*'s involvement. The only people who knew about politics at the *Chronicle* after the recent cutbacks were Sam and Bryony; enough said. Bobbie or Tanya could give me common sense, but I needed more than that. Nigel, not even common sense. I was on my own.

I needed to find out as much about Mikin as possible, so I called Nigel to say I had a test for him. I was going to quiz a Mikin expert and wanted the twenty most obscure facts about Mikin he could find, to see if the expert was any good. His challenge was to come up with questions about things that were so well hidden that only a superhero expert would be able to get them right.

One of the good things about the way Nigel's mind worked was that he never thought about anything other than the task in hand. It never occurred to him to ask why I was making such a strange request. Maybe if I had told him about Mikin's approach and made him make a solemn promise not to talk about it, that would ensure that he didn't inadvertently let something slip in one of his chat room sessions, but given the stakes involved, it didn't seem like a risk worth taking. For the first time since we started working together, I was deliberately keeping him in the dark. I felt a bit of a heel about it.

There was also the Tanya situation to feel uncomfortable about. I was seeing her that night for the first time in weeks, and I was nervous about what our new dynamic would be like. An evening cooking dinner at her flat had been arranged. I thought about cancelling, so I could ponder more, but in the end, decided there was only so much pondering you could do.

Mikin weighed heavily on my thoughts as we bantered and chatted as if nothing had ever happened between us.

'Have you known any spies in your time, Tanya?' I asked. 'Real spies, I mean, not some playboy with a 007 fetish.'

'Probably.' She laughed. 'But they wouldn't be much of a spy if they told me about it.'

'Do you think spies stay loyal, though? Wouldn't being involved in all that deception and duplicity make you more likely to become that way yourself? Like police officers corrupted by the crime around them? History's full of double agents.'

'I really don't know, Duncan, I've not been to spy school. Why are you asking me all this? Is there something new about Act Now!?'

So I told her. Tanya was sceptical.

'Russia's number one apparatchik decides to contact you out of blue?' She shook her head. 'He is fraud or trap. Something's not right about this.'

I told her I agreed. 'But think if it were true. And it's not beyond the bounds of possibility. History is loaded with examples of people betraying causes they once believed in. All I'm risking is a half-hour chat with him. What's to lose?'

'What's to lose? Being sucked into con trick that damages you and story you've tried to uncover. Being finished as credible investigator. That's all.'

'So, you're saying I should ignore him?'

She thought for a moment. 'No. I'm telling you to be careful, that's all. Don't do anything too stupid. And whatever you do, don't give him any money. It still sounds like scam to me.'

As the time of the Skype call approached, I became more and more nervous. I had Nigel's list of twenty questions in front of me and I felt another pang of guilt about keeping him in the dark. My computer beeped, signalling a call request. I pressed a shortcut to a macro that Nigel had written for me that would bring up a caller's IP address. The request was coming through a Tor node, impossible to trace. I clicked Accept.

'Ah, Richard Foxe,' the caller said. 'We meet at last. You have made me quite famous. A little more famous than some here would like.'

I decided to keep things curt and businesslike until I was sure who I was talking to.

'Good to talk to you, Professor Mikin. I must admit I was surprised to hear from you. I'm sure you realise I get a lot of unusual messages in my business. Would you mind if I ask you a few questions, so I can be comfortable I know who I'm talking to?'

'Not at all. Call me Pavel, if you don't mind.' He smiled like he was granting me a great honour. 'Ask your questions of verification. I would be disappointed if you did not. Please go ahead.'

I glanced at the most recent photograph of Mikin that

Nigel had found, then peered at my computer screen. He had shaved off his moustache since it was taken; Nigel would have liked that. I looked again at my photo. He definitely seemed to be the same person.

I started to go through my questions. The names of his brothers, the title of his doctorate, the name of the river in the town he grew up in. As each question was answered promptly and correctly, I got more and more excited. This really was Mikin. After the final answer, I got to the real question I wanted to ask.

'That's all very reassuring, Prof—, sorry, Pavel. No more checking. Now can I ask you the most important question? Why did you decide to talk to me?'

Mikin leant a little closer to the screen. 'I created a thing of beauty. Something that the Cold War failed to achieve. Failed to achieve despite forty years of political manoeuvring; despite all of our threats and coercion; despite unlimited budgets. The ability to subjugate the enemies of my country. And I did it using the most powerful weapon of all, the human mind. Turned the social media technology of the West back on itself and the result is what you see today. What you have found out.'

'And now you want to tell people what you've done?' I tried not to sound incredulous.

'No, I want you to do that. I let you know what questions to ask, who to talk to. But nothing is ever to be attributed to me. You are a brilliant journalist, with a nose for where to go for a story. I don't exist, even as anonymous source.'

This was all moving too fast.

'But I've got to ask why, Pavel. Why on earth would you, of all people, want to do this?'

'Because I've been betrayed. I tell you more about that when we talk next. If I've convinced you of who I am, the next time we meet will be in person. Then we can get started. When can you come to Moscow?'

The words sent a chill down my spine.

'Can I get back to you on that? What's the most secure way to contact you?'

Mikin told me he checked the email address he used to reach me once a day. He was confident that no one knew about it, but didn't like to log on more than necessary, in case it was discovered. That suited me. It meant I had twenty-four hours before he would expect me to get back to him. A little breathing space to figure out what to do. I was staring at the greatest story of my life, but I had been warned off in no uncertain terms about ever returning to Moscow. I wanted the story, but not at such a big risk to my safety.

I told Tanya my concerns when we met to discuss what Mikin had said to me.

'You fly back from Moscow with super-sensitive evidence in your luggage. Why did plane-ticket guys not take it from you? Maybe you are bit overreacting.'

'I'm not prepared to take the risk. Finding out that I was in Moscow and what hotel I was staying at shows someone is pretty smart at keeping tabs on me. I think it's too risky to go back.'

'And Mikin can't come to you? Can you ask him?'

'I could, but it would scare him away. He could hardly keep his leaving Russia below the radar, and if we were seen together in London that'd be the end of him. No, all I can hope for is that I can continue to communicate and get information over the internet. But he's not going to like that; he could well find someone else to work with. I'm sure there would be no shortage of takers.'

'But now that he's reached out to you, he's going to want to see this through. He doesn't know what you'd do if he found another journalist, whether you'd disclose his identity if he walked away from you.' Tanya's face lit up, as a thought struck her. 'What about a compromise? Could I go and meet him? I've not been threatened. I'm in Moscow all the time with my British Council work, so being in Russia wouldn't seem at all suspicious. Any intelligence you got from Mikin will be in Russian, so you're going to ask for my help anyway. And it would be useful to have someone who understands the Russian psyche.'

'"A riddle, wrapped in a mystery, inside an enigma". Isn't that how Churchill described Russia? You're right, Tanya, you would be the perfect go-between, if Mikin agrees. But if you get involved, you need to be part of the team. I split all my Act Now! income with Nigel, fifty–fifty. If Mikin agrees with you being the go-between, you should get an equal share.'

'No, that's not necessary, Duncan. You are friend that needs help. And I don't think I'm Nigel's favourite person. There would be big drama if I muscled into the little bromance the two of you have going on there.'

'Don't laugh this off, Tanya. Some scary people are hiding in the shadows with this story. I need you to take the threat seriously.'

'Living in Ukraine you know to be wary of state. Don't worry, I have head screwed on. I go to Moscow in six days for art fair. Is that good time?'

'Let's discuss it after I get a reaction from Mikin.'

I spoke to Mikin the next day.

'I'm concerned about your security if I visit you in Moscow,' I told him. 'On my last trip, someone found out I was there and made efforts to hasten my departure. That means there's a risk if we're seen together. And you might run the same risk no matter what journalist you chose to work with, even if they weren't currently working on the Act Now! Russian story. As soon as they wrote something after their first meeting with you, they'd be a marked person on any subsequent trips.'

'You raise an interesting dilemma,' Mikin said. 'How do you suggest getting around it?'

'We need to have an intermediary, someone who regularly travels from London to Moscow so they wouldn't arouse any suspicion. Ideally, someone who speaks Russian, who can translate any documents. And someone who I trust completely.'

'And does such a perfect person exist?' His sardonic smile made me think Mikin realised I was more concerned about my own safety than his.

'They do. Tanya Petrenko, an event organiser with the British Council. She's a close friend and has been doing translation support for me up to now. I've told her I have a potential new source, and she'd be willing to meet you. She will be in Moscow next week if you'd like to talk to her, see if she's suitable.'

'I don't like too many people getting involved.'

I saw Mikin clasping his hands tightly, a whitening of his knuckles. His tone was challenging now. 'And Petrenko, you say her name is? So she is Ukrainian? I need someone smart to deal with, someone sensible. Not silly peasant girl, coming to Moscow with her jar of borscht and grandmother's pickled mushrooms.'

'She's smart. And trustworthy. Why don't you meet her and make up your mind?'

'Let me think about your proposition. Your friend might be the answer.' He forced a laugh. 'Maybe I will get invited to her shows, start to become cultured. We'll see.'

Mikin's reservations about Tanya were mild compared to Nigel's. I explained about Mikin and how his answers to Nigel's questions had convinced me he was real and how having him as a source would be a Good Thing – our stories on Act Now! would be even better.

'The best in the world,' I said. He gave his staccato laugh as I talked, spinning in his chair like a child on a fairground roundabout. Then I mentioned Tanya and his face clouded. The revelation that I had already told her about Mikin hit him like a hammer blow. I could see a volcano of resentment building inside him. I managed to tell him the full proposition, that I wanted Tanya to become part of the team and get an equal share, before he finally exploded.

'No! It's you and me. Holmes and Watson!' he yelled. 'Holmes and Watson, Holmes and Watson,' he chanted.

Usually, his tantrums were confined to swinging in his chair, but this time he ran around the room, screaming. He grabbed a printer, pulled it so hard the cable came out, and threw it against the wall. It crashed to the floor, fragments of black plastic going everywhere.

'Nigel, why don't you go into your bedroom, lie down for a bit, try to solve some mathematical puzzles in your head?' I said, softening my voice like I was reciting a lullaby. 'You know you like doing that.'

'Shut up. Shut up! You want to stick it in her! That's why you told her. You want to fuck her. Fuck her, fuck her, fuck her.'

'No, Nigel. She would be our Russian expert; you are the computer expert. She does different things from you. I need her to go to Russia. I can't go and you obviously can't. We need her.'

'I'll go to Moscow. Watch me, I will.'

'You can't, Nigel. It's full of people you don't know. People would bump into you all the time; everything would be unfamiliar. Let her go. Please?'

I thought Nigel was starting to calm down, but he picked up the broken lid of the printer and ran over to me. He swung it towards me with his full force. I tried to turn away, but it hit me on my face and shoulder, a ragged shard stabbing into my cheek, inches from my eye. I fell to the ground and scuttled backwards, my back up against the wall. Blood trickled down my face. I didn't wipe it away, hoping it would shock Nigel out of his rage.

I could see him grabbing onto everything, anything, like he was trying to pull himself back to earth. He started sobbing.

'I don't like her, Duncan. She's nasty. You want her to be on our team so you can do it to her. Tell her to go away.'

'It's nothing to do with that, Nigel. Tanya and I are friends, that's all.' I kept my voice level and was glad that

Nigel was staring at the floor. 'Look, I need to wash this blood off my face.'

I went into the bathroom to patch myself up. Nigel didn't have a first aid kit, so I dabbed my face with toilet tissue until the bleeding slowed, then tore off a corner and laid it over the cut. The blood spread over it and started to harden, but at least it was no longer dripping down my cheek.

When I went back into the living room Nigel was on his computer, playing a game. I picked up the broken pieces of the printer and put them in a black bin liner I found under the sink. 'I'll drop this off in the rubbish bin on my way out. Beyond repair, I'm afraid.'

I could hear sound effects and explosions coming from Nigel's game. He twisted his body about in concentration, totally engrossed in the action.

'Goodbye, Nigel. Don't forget to order another printer. I'll be going now.'

He ignored me, so I left and headed back to my flat to assess the damage. Small scar, no problem, it would heal. I slipped a plaster over it.

★ ★ ★

I worried about Tanya the whole time she was in Moscow. Worried that she would also be found out, and that whoever was behind the threat to me would not be so civil to a Ukrainian national. That the whole thing was a set-up and the story would come crashing around my ears. Worried that even if it all went okay, I'd screw everything up.

She called me after meeting Mikin, told me it had gone well and they were going to meet again before she left for London so he could brief her on what I should be looking for. She sounded thrilled and excited about her big adventure and I hoped and prayed that I wasn't putting her in jeopardy.

'So, what was Mikin like?' was my first question when she returned.

'Impressive intellect. Even more impressive ego. And boy, does he bear a grudge. Want to know what this is all about? He claims he was architect behind strategy to set up Act Now! across Europe as Russian puppet. Now that is done and project has moved into next stage, he's being sidelined as Kremlin bring in new experts. But Mikin didn't want to let go, or if he had to, he wanted juicy reward, like being made Russia's ambassador to the UN, or here in the UK, that sort of thing. When he was told to get back in his box and be policy adviser again, he get pissed off. He say to me if there is no reward for keeping quiet, he want world to know how smart he is.'

'Even if it means destroying his life's work and risking being caught? He does have an ego.'

'His role is to be guide, not source,' Tanya explained. 'He say he never give you any information directly, but will point to right people and right place where you go digging. That way, no one suspects he is guy leaking all the information, they think you are smart journalist. And he has given me this to get started.'

I opened the file that Tanya handed to me. Documentation on the five Western leaders that had been chosen to run the Act Now! organisation when it was getting started. It was clear that the five countries had been coordinated from the start, the leaders frequently photographed together as they attempted to garner publicity for their new cause. Mikin had also supplied a list of key questions that would pinpoint how they got hold of Russian money for each of their start-ups – the exact sums involved and the payment dates; details of how, when and where the leaders met their Russian sponsors. If only ten per cent of the leads ended in a concrete discovery, this would still blow the story wide open.

I had worked hard at building bridges with Alex at *News Today* after the harsh words we exchanged, so when the story that Act Now! stood accused of breaking campaign finance rules broke on the front page of the *Chronicle*, I readily agreed to be interviewed by Simon Green on the following night's *News Today*. Also invited onto the programme was my old nemesis, Damian Zane; it was the first time we had been face-to-face in the studio since I had been outed by him. As we sat across from each other, watching Simon's report play out on the TV screen in front of us, I braced myself for what was to come.

Zane's opening comments were completely unexpected.

'We'll discuss the contents of your report in a second, Simon,' he said as Green asked Zane for his reaction to the story. 'First, I have to deal with the very specific allegations concerning financial irregularities that appeared in the *Chronicle* this morning, courtesy of Mr Foxe here. I ordered an immediate investigation as soon as I became aware of his allegations and can confirm that payments were made into Act Now!'s bank accounts that match the dates and amounts detailed in the story. The funds originated from foreign nationals, which was not disclosed at the time and which, as you know, is in contravention of UK election law.'

Zane sat perfectly rigid. He sucked his cheeks in. 'The funds were accepted on behalf of Act Now! by inexperienced but well-meaning officials within the party in the early days of the its existence, when our oversight and compliance procedures were not as robust as they should have been.' He looked uncomfortable. 'But none of that is an excuse. The two officials have been expelled from the party and the funds received are being returned to the donors as we speak.'

'Richard Foxe, your reaction to that?' said Simon Green.

Bugger. Why couldn't he have commented himself to give me a few seconds to think?

'I have to say I'm surprised by Damian's refreshing candour in admitting that what I reported is true,' I replied. 'It makes a change from the blanket denials and insults I'm more used to having from him. But he needs to go further and confirm who these foreign nationals were and whether they were acting on behalf of the Russian government. And to tell us what other donations of a similar nature have been received since.' I was still reeling from the shock of Zane admitting to my claims, and only just managed to have the presence of mind to push home my advantage and try to force further disclosures.

'You'll understand that I cannot do that,' Zane replied. 'These donations were made in good faith, and it is entirely my party's fault that we did not tell the donors that they could not be accepted without disclosing their identities. They wish to remain anonymous and I have to respect their right to do so. I can, however, confirm they were not Russian nationals and had no connection to the Russian government.'

'None at all?' I interjected.

Zane ignored me. 'I can further announce that I have ordered a full internal audit of our finances to make sure that no other inappropriate funds have found their way into our party's accounts. And I'd like to thank Richard Foxe for drawing this to our attention.' He gave me a nod of acknowledgement, but his eyes had the dull opacity of a shark in the deep. 'We hold ourselves to a higher standard of ethics than the established political parties, and I'm grateful that we have managed to correct this very early, regrettable aberration in our party's history.'

I sailed through the rest of the interview in a euphoric daze. Zane must have hated to come clean after all the vitriol he had poured over me in the past. It was the specificity of Mikin's information that must have nailed him. Vague accusations were one thing, but now that I could point to exactly what and when, there was no room for manoeuvre. He had had no choice but to confess everything. I had hit the first nail into the Act Now! coffin.

Or so I thought. There was a furore of press coverage on the story after Zane's admissions, and I could hardly contain my glee as I watched him try to regain some moral high ground with disingenuous attempts at openness and sincerity. But then the first opinion polls since the scandal broke came along, and Act Now!'s lead remained undiminished. Voters apparently were prepared to forgive their early foibles to let them continue their crusade against what they described as the high-handed arrogance of the old political establishment.

Tanya's next meeting with Mikin led to the naming and shaming of Russian operatives behind cyber-attacks and the attribution of malware viruses to the Russian software companies that developed them. This story also dominated the news cycle, but was dismissed as the actions of a few self-appointed rogue operatives – and again there was no impact on the polls.

Mikin followed up by revealing the identities of the elite group of Russian businessmen with close links to the Kremlin who masterminded the troll factories and who the Russian government had rewarded with lucrative business contracts. That had even less impact. Act Now! could easily say that the awarding of contracts to Russian companies inside Russia was a matter for Russia, and that they had no right to comment or become involved.

The list of revelations from Mikin went on and on. Russian operatives whipping up anti-immigrant sentiment in marginal constituencies; illicit funding of social media campaigns, all with some piece of evidence to back them up. I had a new story every month. There was unwavering accuracy in my predictions, every question I raised pinpointing what rock should be looked under. Mikin was smart; there was a logic to the order in which he revealed things, with each story moving the scandal closer and closer to the Act Now! leaders and their Russian backers. I was shining a spotlight into some unsavoury corners of international politics, and Mikin was right there behind me, making sure it was pointing into the darkest shadows.

My blog became the most talked about and widely read political website in the UK, but it was a pyrrhic victory. Outside of the Westminster political bubble, it was having little real impact on voters' intentions. It was incredibly disheartening.

Then Nigel called, telling me to come to see him, immediately. His voice had a zombie-like tinge that was unsettling, even a little sinister. It didn't sound like he was having a meltdown; just the opposite, he was eerily calm. He said he had found something out, something I needed to know immediately. I set off, full of trepidation about what he was going to tell me.

It sounded serious, and I steeled myself to hear some big news. But nothing could have prepared me for what I was about to find out.

chapter thirteen

Nigel was in his chair, gently swaying from side to side, like a contented baby rocking in its cradle.

'Okay, Nigel, what is it? You're looking very pleased with yourself. What have you found out?'

He looked serious. 'You said it wasn't a Bad Thing. You did. I said it's not like stealing from a shop, and you agreed with me. Didn't you, Duncan?'

The swaying had stopped now. He was approaching an equilibrium point before he went into being agitated. I tried to keep him as calm as possible.

'Nigel, you know I haven't got a good memory. Not as good as you, remembering everything like Sherlock Holmes. Remind me, what's not like stealing from a shop?'

'Hacking. Remember you asked me about it when we first met? And I told you it was easy-peasy, lemon-squeezy? And you said it was alright to do it if it meant you uncovered lies?'

I was getting concerned.

'You've been doing some hacking? Is that why you wanted to see me?'

'That Russian malware virus was super, super smart. The smartest computer coding in the world. Smarter than anything I'd ever seen before. I've been practising writing coding like that. So I could be super smart.'

I started to take deep, calming breaths.

'Have you been hacking into Act Now!'s computers, Nigel? We discussed that, remember? I said that I'd split my fees with you for stories where the things you found out formed the basis of the story. But that it had to be verifiable and you couldn't do anything illegal. I'm sure you've not forgotten.' I spoke with a severe authority, like a headmaster berating a badly-behaved schoolboy.

It had little effect on the smirk on Nigel's face.

'You said it was illegal because it was stealing and I said that it wasn't really stealing because it helped discover lies and lies were bad and could be worse than stealing. If you do a little stealing but find a big lie, then it's not illegal any more. It's a Good Thing.'

'Nigel, tell me what you've been up to.'

'And I knew I'd find a big lie. And I did. She's a big, big liar. Liar, liar, pants on fire.'

'Nigel, you are not making any sense. What are you talking about?'

'Tanya. She was only pretending to be Mrs Hudson, and helping us out. I built a malware virus like the Russians and I put it on the computers at the British Council, where you told me she worked. And then I went snooping just like Sherlock Holmes and found that Tanya Petrenko used to work at the British Council, but she left a year ago. But she didn't really leave, they still pay her salary, but the same amount is paid into the British Council every month from another bank account to cover it. Her phone is only a voicemail account, nobody else can pick it up if it rings. It's the only phone in the British Council like that. The person who took over her job organises all the exhibition openings in Russian-speaking countries. Not her. I've been through the emails – the new person does everything for exhibition openings, Tanya's not even copied in. She does go along to the openings, sends in her expenses, and they're paid from this other bank account. But somebody else does all the work.'

'What does she do, then?' My head was spinning.

'She goes into the office once a day and sends one email on a secure computer. I looked at the time she swipes in, the computer is switched on five minutes later and closed down five minutes before she leaves. She does nothing else. I tried to see what she was writing, but the email she sends is super-encrypted and the computer has its own second-tier firewall. I should be able to get past any normal firewall, but this one is special. I can look at whatever's on any other computer in the British Council, but not that one.'

'There must be some innocent explanation,' I said. 'Maybe this other person's her assistant, and maybe you need extra security when dealing with the Russians.' Tanya had never mentioned an assistant. I was clutching at straws.

'She's a big liar. I knew she was. That's why I stole the data. But it was a Good Thing stealing because I found a big, big lie.' Nigel started to swing in his chair in self-congratulatory oscillation.

I finally snapped, furious at his smugness.

'What gives you the right to go snooping after Tanya? She's one of us. A friend. You don't betray a friend.'

Then I stopped to think. The starkness of her flat, nothing to show her past; nothing lying around from her job at the British Council. I thought about our first meeting, randomly bumping into each other at the National Portrait Gallery. Then the good fortune of her giving me a red-hot tip about the Russians building Britain's nuclear power stations. And then, once I'd swallowed that information, how she went on to become a source of even more intelligence about Act Now! and the Russians.

'But why would a Russian spy want to undermine their own programme? And why would the British Council let them? It doesn't make any sense.'

'It does.' Nigel was as excited now as the time he told me about alien spaceships saving Chernobyl. 'Do you want to know my theory? She's not a Russian spy. She's a British one. MI5 are using her to feed information to you about Act Now!, because they can't do it themselves, prosecute their own government. They needed someone to get all the secrets out in the open, so they'd be forced by public pressure to investigate. That's why you've been getting told everything.'

For a second I wanted to scream in anguish, to release the torment inside me. My mind flailed about, trying to make sense of what Nigel was telling me. Then a new wave of emotion flooded over me; one of fury and anger. First at Tanya for her treachery, as I processed how believable the things that Nigel had found out could be. And then at myself. For being so stupid, so gullible, so convinced that I was a brilliant investigator that I never for a second considered whether I was being used and manipulated. I was so conceited about how smart I was, I never thought about why so much of this stuff started landing on my lap after Tanya showed up.

'Show me,' I said, picking at my nails. 'Show me everything you've found.'

Nigel handed me a pile of printouts he had made of his findings. I picked them up and started reading. I wanted to vomit. Everything Tanya had told me was a lie.

I glanced over at Nigel. His face was blank as he stared into space. He caught me looking at him and something deep inside fought its way through the dysfunctional synapses of his brain.

'I'm sorry, Duncan,' he said. 'She was a bad friend.'

'Is there any way Tanya or her bosses could know you've been snooping around? Any chance at all?'

'No. I've never been able to find the slightest crack in her computer security, so in a way that's a Good Thing, it means I can't have left a trace. Unless someone is monitoring the proxy sources I investigated, we're in the clear.' He looked up and gave me a cheery smile. 'It's the two of us, again, isn't it? You and me, Holmes and Watson, no Mrs Hudson.'

His words cut through me. I could feel my anger bubbling up again, with an intensity even greater than before. Everything, even that night in bed together, all of it a sham. I pulled myself back under control.

'Yes, just the two of us, Nigel.'

I headed over to Tanya's flat, my head feeling it was going to explode with all the emotions raging through me: anger, indignation, betrayal, all fighting for supremacy. But underneath them all, another one was silently, profoundly taking over. Sadness. No matter what her reasons, no matter what she said, our friendship was over. It wasn't that she had lied to me, it was that I could never believe her ever again.

I rang the doorbell. I almost willed her not to answer, to give me a short, precious delay from having to confront her. But after a few seconds I heard that familiar voice saying hello, with the cute little emphasis on the second syllable that always made me smile.

'It's Duncan.'

'Duncan. We are meeting? I forget.'

'No, you didn't forget. I need to talk to you. Can you let me in?'

She must have heard the ice in my voice. She made no reply, the sound of the buzzer unlocking the door her only response. I walked up the stairs, that long climb so often the precursor to an evening of laughter and frivolity. Now the sound of every footstep was like the tolling of a funeral bell.

She was standing at the entrance to her third-floor flat, half-hiding behind the door. As I approached, she must have seen something in my eyes, and the door started to close. For a moment I thought I would be left standing on the outside, but then she stopped, opened the door and stood with her back to the hallway wall. She stared at the floor, no eye contact. Eschewing our regular embrace, I walked grim-faced into the living room.

'What has happened? Are you okay?' Her voice was full of concern. There was a sickly expression on her face as she held her elbows tightly against her side. 'Tell me, Duncan.'

'I've found out that you don't work for the British Council. That you've got security systems on your computer that only a professional spy would have. You've been setting me up, feeding me with information, to try to discredit Act Now!. Everything about you is a lie, isn't it?'

She slid down the wall, pulled some hair across her face and let it hang there. Then she clasped her knees together and hugged herself tightly.

'*Da*,' she said softly.

I turned away. That way I didn't have to look at her. 'So, you've been using me from the beginning? Our meeting wasn't an accident, it's all been part of a plan to manipulate me to do whatever you and your bosses wanted to do? Did they even tell you to fuck me? How can you live with yourself, Tanya? Is that even your real name?'

I stopped. My anger was taking control and I had to stay calm. I had achieved my first objective, proving that Nigel's suspicions were correct. Now I needed to find out why, what game I had been a part of. Then I could slam the door behind me and get on with the rest of my life.

'Duncan, I think you should leave. You are angry, and I don't want to say more. Please go.'

'I need to know. Who are you? Why are you doing this?'

She ran her hand through her hair. 'I can't tell you. I can't.'

'Then all this goes on the internet with your name all over it.' I threw Nigel's folder at her. 'Here, have a look.'

She flicked through the folder. 'This was Nigel, I

179

suppose?' she said, her voice carrying a weary resignation. 'You publish this, and my days in London are over.'

'Then tell me what's true and I might go easy on you. If you deserve it.'

'My name really is Tanya Petrenko. I'm from Ukraine and I used to be model.' She stood up and I could see tears in her eyes. 'I got job at British Council four years ago. All that is true. Then my brother was killed by Russian supporters in Ukraine and my world collapsed. My little brother, who only wanted Russians to leave us alone.' She stared at me, shaking, trembling.

I remained silent, not trusting myself to speak.

She shrugged. 'I quit job. Cannot be fun person when you are dying inside. I plan to go back to Ukraine, maybe be primary school teacher, I have qualification. But before I left, this guy I never met before at British Council, he told me if I wanted my brother not to have died for nothing, there was something more important I could do for his memory. Find out Russian plans for UK from top Russia guys with big mouths. Who like Ukrainian girls.'

She walked into the living room and crumpled onto the sofa. I sat down opposite her, steeling myself to stay silent.

'I tell them I'm no whore,' she said, shaking her head. 'But he was convincing. He knew I was, well, not exactly schoolgirl virgin. He said, we make opportunity for you to meet guys. You like them, great. You don't like them, no problem, say goodbye. Never would I have to do something disgusting. I say yes, for one year. For my brother. When year up, they offer me new job.'

180

She looked me straight in the eye, her gaze burning with growing intensity. I looked away.

'When Act Now! win election, MI5 had big problem. They knew Russia was behind new government, but for security service to make accusation would be catastrophe. They need someone else to tell story, then they can say they were forced to investigate. Only once they are ready to prove everything, would they dare to bring down government. They draw up list of people to help with story. But they must never know they were part of plan. I'm told to meet three guys, write report, then they choose the one to give stories to. They chose you.'

'You knew who I was before we ever met at the art gallery?' I needed to hear her say it.

'*Da*. They knew you visited there. When you left your Soho House club they tell me to go there, pretend to bump into you. The first few times we met, I was doing my job. Then I become unprofessional, start to like you too much. I tell my bosses that we need to use another guy, but they tell me no.'

'And were you doing your job when we slept together?' I tried to keep the venom out of my voice.

'No. Unprofessional behaviour.' Tanya gave a thin smile. 'I wanted to. You can believe me or not.'

'So how much of our time together was "unprofessional behaviour" and how much was doing your job?'

'All I had to do was get information to you that you believed you were finding out for yourself. You passed first test, realising the importance of what I tell you and using smart IT guy to help you find more. They promote you to next level, get Dmitry Vlasov to give you files. He had contacted MI5 saying he had information, they told him they would send you out to Moscow to get it, but you did not know MI5 were behind you. Dmitry promised he would play along so that you believed everything you were finding out, you were doing by yourself. You could not betray MI5 operation, if you didn't know you were part of it. Then you passed third and final test.'

There was a sour taste developing in my mouth; metallic, bitter. I went to ask for a glass of water but stopped myself. I wanted this to be over as quickly as possible.

'What was the third test?'

'Courage. If you did good job of publicising what Dmitry found out, they were going to give you crown jewel of their intelligence, Pavel Mikin himself. But to be chosen for that, you needed to be not only be good blogger. You needed to be brave.'

'And how did you test my courage?' I had to keep forcing myself to talk to her.

'Plane ticket to London. Making it business class was nice touch, wasn't it? Classy.' Tanya almost went to smile again but caught herself just in time. 'The plan was, that after you got information from Dmitry and guy from troll factory, MI5 would play stunt of leaving you ticket on next plane back to London. To see if you were street smart enough to run, but also brave enough to take evidence with you and write story when you got back. You passed on both counts.'

'And my prize was Pavel Mikin getting in touch?'

'Exactly. MI5 had turned him into double agent and he was my new job before you; I was his handler, based in Moscow. But they daren't risk publicising themselves what he was telling them, the constitutional repercussions would have been unprecedented. Fan would be hit by shit. You had to be completely convincing that you were independent investigative journalist. And you were convincing, because that's what you believed you were.'

'You and Mikin must have enjoyed a good laugh about my gullibility when you saw him in Moscow.'

'No, Duncan.' My jibe had rankled her. She stood up. There was a sharp tone in her voice. 'Stop feeling sorry for yourself. You were lucky one to be chosen. I don't hear you complaining that you are now famous blogger, not scrabbling for crumbs from the table. That the world waits to hear what the next big scandal is you tell them. Maybe you should not complain so much.'

Her words had a ring of truth to them. But I wasn't going to give way in my anger. 'You lied to me. And you were good at it. That didn't happen by accident.'

'I hated every second of lying to you. MI5 knew that you wouldn't want to go back to Moscow because of the plane ticket threat and so you'd agree with using me as an intermediary as the only way forward. When you agreed, I was able to work directly with Pavel as his handler again, to get information to you, and you would think it had been your idea.'

'I want you out of my life, Tanya. I never want to see you again.'

'I understand.' Her voice was toneless, her movements lacklustre. 'When I got to know you as friend, I worried this day would come. I ask myself many times if I should tell you. But you wanted these stories. They made you top blogger. Why not help you achieve your dream? That was what I told myself. But I also said, if day comes you find out, then no more lies. My bosses, they told me if that ever happened to say nothing, get away from you, terminate the operation. But I have to look you in eye this once and tell you truth.'

Her despair was unsettling, and for a second my bitterness started to waver. Then the hurt returned. 'Well, you haven't tried to deny everything. Thanks for that at least.'

She shrugged. 'You owe me nothing, I know that. I've said more to you than I should have. Tell the world what you think you should tell. But I'll have to deny it. I have no choice. Then there will be big question mark over story. Best you say you worked it all out, after Nigel found out about British Council. That would be big help for me. The story will be the same.'

I left and went back home to start writing up the story. The first draft was useless, full of venom and hatred, all directed at Tanya. I started again, keeping things calm and neutral; focusing on the story, not my feelings. I began to reflect the more I wrote. Was I behaving like a petulant child, making it all about me? Would I have preferred not to have been duped, to never have had the chance to expose the story? Maybe I did owe her something. I decided to give Tanya her wish, telling what she had done without revealing her name. I could always change my mind later.

I finished writing, and promised myself I'd sleep on it and put it online in the morning. I staggered off to bed, my head still spinning. When I woke at three and wandered back into my study, the article was still on my computer screen. I knew I should check and double-check what I was saying, maybe even get a lawyer to look over it, it was so controversial. But I was never going to make myself safe from repercussions if I broke this story. I either should do it now, or give up blogging and never mention it again.

I read through the copy one last time. I thought again about waiting, getting the story published by the *Chronicle*, or *News Today*, letting them take the brunt of the repercussions. But after the revelations that Mikin had fed me, my blog was big time now; over a million people would be reading what I posted. I hit Submit and watched the document being uploaded, going out live across the world. The computer gave a dull ping as the task was completed. I fired off a quick email to Alex at *News Today* with a link to the post. 'Latest Developments', I called it. The release of tension now that the story was live was almost palpable, and in its place came a wave of exhaustion as I was finally released from the pressure of the last few hours.

I drifted back off to sleep, trying not to think about what the world would be like when I awoke.

chapter fourteen

About seven in the morning, I stumbled into my study to see the reaction to the article. I stared in disbelief at my computer screen. The blog had disappeared.

For a moment, I thought I must have screwed up last night when I was tired. Then I checked my emails. A few alerts straight after I posted it, showing that it had been seen and that people were responding. The last one was four minutes after the first and then nothing until 5:18 this morning. When there was an email from a legal firm. The heading was *Interlocutory interim injunction on Richard Foxe article*. I clicked on it, full of trepidation.

I couldn't believe what I was reading. In the middle of the night an injunction had been sought and granted, instructing my website hosting company to take down the article. There was to be a follow-up hearing in the High Court at two o'clock this afternoon to extend the ban from its initial forty-eight hours and to make it indefinite. A second superinjunction prevented me from posting to say anything about what was taking place.

There was also an email from Alex from half an hour ago, saying she'd clicked on the link and got an error message, and asking me to resend. I banged my fist on the table. Whoever was behind this had finally gone too far. We didn't live in a police state. When the injunction was overturned, the credibility it would give to my claims would mean they would be everywhere.

I texted Alex, asked to meet her urgently, promising she wouldn't regret it. I couldn't risk going into details in the text because of the superinjunction, and hoped that she wouldn't ignore me. I needed a powerful ally if I was going to tackle this and get the injunctions overturned. Alex texted back, suggesting we meet at eleven. I texted that I'd be at her offices at ten. If she could see me earlier, that would be great. An exasperated emoticon was her only response.

I got to her office and kicked my heels in reception until I was ushered into her office at ten thirty.

'This had better be important, Duncan. I've had to leave a staff meeting.'

'You won't regret it, I promise. I'm sitting on the biggest story of my life, but I've been gagged by Act Now!.' I placed a printout of the email in front of her. 'I posted an article last night, about someone who I thought was a friend and supporter, but it turns out they were working for MI5, feeding me leads and information that MI5 didn't dare publish themselves. It was MI5 that sent me that plane ticket in Moscow, as a sick test of my courage. I thought it had to be someone here who had leaked that I was there. I was wrong. I owe you and *News Today* an apology.'

'I should bloody well think so,' replied Alex. 'But we'll save the hearts and flowers for later. Why would MI5 feed you leaks? Aren't they supposed to be about stopping leaks, not starting them?'

'That's what so important about this story. MI5 suspect that Act Now! is being controlled by the Russians, but they can't just come out and say it. For the security services to accuse the sitting government of treason would plunge the country into a constitutional crisis. They wanted someone else to reveal what they found out, so that the clamour for them to investigate would become overwhelming. And that someone else was me.'

'You?' Alex gave me an incredulous stare. 'You're working for MI5?'

'Not exactly. One of their operatives was ordered to get close to me, feed me the information MI5 had, connect me to their sources, without me ever suspecting a thing. I was their patsy, their fall guy. The perfect foil to get their message across, because I was blissfully unaware that they were using me.' I paused for a second to let the anger inside me subside. 'When I found out what was going on, I wrote it up in a blog and posted it last night. It was live for less than an hour before it was taken down under a temporary gagging order, which is going to be reviewed in the High Court this afternoon. I've got about four hours to put together a defence before they decide whether or not to make it permanent. I can't believe that this could happen in our country. I'm appalled.'

'Let me see,' Alex replied. She picked up the email. '"Order under the Dissemination of Terrorism Act", it says.' She frowned. 'That legislation was brought in to stop terrorist grooming videos and atrocities being posted online. It was never intended to be applied to a case like this. Right, we need Barbara in here for this.' She saw my questioning look. 'In-house lawyer. I should have called her the second you said you had a gagging order.'

Barbara turned up, a severe-looking woman with bouffant hair, dressed in a grey business suit. She shook my hand like she was handling a dead fish. Alex introduced me, said I was the blogger they had used for the Act Now! troll factory story and was on the programme that forced the government to confirm they'd received illegal campaign contributions. And that my follow-up investigation had resulted in me being served a gagging order and a superinjunction.

'So I immediately insisted Duncan stop what he was telling me, until I had a lawyer present.' Alex shot me a look, daring me to contradict. 'So here we are.'

The way she said it, I could sense the two of them had crossed swords before.

'You did right this time, Alex.' I saw Alex bristle at that.

Barbara turned to me. 'For the purposes of this conversation, Mr Jones, you are a freelance consultant who I am interviewing in my capacity as in-house counsel, and this conversation would have to be disclosed in any legal proceedings. Ms Richards is here as note taker.' I made sure I didn't catch Alex's eye.

Barbara picked up the email and the superinjunction document and read through them slowly. Alex and I stared ahead, not saying a word.

When she finished, she addressed us both.

'Technically, they are completely within their rights to do this. It's an interpretation of the new law that was raised as a concern by legal experts at the time it was passed, but there was such public outrage over the atrocity that sparked it off, the protests fell on deaf ears. As things stand at the moment, if the Attorney General says something posted online is a threat that could lead to public disorder, then it's a threat that could lead to public disorder and it gets banned. The ban only gets lifted when the Attorney General says so, or if the government's Security Committee votes to repeal it. And neither's going to happen as long as Act Now! is in power.'

'We've sleepwalked our way into a police state,' I said. 'Can't we publish anyway and take the consequences?'

'Anything published will be pulled immediately,' said Barbara. 'And if it's done with the knowledge that the banning order is in place, there's immediate incarceration of everyone involved. That's what happens when you pass legislation in a hurry while passions run high. You might be prepared to go to jail over this, but I'm not. I've got to keep the TV station on the side of the law, even if I don't agree with it.'

'But this is the twenty-first century,' I protested. 'Surely it's impossible to keep a lid on scandals anymore? Won't this story get out there, somehow, in the next few days?'

'On the lunatic fringe of the internet, where people won't notice it and even if they do, won't take it seriously.' Barbara paused. 'It pains me to say it, but as things stand at the moment, there's nothing we can do. And I have to insist that while these orders remain in place, you agree to abide by them. In particular, you are not to discuss the injunction or the details of the article that precipitated it with anyone at *News Today*. You are to have no further meetings or discussions with Ms Richards, unless I am present. In fact, it would be better if there was no contact from you on any matter until this is resolved.'

'Barbara, we can't do that,' Alex protested. 'The freedom of the press is at stake here. Let's at least provide Duncan with some legal support for his hearing this afternoon. He gave us a major scoop on that Act Now! financing story, and he's offered me an exclusive on this story. I'm sure that offer still stands.' She looked over at me and I nodded. 'We need to do everything to get this overturned.'

I became a bit of a spectator as Barbara and Alex locked horns, two alpha females duking it out for supremacy.

'We have a duty of care to help reporters deal with the aftermath of stories we've sanctioned,' Alex said. 'Especially when that responsibility coincides with an attack where the very freedom of the press is at stake.'

'And it's my duty to stop the station from becoming entangled in court hearings,' Barbara snapped back. 'The only obligation we have to this reporter is a moral one at best. At worst, we could be becoming a party to litigation based on entirely spurious conjecture. We have no way of knowing that any of what Mr Jones claims to be true is not just a figment of his imagination.'

'You do know I'm still here, listening to both of you, don't you?' I said.

Barbara looked daggers at me, a scowl of such ferocity that it took me back to my school days. 'I'm glad you find this amusing,' she replied. 'Can you please enlighten me as to how you came across the evidence that this operative of MI5 is who you say they are?'

'My IT guy used the same hacking techniques that we discovered the Russians were using on Act Now!'s opponents, and hacked into the British Council's computers. He found that the person who was feeding me information was lying. She was using the British Council as a cover, and the only work she did there was to file a daily report to MI5 on a secure computer in the building about the latest status of my investigations.'

'And what's this person's name?'

I hesitated. 'I'm not ready to reveal that just yet.'

Alex looked astonished. 'You want to protect the person who betrayed you? What's going on, Duncan?'

'I don't name sources. I'm not ready to do that yet.'

Alex shook her head in disbelief.

Barbara continued her questioning. 'So this story is based on evidence that you obtained illegally?'

I gave a slightly shamefaced nod. Got no reaction.

'Have you seen the reports she sent from the secure computer? You can confirm they are about you and that the recipient was someone in MI5?'

I bit my lip and shifted uneasily. 'No, I haven't seen the actual reports or the recipient. But when I confronted her about this, she confessed everything. That's why I'm hesitating about naming her. I don't need to reveal her identity or that she confessed. With what my partner has found out, I can prove that she provided me with information and that her cover story was a lie.'

'But I presume you recorded this confession? Or got her to sign a document admitting to all this?'

'No, of course not. I went straight to her apartment after I was told of her deceit. I wasn't thinking straight,

192

I didn't think to take along a voice recorder. Anyway, she will have signed the Official Secrets Act. Her confession would get her in a lot of trouble. That's why she'd have to deny it.'

'Duncan, what the hell is going on here?' Now it was Alex's turn to read the Riot Act. 'This woman deceives you, treats you like a fool, then you look after her and protect her from any comeback? Why on earth would you do that?'

'I don't know. Seems the right thing to do, I suppose. She didn't have to confess.'

Alex and Barbara looked at each other in disbelief.

'Duncan, is there something you're not telling us?' Alex said eventually. 'Is something else going on here?'

I shook my head. There was another pause, a longer one this time.

Finally, Barbara spoke. 'I'm afraid all this does is confirm there is no way I can sanction this station becoming a party to these proceedings. I can give you a recommendation for a lawyer to speak to, but if you brief him, that will be on your own cost. Alex, I know you have a fondness for lost causes, but this is one lost cause that we have to stay well away from. Is that clear? Show Mr Jones off the premises, Alex.'

And with that, she left.

'Well, you excelled yourself there, Duncan,' Alex said, as she walked me to the door. 'You even had me questioning whether your story was a crock with that description of events.'

'It's complicated,' I replied. 'There's some personal stuff between her and me, which is why she confessed so readily.'

'And how old did you say she was?'

'Early thirties. Not that it's relevant.' I decided to change the subject. 'So have you and Barbara have had some issues in the past?'

'Fuck off, Duncan.'

'Right. Well, I'll just fuck off then. Thanks, Alex.'

I phoned the legal firm Barbara recommended and, after answering a few questions from their receptionist, was told I should talk to their criminal lawyer, Tristian Hawtrey. As I heard the words 'criminal lawyer', I had the sensation of things moving too fast to process. I went straight to their offices and asked for Mr Hawtrey. He was younger than me, but had the supercilious air of someone born to privilege, and spoke in a condescending Old Etonian accent. And it had been years since I'd seen someone in a pinstripe three-piece suit who was not on their way to a racecourse. I took him through the chain of events, having to explain to him what was meant by searchbots and filter bubbles. When he asked me to define what a portal was, I really began to worry.

'To get this order taken down, we have to go before a judge. For that, you'll need a barrister, and I would recommend Jeremy Hobbs. Sound chap, and he's up to speed with the panoply of social media.' That reassured me a little, and we headed off to Chancery Lane. We were shown into a cramped office, dominated by a large bookcase overflowing with legal journals, papers scattered on every surface. It did not exactly project the occupant as having the clear and uncluttered mind I was relying on to get my injunction overturned.

Jeremy Hobbs stood up to greet us. Not exactly the

young, thrusting computer-literate hotshot I was hoping for. His eyebrows extended horizontally a good two centimetres and strands of hair dangled from his nostrils, like he'd inhaled a Portuguese man o' war. He nodded to Tristian and then addressed me. 'Mr Jones, please take a seat. Tristian, good to see you again.' He pointed to an old leather captain's chair, with a worn green cushion and scuffed oak legs. In the absence of another chair, Tristian stood at the back of the room.

'You've had an Order under the Dissemination of Terrorism Act served on you, you said on the phone? Can I see the Order and the article it relates to?'

His words were low and melancholic; he would have made Eeyore sound like a ray of sunshine. He read the two documents carefully.

'Shocking,' he concluded. 'The Dissemination of Terrorism Act was never intended to be used in this way.'

'We can get it overturned?' I tried to take heart from his words and ignore his lugubrious delivery.

He sighed. 'Depends on the judge. Not much time to prepare. But if common sense were to prevail, then I would hope so. It will cost £6,200 for me to represent you, up to and including the hearing today. That is, of course, on top of Mr Hawtrey's solicitor's fees. I take it that will be in order?'

Tristian had told me his bill was going to be around two grand. Eye-watering sums, but the clock was ticking and I didn't have a lot of options.

'Yes. Please go ahead. What happens next?'

'I'll need a sworn affidavit from you covering the facts of the case and your assertion that everything you state in your article you know to be factually correct. If anything is conjecture and hearsay, you need to clearly identify that, although the hearing this afternoon is strictly to do with the necessity and legality of the injunction, not the validity or otherwise of the allegations you are making. These would be contested at a later date.'

Jeremy stood up as a signal that the meeting was at an end. 'I'll prepare my submission while my clerk drafts your affidavit. I'll see you on the steps of the High Court at one thirty. Here's my card with my telephone number if you need to talk to me before that. Do you have any questions?'

His clerk came in, a bookish young woman with horn-rimmed glasses.

'Janet, Mr Jones needs to prepare a sworn affidavit. Can you assist him and track down a notary to witness it?'

She gave a demure smile and said it would be done straight away. Jeremy ushered Tristian and me out of his office and I went off to prepare the documents.

★ ★ ★

I arrived at the court in plenty of time. Tristian had said he'd get there as soon as he could, as he had a prior engagement. Jeremy arrived at 1:45, fifteen minutes late, no apology. Customer service was apparently not a high priority in this part of the world.

'We'll have to go straight in,' Jeremy informed me. 'Doesn't do to keep the judge waiting.'

I scuttled along behind him as he strode purposefully through the labyrinth of corridors before arriving at the designated courtroom. It had the full paraphernalia of criminal dock, witness box, jury bench and judge's chair, an empty public gallery behind us. I started to feel intimidated. The other lawyers were already there, six of them, their leading silk in his magisterial pomp, exuding gravitas and confidence.

Jeremy was flicking anxiously through his papers like he had lost something, his eyebrows leaping up and down like dancing caterpillars. Tristian arrived, nodded a hello, then sat behind me and stared into space, like he was in a trance. It felt like Raith Rovers were taking on Real Madrid.

Janet sidled in at the last minute and handed Jeremy a lever arch file. He opened it up and looked relieved when he glanced inside. I was glad he wasn't defending me in a murder case. The judge arrived with due pomp and ceremony and after the formalities were over, Jeremy stood up and mechanically and laboriously read out word for word what was in the folder in front of him. Impenetrable legalese about the mechanics of going to trial, as far as I could tell.

'And so, I humbly submit to Your Lordship, that due process should be allowed to take its course. My client should be allowed to publish his accusations freely and openly, fully aware that any mendacity on his part will ensure the full force of the law is brought to bear on him and he will be punished accordingly.'

Not exactly the ringing endorsement of the veracity of my story and the impassioned defence of free speech I was looking for.

'I thought he was supposed to be on my side,' I

whispered to Janet. I was sure I detected a flicker of amusement trying to break through her ice-maiden expression.

The opposing barrister rose up with regal splendour to make his arguments.

'The Crown is of the opinion that this article by Mr Jones is nothing more than a reckless canard, a flight of fancy which attempts to undermine the nation's security and is an indiscriminate and irresponsible attempt to sow discord and animosity towards the government.' He enunciated every syllable, making every word appear to be dripping with deep significance. 'I respectfully submit an affidavit from the Attorney General stating this to be the case. Under section two, clause one of the Dissemination of Terrorism Act, I would ask Your Lordship to extend the current order, until the threat to public order represented by this article can be addressed by the court in due course by full legal process.' He nodded his agreement to himself and settled his ample posterior back in his seat.

'All rise,' said the usher.

Totally nonplussed, I got to my feet as the judge left.

'Was that it?' I asked. 'Isn't there, like, a cross-examination or something?'

'No, that would be for the trial,' replied Jeremy. 'But risky strategy that, relying on the judge to interpret the Act in that way. Now we wait.'

'For what? Between the two of you, you've uttered less than a thousand words.'

The courtroom door opened. 'You're right, Mr Jones. The judge is returning,' Jeremy said.

The usher called for us to stand as the judge re-entered

the courtroom. He sat down and glared at the barrister for the Crown.

'Your argument, Mr Davidson, relies exclusively on the Attorney General's affidavit that the article under discussion is in breach of the Dissemination of Terrorism Act. And under the provisions of that Act, the affidavit of the Attorney General is, *de facto*, grounds for the injunction to be upheld, along with the conjoint injunction barring discussion of the banning order.'

Davidson bowed his acknowledgement.

The judge scowled again. 'This is a perilous and sinister path the government is going down. When this case comes to court, and if the scenario of the defendant being found not guilty prevails, I would expect the consequences for the government to be very severe indeed. However, in the meantime, my hands are tied due to what I would characterise as the draconian provisions of the Act requiring the injunction to be extended if so requested by the Attorney General. I hereby extend the injunction for another four weeks, after which we shall reconvene to see if the Attorney General sees fit to withdraw his affidavit.'

The judge turned to me.

'Mr Jones, I continue this injunction until further proceedings in the case.'

With that, he stood up and left.

I staggered out of the courtroom in a state of shock. 'So, if in four weeks the Attorney General hasn't changed his mind, it gets extended again? And then again and again, until one day they bring me to court and decide whether I'm telling the truth? Is that what just happened?'

'I'm afraid so. Shocking really.'

I wished Jeremy had put more outrage into his voice.

'But of course, I will be happy to represent you at the next hearing, and perhaps we might get a more sympathetic reaction from the judge if the other side doesn't do any more than restate the same case again.'

'I hope so.' A horrible thought struck me. 'But that won't require an extra fee, will it? After all, today took all of ten minutes and five of them were spent waiting for the judge to pop in and out of the courtroom.'

Jeremy looked offended. 'I'm sorry to say, yes, I'm afraid it will. The fee for today's hearing was not predicated on the length of the hearing. I'm able to make some accommodation to reduce the fee to £5000 for the next hearing, but unfortunately, yes, there will have to be another fee.'

'And five grand for the one after that? And the one after that? Every four weeks until it comes to trial?'

'Worst case, yes. And if you decided to escalate this to the court of appeal, I'm afraid the costs would be even more severe. But I doubt if the judge will keep extending the injunctions indefinitely.'

I returned home, despondent and depressed. I fired an email off to Bobbie to see if we could have a chat. It was after eight before she got my message; spring's a busy time up in Scoraig, apparently. I could see she shared my pain over the Tanya revelations and my distress at being gagged by the State from telling my story. Even more so, being made bankrupt if I wanted to keep fighting it every four weeks.

'Tanya always did seem too good to be true,' she said.

'But I'm appalled that we live in a country where the truth can be silenced so easily. How did that happen?'

'I suppose the communication age has been a victim of its own success,' I replied. 'It became so easy for anyone to say anything and the consequences became so problematic, that there eventually had to be controls put into place. And Act Now! saw it as a chance to create a police state without anyone realising it. I need to give up on this and move on.'

'I've never known you to be so defeatist, Duncan. That's not like you.'

'I know, but everything about this sickens me. Being deceived by Tanya, being manipulated by MI5, the bully boy tactics of Act Now!, rip-off lawyers and ineffectual judges; sometimes you've got to realise that the odds are stacked against you. If the law's geared up to stopping me from talking, and they've got the full might of the State behind them, there's not a lot a one-man-band can do to stop them.'

'One thing's for sure. You can't keep shelling out money on legal costs.'

'Tell me about it. These bloody lawyers would drain me dry.'

We finished on that unsatisfactory note, and I headed off to bed. In the middle of the night, a noise encroached on my subconscious. It was a Skype notification ping, and I staggered blearily into my study. It was Bobbie. Three o'clock in the morning. I clicked Accept.

'Hi Duncan, sorry to wake you.'

'It's all right. I had to get up anyway, my computer was making a noise.'

She ignored me. 'There is another way you could get the story out. One that a lawyer might not have thought about. And one you've proved you're good at.'

My eyes were starting to focus now, and I could see Bobbie had a glimmer of a smile on her face.

My interest was piqued. 'And what's that?'

'Write the truth as a novel. *Roman-à-clef*, remember? When you used my story about Michael as the inspiration for that bloody book of yours which brought the world crashing down. Get your author hat back on, tell the story as a work of fiction, get it talked about and eventually the true story will come out, like it did all those years ago.'

'Except that the story led to an innocent man going to jail. In case you had forgotten.'

'That's not nice, Duncan. I'm only trying to help. What I'm saying is write a story, have people speculate about the truth. Don't say it is the truth, but don't deny it either. It might knock a hole through this ban you're under.'

'It's a nice idea, but it would take too long. A year to write, even longer to get it edited and published. And that's assuming I've even got it in myself to write something. I've not written any fiction for twenty years.'

Bobbie shrugged. 'Just a thought.'

Then I felt a surge of excitement.

'Wait a minute,' I said. 'Who says it has to be a novel? It could be a play, even a radio play. I'd only have to write ten thousand words, not eighty. That could be done in months, if not weeks.'

Bobbie nodded at my enthusiasm. 'And you could do that? Write it as a play, I mean?'

'I could try. There's a lot of technical differences, but I've been around the block enough times to give it a go. And I was involved with the screen adaptation of *Escape to Danger*.' I paused. 'Yes, I could do it. Let me check with the lawyer, see if it could be published and performed. Then at least I'm trying something to get the story out.'

When I checked, my cunning plan turned out not to be so cunning after all. Simply performing a re-enactment of my blog, changing the names and a few details here and there, didn't get around the injunction, my lawyer told me. Despondently, I told Bobbie the bad news.

'He said it had to be fundamentally different. To the point that nobody could reasonably assume that what I was saying was that Act Now! was under the control of the Russians. Which sort of defeats the point of the exercise. I could try to write something allegorical, like Orwell's *Animal Farm*, but the more obtuse I make the connection, the less likely it is to do the job I want it to do. And I'm not that sort of writer, I'm more of a real-life drama sort of scribe. Bit too old a dog to learn new tricks.'

Bobbie made me promise to at least give it a try and so the next day I headed off to Soho House, found my favourite nook and sat down brainstorming idea after idea about how I could tell my story. Nothing. After two hours, my head was exploding and the size of the pile of torn-up sheets of paper thrown into my rucksack was depressing. I needed to clear my head, and headed off to the National Portrait Gallery.

I almost subconsciously headed up to the Tudor Gallery. Henry was still there, and the portraits of Elizabeth I. The courtiers were looking as fierce and cunning as ever, taking on new significance as I thought of the dark forces behind the current government. Some things never change.

The room had bittersweet memories – of my first encounter with Tanya and how completely I was taken in. Did I really think that my knowledge of Elizabethan England had been the reason a friendship developed? I thought of her jibe when she described my novels set in the 1970s as historical fiction. Despite everything, it still made me smile. Some of that chemistry must have been genuine, even back then, I tried to convince myself. I looked at the portrait of Sir Henry Lee, his eyes blazing with psychotic ruthlessness.

'You'd fit right in with Act Now!,' I told him.

That was the thing about historical fiction these days. Much of it was really about the present. The thought unsettled me.

I'd gone there to clear my head and all that was happening was that old memories were coming back, clogging up my thoughts, tearing at my emotions, making it impossible to think straight. I needed to escape. I headed down the stairs, passing through the post-war gallery on my way out. I stopped for a moment at the Clement Attlee painting. 'A modest man, who had much to be modest about,' was how Winston Churchill described him. But the painting showed something different. Attlee staring straight at the painter, a steely glint in his eyes, the grim determination of the man who had picked Britain up from the ashes of the Second World War and built the foundation of the Welfare State. All from a man who had the outward appearance of an introverted bank manager.

I allowed myself a few minutes of contemplation of the painting and the man it was revealing to me, my favourite pastime in the gallery, the one I had been indulging with Peter Capaldi when Tanya first came along. I flipped open Attlee's Wikipedia page on my phone to read more. Won the 1945 general election against all the odds, standing for Labour against Churchill, the war-time hero, and formed a majority government. Dark rumours from the establishment that other forces must be at work, it couldn't be simply the will of the people that had swept Labour to power on a tide of populist measures which had appealed to the returning troops and their families. The main rumour being that Stalin was somehow behind the election victory, that it was part of the Soviet drive to achieve world domination.

I reeled at the parallels to Act Now!. A political party gains power unexpectedly for the first time with a wave of radical populist measures that are secretly being orchestrated by the Russians. Not true in Attlee's case, but a story that could be told as a work of fiction, almost exactly mimicking the events of the twenty-first century.

'I'm sorry to do this to you, mate,' I said to Attlee, 'but I can't be done for libelling the dead.' I almost detected a twinkle of complicity in his eyes.

I went back to Soho House, sat down at my computer, and set off exploring the depths of my imagination to make the story come to life.

I had become a writer again.

chapter fifteen

The Ubiquitous Chip had hardly changed since it first opened in 1976, offering a radical alternative to the then typically stodgy and unhealthy Glasgow cuisine. Chips in Glasgow were still ubiquitous, but on the cobbled alleyway of Ashton Lane in the city's West End, the restaurant had inspired a host of neighbouring cafés and restaurants, creating an eclectic bubble of international gastronomy, tucked away behind the busy thoroughfare of Byres Road.

It had been three months since I'd first started writing the play and now I was ready to meet with Bobbie to discuss getting it performed. My train from London had arrived on time, but she had texted me to say that a jackknifed lorry was slowing her progress as she drove down from Scoraig. I took another sip of sparkling water and enjoyed the guttural Glaswegian banter all around me.

'I telt him he was aboot as welcome as a fart in a spacesuit', I heard one guy say to his fellow diners. A well-travelled Billy Connolly one-liner that always made me chuckle.

It had quite an impact on me when Bobbie walked in. We try to meet up at least once a year, but it had been a while since I'd made the long drive up to her remote

Highlands home. Seeing her in Glasgow, our old stomping ground, with ghosts and memories in every corner, was overwhelming. Our embrace went on for thirty seconds, maybe more. When we separated, we smiled at each other like embarrassed teenagers.

'Any more of that and they'll be telling us to get a room,' I said.

'I've been thrown out of better places than this,' Bobbie replied. 'In fact, I have been told to leave here once before. A sense-of-humour failure at you writing about my debauched existence, and look where that led us.' She laughed. 'I hope history's not about to repeat itself. Duncan, Duncan, what am I to do with you?'

I tried to look sheepish. 'We're a bit older and wiser than we were back then. Well, older anyway. But there's a difference. This play was your idea. You've got me into this mess, so you can get me out of it.'

Bobbie rummaged in her bag and retrieved a printout.

'Well, I've read it,' she said. 'And it's great. Forget its purpose is to bring the Act Now! story out into the open, it's a bloody good play. So, what's the problem with getting it performed?'

'Legality. Despite what my lawyer said about it being okay to put on a play about Clement Attlee being a Russian stooge, I've pitched it all over London and no one will touch it with a bargepole. The legislation behind the superinjunction is unbelievably strict. People have no idea what sort of repressive police state we live in now. So that's when I thought of Scotland.'

'Let me get this straight. You want to put the play on in Scotland, where Act Now! isn't the government,

207

and hope that the different legal system waters down the injunction's impact? And you want me to dust off my little black book and see if I know of any theatre directors who might like to take the risk of heading to jail with you by deciding to stage it? At least you told me beforehand, rather than dropping a bombshell like the last time we met here.'

'So that's a no, is it?' I tried not to look too disappointed.

Bobbie laughed. 'When did you get so defeatist in your old age? If you can come out of retirement and write something as great as this, who's to say I can't do the same? Here's my proposition. I'll come down to Glasgow and direct the thing. I've spoken to Davie, and he's happy for me to give up three months of the croft to do this. I know a great church in Cowcaddens that will work as a venue, and there's no shortage of acting talent. The only thing I need from you is to cover the financials; there's not enough left over from a crofter's income to fund these sorts of indulgences. But this story captures the zeitgeist of the moment. If you say your media contacts are champing at the bit to give it publicity, it should be a smash. What do you say, Duncan? Want to do this together?'

I said yes. Bobbie said she would need £5,000 up front, but wouldn't take a salary as director. Once the play was up and running and the advance was paid off, we'd split any profits from the run fifty-fifty.

When I got back to London, I got Alex and Sam together at a neutral venue, a hotel lobby in a discreet part of Knightsbridge. I got there first, in case either of them felt uncomfortable sharing a story with a media competitor.

'I hope this is okay with you both,' I said. 'You've been very supportive of the Act Now! story and you were the first two people in the media to know about the superinjunction.'

Their faces remained impassive, neither wanting to reveal their hand to the other.

'The injunction's only temporary, but the government have been asking for it to be reapplied every four weeks, and the judge is powerless to prevent it. I've tried fighting it, but all that does is waste legal fees. Theoretically, the case will eventually come to trial, but there seems to be no urgency about progressing it. I could be stuck in this limbo for years.'

'Shocking,' ventured Alex.

Sam mumbled his agreement.

'But I've got a way around it,' I said in my most confident voice. 'I've finished writing a play, called *The Art of Deception*. Tells the story of the Russians being the guiding force behind the Labour Party coming to power in 1945, with uncanny parallels to what's happening now. My lawyer says it's on rock solid legal ground, no problem with it getting performed.' I crossed my fingers behind my back as I spoke. 'It's booked for an eight-week run in Glasgow starting next month and I thought you could each send someone to the premiere, run a story about it, and that would spark off a discussion about whether any of it could be true today. Maybe coordinate what you'd both be doing for maximum effect. The more it gets discussed, the more we get the story out in the open. What do you think?'

'Well, it's a clever plan,' said Alex. 'But are you sure

people will see the connection between Act Now! and Clement Atlee? It's a bit of a stretch.'

'Not if I say the play is by Richard Foxe, rather than my author name,' I replied. 'Think about it. Richard Foxe is always being talked about, because of all my revelations about the Russians. Then someone who's thought of only as a political blogger surprises everyone and writes a play, not based on current events, but a piece of historical fiction. That's even more unexpected. It's bound to spark off conjecture, and there's only one way the speculation can go – that *The Art of Deception* is an allegory on current events. Before you know it, everyone is talking about whether MI5 have recruited a spy to fool a journalist into telling the world the Russians are behind Act Now!. I think it can work.'

'It might,' said Sam. 'I could certainly have our arts correspondent write a review. But getting it onto the political pages is going to be more difficult.'

'We'd need to have a news story to report on,' agreed Alex. 'Something linked to the play that would allow us to do more than hint at it being a comment about Act Now!. A piece of evidence, for example, that we could report on without breaching the injunction, that asks questions about the issues raised.'

'I do have evidence. The stuff that was on my original blog. The details around the hack into the British Council computer that showed a Ukrainian spy was working for MI5.' I sighed. 'I know, I know. All of that is covered by the injunction.'

'We would need something new,' said Sam. 'You could name your source, for a start.'

'She asked me not to, said it would destroy her life

in London,' I said. Then I thought about it. 'I suppose I could get back in touch with her, ask her again. But even if she said yes, if I went public on her identity I'm pretty sure that would be breaking the terms of my injunction.'

Sam shook his head. 'Then the only way to break the story is for us to interview your source. That would be a legitimate news story and the interview would be outside the scope of the injunction because it wouldn't involve you. I could maybe get that past our lawyers.' He looked over at Alex for agreement.

'I'm not so sure, Sam,' she replied. 'But if this source did agree to be interviewed, it might be better with your paper, and we pick up on the aftermath.'

I hadn't given up hope that Sam might go along with my idea, without Tanya having to do an interview. I tried again.

'You couldn't use all the publicity from the play, and just come out and say a Ukrainian spy is helping MI5 disclose what's going on?'

'Too risky,' said Sam. 'You've got the evidence from your British Council hack, but that could all be faked. I'd need some corroboration if we were to run the story. Your Ukrainian going on the record, with all the risks to her that that entails, is the only way the story is strong enough for my paper to take the chance to run it.'

Alex nodded her support.

I forced myself to be objective. All I could do was give Tanya the arguments for doing the interview. It would be up to her if she said yes.

I sent an email to Tanya, got no reply. Followed up with a text. Nothing. I told Alex and Sam that it was obvious she didn't want to talk, but they told me to try harder. I realised I would have to doorstep her. A bit more confrontational than I felt comfortable with, but I had no choice. I headed round to her flat to catch her first thing in the morning.

A stranger opened the door, told me the previous tenant had moved back to Ukraine, and left no forwarding address. I felt a peculiar resentment. Tanya had apparently wanted to get on with her life without me, but I was hurt that she hadn't told me she was going to disappear. Then I smiled at my hypocrisy. I had told her I never wanted to see her again and now I was upset that she had taken me at my word.

I called up Nigel to see if he could help. There had not been much for us to work on together since I dialled back on the investigative journalism to focus on writing the play, but I'd made a point of keeping in touch with him every couple of weeks. He was beginning to realise that if we talked about whatever was obsessing him at that moment for more than ten minutes, it was a Bad Thing and would mean that I would be getting bored and he should let me change the subject.

We talked about other Bad Things, the fact that the government wouldn't let us tell our story, that Tanya had lied to us and that Act Now! had been able to shrug off all the scandal and continue to ride a populist wave in the opinion polls. Now I wanted to talk about another Bad Thing, that Tanya had disappeared and I needed to track her down.

'It's not a Bad Thing that she's gone away, it's a Good Thing,' said Nigel when I told him the news about Tanya. 'She was a liar and made you look silly. I hate her more for making you look silly than for being a liar and I really hate liars. That's how much I hate her.'

'She thought she was doing a Good Thing helping us find out stuff. We shouldn't hate her. The TV and newspapers want to talk to her, or they won't tell people about what we know. And she might be in trouble. Yes, I was furious when I found out she was deceiving us, but I've come to understand her point of view. Can you help me find her?'

'Only if you make me a solemn promise that she won't be part of the team again. Just you and me, that's how it should be.'

'Solemn promise. So how would you track her down?'

'I need clues, like Sherlock Holmes. Can you tell me her full name, date of birth, parents, where she lived in Ukraine? Everything you know about her.'

I wrote down what I knew and realised it didn't amount to much. Petrenko was one of the most common surnames in Ukraine, and she had never mentioned the town where she lived before she left to become a model. I knew her age and birthday, and that was about it. Her mobile phone number turned out to have been discontinued, she'd never had a Facebook profile, and she had switched off video calling. She was serious about disappearing. It didn't look good.

I wracked my brains for something else that could help track her down. I remembered she'd said to me she trained as a primary school teacher before becoming a model. She had a friend that she kept in touch with in Kiev, but she never told me her name. Nigel said that his hack into the British Council website had been discovered and more security had been put in place. He promised to keep trying, but he didn't sound particularly hopeful.

He called me a few days later.

'Tanya Petrenko is her real name. Or if it's not, someone is being super sneaky. I went back to 2010 when you said she was a model, and her name and photo popped up on some Paris fashion shows and some photoshoots for ladies' clothes. Check your messages – I've sent you some pictures.'

It was strange looking at Tanya's modelling shots, – the haughty, dour expression that seems to be the done thing in the fashion industry. Nothing like the vibrant, effervescent Tanya that I knew. Groomed to within an inch of her life, full of confidence and charisma, and definitely Tanya.

'It's her, alright,' I said. 'That's a result. I suppose with her working at the British Council before MI5 recruited her, it would have been too problematic to suddenly give her a false name. Well done, Nigel.'

'That's not all. I managed to find a register of primary school teachers in Ukraine. Easy-peasy to hack into, but trying to read Ukrainian using Translate was trickier. There are seventy-one people called Tanya Petrenko working as primary school teachers, and I know the towns they work in, but not the name of the schools or the teachers' home addresses. There's no way of narrowing them down. That's too many, isn't it?'

It was. I couldn't cover the whole of Ukraine, but presumably there were some in Kiev. I could try flying to Ukraine and visiting them, hope they spoke English and might know my Tanya. Maybe the coincidence of having the same name as another teacher might mean they'd remember a Tanya Petrenko who moved to London. But it was a long shot. Probably too long a shot to be worth taking. I encouraged Nigel to keep looking, but it seemed like Tanya had disappeared for good.

In the meantime, the play premiered in Glasgow with a nerve-jangling opening night. I had based the story on a fictitious Lee Symonds, a bold and ambitious twenty-something woman who joins the civil service in 1945, just as Attlee's Labour Party sweeps to victory, defeating Churchill in an electoral bolt from the blue. Spurred on by her American lover, Lee agrees to spy on the British government for the Americans, who have a hidden agenda in making sure the electorate's burgeoning Socialist ambitions don't play into Soviet hands. Not a hint about the world of superinjunctions and gagging orders, but with Richard Foxe as the name of the playwright, it wouldn't take too long before the parallels to today were being drawn.

Afterwards, I was surprised to find Bobbie in tears.

'What's the matter?' I said. 'It wasn't that bad.'

'Oh, piss off, Duncan.' She smiled at me as she wiped her face. 'You've really done it to me, haven't you?'

'Done what?' I was genuinely confused.

'Reminded me of this life. Doing the rehearsals these last few weeks I've been happier since, well, I don't know when. And when I stood at the side of that stage tonight, all I could think about was, in eight weeks this will all be over. I'll be back to living in Scoraig again, back to the grind and monotony of living in that damp, draughty croft, shut off from the rest of the world.'

I was shocked. 'I thought you loved it there. And you and Davie seem happy.'

'We are. But it's typical of me to run off to the back of beyond whenever there's a crisis in my life. And now I'm stuck there. Crofting is Davie's life; he'd never want to move.'

'Couldn't you get a farm somewhere else? Somewhere less remote?'

'Where's the money going to come from? And even if I could, what if I have another panic attack? Where I live is a different universe from all the stuff that scares me, a different world from Michael Mitchell, Act Now!, and all the other evils in the world. Even if I could convince Davie to give up everything we've built together in Scoraig, come back into the twenty-first century, what happens if it all goes wrong because of me? I'd never forgive myself.'

The conversation put a dampener on the evening, and things didn't get any better. The reviews of the play itself were excellent, but *News Today* confirmed that, without Tanya, they couldn't cover it as a news story. Sam stuck his neck out and ran a piece in the *Chronicle* that featured a full-length article on the play and an interview with myself, pored over by the paper's lawyers so I could say as much as possible about how true it might be without running foul of the law.

Today, as the world finds itself at the mercy of strained political relations and ever-shifting borders and alliances, The Art of Deception *explores another time wracked by similar fears and mistrusts and provides a fascinating insight into a time and place where the fulcrum of power rested on a pinpoint. With the author being none other than the political blogger Richard Foxe, one can only wonder how much of this story is meant to be seen as historical fiction, and how much is really a commentary on current political events.*

The Scottish press were also big on speculation, and by the end of the first week there could be no doubt in anybody's mind that there was no smoke without fire, and that Act Now! had some explaining to do, to answer the question of whether all the rumour and speculation was true.

Damien Zane went on the record as saying he wished the show well, but underneath the good-natured reaction that Act Now! was trying to portray, the real dirty tricks began. Act Now! dug up my past yet again, and the fact that Bobbie was directing the play brought her into the firing line as well. Back in London, when a local radio station invited me to their studios to talk about the play, I couldn't wait to come to her defence.

'People have said that you are a vulture, Richard Foxe, writing works of fiction that are based on real people and events and seeing lives ruined as a result,' said the presenter. 'Didn't you learn your lesson twenty-five years ago with the Michael Mitchell case? And now you and your partner in crime from back then are doing it again, criticising Clement Atlee, the prime minister who created the National Health Service, and casting aspersions on the current government? Shouldn't the two of you be ashamed of yourselves?'

I defended my right to create a piece of political satire,

saying that the big problem with writing historical fiction these days is that history keeps repeating itself.

'But that's the point, isn't it?' the radio show host persisted. 'The play shadows real-life events remarkably closely until the penultimate scene when the young woman is revealed as a spy, working for the CIA who are seeking to discredit the British government. Do you think what's happening in real life is more unbelievable than that?'

'You might think that, I couldn't possibly comment,' I said in my best *House of Cards* impression. 'There are things going on in politics today that bloggers like myself would love to talk about.'

'Like what, exactly?'

'That's just it, I can't say. I'm not allowed to. Act Now! says they've shown a sense of humour about my play. But ask them, if they really find it so entertaining, why don't they let the real story come out? I wrote this play, hoping to raise questions in people's minds as to whether such as a dystopian scenario as I depicted could be true in today's world. Because if it were true, I wouldn't be able to sit here and talk to you about it. That would be banned by a court order under the Dissemination of Terrorism Act.'

The radio show host remained blissfully unaware of what I'd just managed to get away with saying.

'There we must leave it, folks,' he cheerily announced. 'Is Act Now! under the control of the Russians? Does the CIA have beautiful female spies trying to bring down the government? I don't know the answer, but I do know that *The Art of Deception* is running in Glasgow for the next eight weeks, and if the reviews are anything to go by, it'll be transferred to the West End sometime soon. Thanks to the playwright and blogger Richard Foxe for coming in today and shedding some light on what might or might not be the inspiration behind the play.'

I headed off home, pleased with myself. With every piece of publicity, the story was, little by little, creeping out into the public domain. The strategy was working, and I was convinced that the constant chatter and speculation about how much of the play was true would make it more and more impossible to keep the real story secret.

I couldn't have been more wrong. That evening there was a knock on the door and two uniformed policemen were standing in the hallway.

'Duncan Jones?' I nodded.

'We have a warrant for your arrest for contravening an injunction granted under the Dissemination of Terrorism Act. Please accompany us to the station.'

'Arrest? You're arresting me? For what?'

'We'll discuss that at the station.'

I was firmly, even a little forcibly, taken to the police car waiting outside. As the car drove off, the blue light was switched on and the siren blared as we sped off to wherever I was going. It didn't seem real; I kept expecting to wake up.

I was staggered to discover that I was to spend the night in a jail cell before appearing before a judge the next day.

'Is this strictly necessary?' I said. 'You know I'm not going to run off somewhere and I'm hardly a threat to society. Can't I post a surety or give an undertaking I'll be there? Locking me up seems a bit excessive.'

The custody officer looked sympathetic. 'I'm sure you're not going to run off, Mr Jones. But the powers that be are insisting on you being detained, quoting a risk that you would breach your injunction again if you were left to your own devices. You can make one phone call to your lawyer, but other than that you are to be kept in isolation until your hearing.'

As the cell door clanged behind me in the police station, it brought the stakes home to me. I tried to convince myself that one night in jail wouldn't be too bad. An experience to dine out on, and it would improve my street cred no end. As I tossed and turned on the hard mattress trying to get some sleep I was actually starting to be thrilled at my new-found status as a martyr for free speech.

Tristian Hawtrey came to see me the next morning, looking concerned. I gave him a cheery greeting to lighten the mood, made some joke about posting a negative review on TripAdvisor about the lack of facilities. He did not play along.

'I've been through the transcript of your radio interview, and it is possible that it could be considered that you have breached the terms of the injunction,' Tristian said. 'That's a serious matter.'

'How serious? Could I be fined or something? I'm pretty broke at the moment.'

'More serious than that, I'm afraid. The Dissemination of Terrorism Act was designed to deal with serious cases of terrorist grooming and to outlaw the posting of inflammatory messages by extremists, or videos of atrocities. In a normal situation, what would happen is that you would be charged with contempt of court and given twenty-four hours to turn up in court, where a judge would decide the case. But this Act allows the Attorney General to make the order for arrest directly, and set the sentence, without involving a judge. You go to court, but that's purely for a judge to ratify the sentence and to allow it to be processed. He has no powers to overturn the order. And the hearing is heard *in camera*, which means no journalists or members of the public are allowed to attend. Theoretically, contravening an order under the Act could result in twenty years in jail, life in some cases.'

He saw my jaw hit the floor.

'Now we're obviously not dealing with that sort of case here, but you have to be aware that you have been charged with a very serious offence, at least in sentencing terms. We need to handle this hearing extremely carefully. I've taken the liberty of getting in touch with Jeremy Hobbs already. He will be at the court to represent you, but you have to realise there's not a lot he will be able to do.'

Suddenly, my martyrdom did not seem quite so glamorous. I was sure Tristian was being unduly pessimistic, and I told myself that once this was over, I'd start looking for more of a glass-half-full sort of person as my lawyer. It would be time well spent. Legal battles looked like they were going to be the norm rather than the exception going forward.

My solicitor and I travelled separately to the courtroom, me in a Black Maria, feeling like a caged animal as I peered through the metal grille separating me from the police officers in the middle part of the van. Two guards plus the driver seemed a bit excessive. The van pulled up outside the court and I was escorted inside, to the same courtroom I'd been in for the earlier attempts to have my gagging order overturned. I was an old hand at this now. I went to sit down next to Jeremy and caught his embarrassed look.

'I'm afraid you sit there,' he said, gesturing to the dock.

'Oh. Right,' I replied. I looked at the two policemen, who hadn't left my side. I went over to the dock, and one of the policemen told me to stand beside it. There was a signal from a court clerk, the door was opened and I walked up the steps and sat down, facing the court. Behind me was a spiral staircase, leading down to an ominous-looking door. My early bravado had now completely disappeared.

'Be upstanding in court!' boomed the clerk, and the judge appeared, a stern-looking gentleman of uncertain age, resplendent in ceremonial trappings. He settled down into his chair, and the proceedings began.

Prosecuting counsel went through the background to the case. I had been subject to a gagging order. I had tested the patience of the Crown by attempting to circumvent it by staging a play paralleling the events covered by the order, and had revelled in the ensuing speculation and notoriety. During my radio interview the day before, I had flagrantly broken the terms of the order, encouraging listeners to believe that the play was based on current events and alluding to the gagging order in contravention of the superinjunction. This had all resulted in an order from the Attorney General that I be detained for six months under the Dissemination of Terrorism Act.

Jeremy had advised that the best response would be for me to apologise for my intemperate comments on the radio and to give an undertaking to the Attorney General not to do so again. I was having none of it. I told him he had to attack the morality of preventing someone from speaking out about what they believed to be true. It was a high-risk strategy, and the prosecuting counsel's words showed me that Jeremy's misgivings had turned out to be well-founded.

The judge took less than thirty minutes to retire and consider the arguments.

'Duncan Jones, you have the arrogance to think you can pick and choose which laws apply to you and which do not ...'

This was not going to end well.

'Laws are a sign of civilised society. They are made by common consent and must not be trampled on by individuals. But you think you are above such restrictions; so that no matter what actions a court takes, if you don't agree with them, you can flout them at will. And you will continue flouting them, whenever a chance presents itself. I have to demonstrate to you that the courts will not tolerate being treated in this way. I am ratifying the Attorney General's order, sending you to prison, where there will be no opportunities to speak to the media or commit further transgressions until due legal process brings you before this court to be tried for contravening the Dissemination of Terrorism Act and related offences. I would hope that you will treat this time as an opportunity for reflection, so that when ultimately released you do not simply reoffend straightaway. I can assure you that this will only demonstrate a need for a longer period of detention. Commensurate with this sentence I am imposing reporting restrictions, banning further discussion of the play known as *The Art of Deception* in whatever forum until your trial. Furthermore, all performances of the play itself are covered by these restrictions and must cease forthwith. That is all. I ratify the sentence of six months' imprisonment, with the prospect of early parole solely at the discretion of the Attorney General. Take him down.'

My life collapsed around me. Incarceration and financial ruin. I would lose all the money I'd put up for the production and with further court cases looming, legal bills would be mounting.

I took one last look around the courtroom as the door to the dock opened and a policeman stepped inside. He escorted me down the spiral staircase to the netherworld below. The policeman knocked on the door at the bottom, and after a few seconds, I heard it being unlocked. A matronly-looking woman beckoned me to enter. I stepped inside, leaving behind the courtroom, with its tasteful warm beech and contrasting blue panels, and into the dingy and forbidding world below.

The woman introduced herself as Doreen and led me down some further stairs encased on all sides with steel mesh. She showed me into a small, windowless room, bare apart from a padded bench.

'This is the holding cell,' she explained. 'Make yourself comfortable, and I'll be back in a mo.'

With that, the heavy door with its iron-barred viewing panel was slammed shut. I slumped down onto the bench, my head in my hands.

Doreen came back a few minutes later.

'I've brought you a nice cup tea,' she said with a cheery grin. 'How do you take it?'

'Milk, no sugar,' I replied automatically.

It was surreal, this friendliness and courtesy, and I was still in shock that I was now a convicted prisoner. The door opened and another jailer walked in, armed with a sheaf of papers.

'This is Harry,' Doreen said. 'He's got some forms to be filled in. Drink up your tea and let's get on with it. You'll be wanting to have your legal, I'm guessing.'

A 'legal' turned out to be a visit from Tristian, for which I was moved to a larger cell.

'I'm as shocked as you are,' he said by way of an introduction. 'The ban on the play is a scandal, quite unprecedented. The important thing is to stay calm and don't entertain any thoughts of suicide.'

I finally snapped.

'This should not be happening to me. I want out of here. There must be something you can do. There must be.' I could feel tears, and forced myself to stay in control. 'Speak to the media, to politicians, to anyone who can help me.'

'I can ask Jeremy Hobbs to make a submission to the Attorney General that you will give an undertaking not to repeat your accusations, now or in the future. As you recall, it was what we recommended in the first place. If you're willing to sign such a document, there is a chance, only a chance mind you, that you will be released. Would you want me to do this?'

I was terrified of what lay ahead. I was sure the next

six months would not be all cups of tea and friendly faces. Shamefacedly, I said yes.

He left, saying he would get started on the submission straight away. As soon as he left, Harry, the form-filler, reappeared. He produced a set of handcuffs.

'Sorry to do this, mate, standard procedure,' he said. 'I've to take you to the cage for a few minutes until you go into the sweatbox.'

The cage was aptly named – a brutal, animalistic, iron-barred crate where all that day's convicted prisoners were held after sentencing. Some prisoners' anger was completely out of control as they threw themselves against the bars like wild animals trying to escape; others were in almost catatonic misery. I watched one prisoner throwing himself against the bars of the cage with such force that blood started to trickle down from a cut on his forehead. One of the most muscular and heavily-tattooed guys I had ever seen was crouched against one side, sobbing like a child. The most terrifying and dehumanising place I'd ever seen, a scene of absolute rage and anguish. And I was part of it.

The courteous behaviour I'd received started to make sense. Everything about my life had changed in the last few minutes, and the disorientation was intense. Doreen making me a cup of tea wasn't because she was a kindly old dear; it was probably some Home Office protocol designed to reduce my mental shock, help me to transition. Whoever the bureaucrat was that had mandated that procedure, I was grateful to him. These had been a few precious minutes of humanity in the new barbaric world in which I found myself.

It became evident that the promise of being only a few minutes in this cage was optimistic in the extreme. There were about ten of us locked up, and no one seemed to be going anywhere. I headed over to a corner, squeezing past a stupefied black kid who didn't look old enough to be in this company. I felt ashamed that I was using him as a human shield from the belligerent hard men at the far end of the cage and wondered for a second if I should apologise for my actions. I glanced over at him, saw his lips move as he muttered away to himself, too softly for me to make out the words. I decided to leave him to whatever internal agony he was going through.

A fight broke out. Four members of what appeared to be a gang had rounded on a fifth member, accusing him of being the reason they had been caught. He was knocked to the floor by the first punch, then squirmed up against the bars as they started kicking him. He tried to defend himself, then he simply covered his head with his hands and took what was coming to him. There wasn't enough space for the four gang members to kick him all at once, so they operated a bizarre rota system, each taking one kick and then joining the queue for the next one. After about two minutes they got bored, told him once last time that he'd fucked up all their lives, and stomped over to the other side of the cage.

Nobody from the outside intervened, this was the new normal in the world I was in now. I looked in vain for a clock on one of the walls outside the cage. Time had no meaning here. I squeezed even further into my corner.

Eventually, I found out what a sweatbox was. A big prison van with tiny white compartments that a miniature cat would have difficulty swinging in. I cursed my height as I tried to find some way of folding my legs so that I wouldn't cut off all blood supply to my feet. I'd just about succeeded, when, with a lurch, the van pulled off. The windows on the van were high up, too high to see out of, and as we drove off I tried to imagine what part of London we were travelling through. I knew we were heading east and as the light coming through the windows suddenly changed, I realised that meant we were going through the Blackwell Tunnel under the Thames.

To whatever hell awaited me.

chapter sixteen

Hell was a place called HM Prison Belmarsh, a sprawling modern jail in southeast London. When I was told the name, I thought it must be a mistake. I'd only ever heard about it as a high-security place where the most dangerous prisoners were sent, usually for life. But it is also a holding prison, where newly convicted prisoners from London and surrounding areas are held for a few days before being dispersed to jails around the country, those more appropriate for their crimes. I hoped they wouldn't get the two confused.

I stepped out of the prison van, clutching my bag of personal possessions the way a child clutches their favourite blanket. Colossal concrete walls, topped with coils of barbed wire, glinting metallic blue in the evening light. Stern glares from the prison guards, blinding lights above us gave every inch of the courtyard an icy hue that seemed to suck the colour out of everything.

Bitterness and suppressed violence hung heavy in the air. It channelled through me, filling me with anger and resentment. I queued with the other new arrivals, waiting to be registered. A pounding headache seared through my brain; every sound stabbed into my eye. I never got headaches.

I handed over the forms given to me at the Old Bailey to a guard at the reception desk and stood stock-still, waiting to see what would happen next.

'Step back from the desk,' he barked, and I jumped back two paces, head bowed in a submissive posture that I hoped would avoid any further antagonism.

I was allocated my prison number and then put in a communal cage again. The other inhabitants were more subdued this time, the intimidating atmosphere having a sobering effect on us all.

'Jones – property!' shouted an officer, gesturing me to a room next to the cage.

I emptied the contents of my bag on the table and watched as half of them were confiscated as being in contravention of some arcane prison regulation or another. For the next hour or so I stumbled through the formalities of admission: the fingerprinting, mug-shot photography and inevitable strip-search. A moment of incongruity as a cute black and white spaniel came up to greet me, its tail wagging a welcome. As it sniffed its hello, I realised it must be there to smell for drugs. I resisted the urge to give it a pat and as the guard pulled it away it eagerly greeted the next guy in line.

I was told to bend over and cough, then given a light blue T-shirt and scratchy grey tracksuit before I was escorted to the first-night wing. My cell had a single bed up against one wall; a WC was in the corner with the lid removed. I lay down and stared at the ceiling.

How could this be happening to me?

The night was when the horrors began. All the new arrivals had been put in a wing away from the rest of

230

the other prisoners and as the lights went out, random yelling started. Screams into the night, a few nonsensical words, some half-sung syllables; it sounded like wild animals bellowing on a Serengeti plain. The name of one new inmate had been singled out for some reason and a demonic sign-song echoed across the jail from cell block to cell block – chants asking what should be done to him tomorrow, in response the most chilling suggestions in anatomical detail. I lay there feeling lonely, frightened and vulnerable. I couldn't begin to imagine what the recipient felt like.

I barely managed more than an hour or two's sleep. Each time the prisoners' cries began to fade away, someone would give a long howl and the next round of chanting would begin.

Early morning, and I was in a drowsy half-sleep when there was a pealing bell, followed by a shout of, 'Unlock! Everyone out!' I jumped off my bed, looked out of the iron-bar door and saw three prison officers marching along the corridor, unlocking each door. When my turn came, I stepped out of my cell, blinking in the light as I took in the sight of a straggled line of prisoners; some coughing and spluttering, others standing rigidly in a show of macho defiance.

The prisoner standing next to me looked me up and down.

'Nonce, are you?' he growled.

I froze in apprehension. These were the first words spoken to me by a fellow inmate. The barrier I had been building in my mind to keep myself separate from all this, trying to treat it as an out of body experience, shattered in an instant. I remembered the advice I had read about how to survive in prison. Keep your head down; don't draw attention to yourself; say as little as possible about who you are and why you are in there. I thought back to the taunts I'd heard in the middle of the night.

I stared straight ahead in silence, took deep calming breaths while I thought about what to do. I didn't want to speak, but even more I didn't want to be labelled a paedophile.

'I fucking knew it,' the inmate said, after waiting a few seconds for me to speak. 'You fucking hoity-toity fucking D-cat fucking old farts are only ever here for one thing. Hope you enjoyed playing with the family jewels last night. You won't be hanging on to them for long.'

I looked around and saw most of the other inmates engaged in desultory conversations with their neighbours, like the awkward small talk you get at social gatherings you never wanted to attend in the first place. Some level of interaction was apparently allowed. I looked along the line to see how the roll call was progressing. Slowly. If I stood here in silence while this guy projected a more and more depraved image of me, it could be all around the jail that I was a monster.

'No, not a nonce. I'm a journalist. Richard Foxe. I broke a gagging order so I've been sent here for six months.'

The inmate laughed. 'That's a shit-and-a-shave. You'll be out in no time.' He looked over, sized me up again. 'You a storyteller, man? You'll fit right in. Everyone's got a fucking story why they shouldn't be in here.' Then he looked serious again. 'Richard Foxe? I'll check you out, man. You better not be shitting me. I take exception to nonces shitting me. Very grave exception.'

I kept silent for the rest of the roll call; I'd said enough. The guy asked me a few other questions and when he saw I wasn't going to say anything, he spat on the floor in disgust.

'Mister high-and-mighty fucking journo. You'll get taken down a peg or two in here; you and you fucking airs and graces.'

I was relieved to be locked up in my cell again. Breakfast was on a tray, eaten in my cell: small plastic bag of cornflakes, warm milk, stale bread roll. Then nothing. The start of endless hours of mind-numbing boredom. I spent most of that day languishing in my cell, with a few spells of association, 'sosh' it was called, seemingly at random to alleviate the monotony.

At the first one, I went up to the inmate who had spoken to me earlier.

'I'm not being rude or standoffish. I want to be low-key in here. Keep myself to myself. Hope you understand.' He grunted; he didn't seem to care.

A guard came to my cell in the late afternoon.

'Jones. Induction. Follow me.'

Glad of some activity, I followed the guard up three flights of iron steps and was taken into a room with a desk and chair on one side, a single chair on the other. I was told about getting clean sheets and clothes, how to find the library, given a meal slip to fill in for the week. I looked at the choices. Chicken pie, cauliflower curry, bacon chop – there were a few things I thought could be okay.

'Choose carefully, Jones, it's the same every week while you are here,' said the guard.

At the end of my first week, the inmate who spoke to me on the first day sidled up to me at our mid-morning sosh.

'You're famous, mate,' he told me. 'Some geezer was on the telly last night, talking about prison reform, and the conversation turned to talking about you and your Act Now! stories. The bloke said he knew you, and fuck me if he didn't go and blurt out that they were holding you here for breaching some terrorist order. And didn't just blurt it out, went into all the details, made a big bad-ass fucking speech about how what was happening to you was totally out of order. The shit hit the fan, and the whole story was on the front page of one of the newspapers this morning. The *Chronicle*.'

He had just used one of the blue-box phones that allow prisoners to make calls to approved numbers in the outside world and his girlfriend had told him I was on the news. She remembered my name because he had her check me out after our first conversation. I had shied away from the payphones. I'd made a few calls the first couple of days I was there but found it more distressing than helpful, so I'd turned instead to writing long letters to the people who I thought cared about me. Now I needed to call Tristian, to see if he knew what this was all about.

But at that moment the end of sosh was called and I was escorted back to my cell, told to make my call next time. I lay in my cell, staring at the ceiling, trying to work out what this could all mean. It didn't make any sense. I'd never written about penal reform and didn't know anybody working in that area who would know me well enough to risk outing my story in public. And even if they did, the interview would have been pulled off air and there would be a gagging order on the channel reporting it. For the rest of the morning my mind was a whirl, as I waited to find out what on earth was going on.

The seconds had never passed slower. I yelled as guards went past my cell door, asking them for news, but they ignored me. When my lunch tray was dropped off, I pleaded with the officer to tell me if he knew anything; but he shrugged his shoulders, didn't say a word. I tried to read a book I'd borrowed from the library but couldn't focus on the words on the page. In the end, I did press-ups, jumping jacks, anything to keep me occupied. We had sosh with our evening meal; I could make my call then. Only a few hours of this uncertainty to endure.

At three o'clock I was informed I had a visitor and was escorted to the empty visiting room. There was Tristian Hawtrey, a big grin on his face.

'Developments, my dear boy, developments,' he said, as we sat across from one another at a formica-topped table. A single officer stood in the corner, keeping his distance.

'What's going on?' I asked. 'I heard that there was something on TV last night and my name came up. I was told the whole programme suddenly got hijacked by revelations about gagging orders and me being in custody. The gagging order means that no one's supposed to talk about my case. So how come someone's done just exactly that?'

'It's incredible. They had this guest on *News Today* to talk about the rising number of people in prisons in the UK and what can be done about it. He campaigns on wrongful imprisonment, and suddenly he went on about how one of the biggest miscarriages of justice in the UK was happening now, right under our noses. That's when he started talking about you.'

'And they let him? They didn't pull the interview?'

'Obviously not. Apparently the editor had been told to stop the interview by the station's lawyer, but she refused. By the time the station's bosses were alerted, the story had been broadcast. The station put out a statement, regretting the incident and saying the news editor, Alex Richards, had been fired. Then this morning, the *Chronicle* put the story on the front page with a hard-hitting editorial about Act Now! being a threat to liberty and the UK way of life, and the editor there was arrested.'

I felt overwhelmed, like the room was closing in on me.

Tristian glanced over at the guard and then looked back at me.

'Now that there have been two high profile news events about your case, the rest of the media feels free to talk about what's going to happen to *News Today* and the *Chronicle*, while steering clear of the specifics of your case. Press freedom, and in fact free speech generally, are the story. But that doesn't matter. People are talking about it, finding out in their millions what's happened to you. Act Now! can't lock everyone up.'

I couldn't help myself; I broke down in tears, then pressed my palms into my eyes. I held them there for twenty, maybe thirty seconds as I blacked out everything around me, forcing myself to bring my emotions under control. The risk that Alex and Sam had taken to break the story. They saw what had happened to me and were prepared to see the same happen to them for what they believed in. And this guy who did the interview – I owed him even more.

'Who was it being interviewed that sparked all this off? Do I know him?'

My solicitor shifted uneasily in his seat.

'Yes, I do believe you do.' He took a deep breath. 'It was Michael Mitchell, Duncan. He was the one calling for you to be released. You can see why it's had so much impact.'

Michael Mitchell. The guy who was put in jail in the 1980s because of the book I wrote. Michael Mitchell, the guy who had his thugs terrorise me and beat me up, while he tried to track down Bobbie as she tried to hide from him. Michael Mitchell, my saviour.

My heart froze, then pounded.

'Him? He's the one behind this? That's unbelievable.'

'Quite. There has been frenetic activity all morning, as you can imagine. This is all very positive, but don't get your hopes up. The court's ratification of the Attorney General's order still stands, and you remain in custody. I'm asking the clerk of court to bring forward my appeal against it. I hope I'll be successful, but there are no guarantees.'

We talked for another ten minutes, then I was escorted back to my cell. I had been trying to come to terms with being in jail three months, maybe more. Now I could be out in a few days, a week at the most. I thought back to what I was doing the day before my hearing. The memories were still fresh in my mind. That was the time I had left.

I called Tristian the next morning, and he gave me the good news that the appeal against the order would be heard after the weekend and that the debate about my treatment was continuing unabated.

'Try to stay positive through the weekend,' he told me. 'I don't want to get your hopes up, but if I were a betting man, I'd be placing a wager that you'll be out of here Monday afternoon.'

First thing on Monday morning, as I was escorted to the sweatbox to be driven back to central London, I felt my identity return. I'd been given my bag of belongings to take with me, as seconds after the hearing concluded I could be a free man again. I clutched it close to my chest like a talisman.

I was escorted into the court. Tristian and Jeremy were already there, along with the usual formidable team from the government's side. The public gallery was empty, as the hearing would again be held *in camera* under the terms of the Dissemination of Terrorism Act. No matter, I could tell the story on the steps of the court afterwards.

Jeremy was more focused than I'd ever seen him before.

'My client has been incarcerated for simply telling the truth,' he told the judge. 'And the public outcry that this could be happening in Britain today is testament to the heinous unfairness of the manner in which this piece of anti-terrorist legislation has been applied. I would hope that prosecuting counsel is here today to tell the Court that the Attorney General has rescinded his order and that my client can go free. But if he is not, I would seek to right this terrible wrong by asking Your Lordship to

238

strike down the order as an affront to natural justice. I will now quote the precedents for such a decision to aid Your Lordship's deliberations.'

Jeremy recited case after case of precedents for the judge to overturn an unjust law. Finally, I could see how he earned his money.

The prosecuting counsel decided to go on the offensive.

'Jones flagrantly and knowingly flouted an order amply justified by current events and permitted under terrorism legislation. Contrary to what he would have us all believe, we live in a fair and civilised society, where any grounds for appeal against the court's decision will be fairly and judiciously decided upon. But once again, Jones has decided that such rules do not extend to him. Rather than follow the correct course of action, he has conspired with his friends in the media to try to whip up a public frenzy to publish tendentious and frankly illegal accounts of his banning order and subsequent incarceration, in the hope that the pressure of misguided public opinion will force the government to order his release. For Your Lordship to legitimise these actions by striking down a lawful order obtained after due process, would be to give in to the principle of mob rule and allow the court of public opinion to take precedence over the courts of the land.'

I gulped. This didn't sound like it was going to plan.

The prosecuting counsel raised his voice as he concluded his remarks, his stentorian words echoing around the room.

'Given that the original order seems insufficient to temper Jones's contempt for this court, the Attorney

General has issued a new order, extending Jones incarceration for another six months and has further ordered that the media outlets involved in this breach of the injunction, *News Today* and the *Chronicle*, appear before this court to answer for their actions.'

The judge agreed.

I don't think the look of shock on the faces of Jeremy and Tristian was for my benefit; I detected real human emotion breaking through their professional veneer. The numbness and devastation I was feeling paradoxically acted as a kind of buffer, shielding me from the incipient madness I could easily have descended into.

I made the now familiar journey down the stairs to the prison cells below and back into the sweatbox.

To return to hell.

chapter seventeen

There was no sympathy from the guards as I was processed back into the system – they asked the same questions and I gave the same answers.

I was sharing a cell this time, with a career criminal in his seventies who lay in his bed, said nothing, and farted all day. It was fine. I didn't want to talk to anyone.

Tristian came to see me the next morning, told me that the perceived wisdom was that it had been a political calculation from Act Now! to resist any pressure to release me, weighing the hit they would take in the opinion polls against the risk of me being freed to be a nuisance to them again. Under the law as it stood, any judge had no choice but to support them. Their drop in popularity would be minimal, they calculated, and it looked as if they were right.

My predicament, what was known of it, mattered to some people, but not enough to make a difference. Act Now! was still doing well in the polls, the public willing to forgive anything from a party that seemed to be on the side of the people rather than the establishment.

News Today was fined £50,000, the *Chronicle* £200,000 because they led with the story, and that had effectively put paid to them making any further comment on my case. At least there were no new prison sentences. Sam and Alex had their liberty, and that was some comfort.

Tristian said that Bobbie had called him, saying she was heading down to London to visit me, but I asked him to tell her not to. I needed time to reflect. An emotional reunion with Bobbie, no matter how well-intentioned, was something I didn't think I could cope with. I needed time out from the human race.

I spent the next day going over and over in my head what had happened. With my sentence now twice as long, I tried to forget my earlier calculations and focus on defining in my mind what the new date of my release was, now probably six months away. Six months. The length of time since I had gone to Moscow; aeons ago. I focused instead on my birthday and Christmas: they were six months apart, and it never felt long. It was little comfort.

A few days later, I was told I was being transferred to an open prison. A slip of paper was posted under the door of my cell, telling me I'd be moved the next morning. There were an hour or so of transfer formalities to go through, then I was driven with two other prisoners to a prison in the Kent countryside.

The new regime was considerably more relaxed. I was amazed to find that I even had a key to my cell. I was in a D-cat jail, where the inmates were assessed as low risk. That suited me just fine. I vowed that I would stop trying to fight the system, serve out my time and then pick up the pieces of my life when I got out. After a flurry of activity following my appeal hearing, communication with Tristian had dried up. That was the legal process finished with me, until my first parole hearing.

I kept up to speed with the news and political events, but had no contact with Alex and Sam after their punishments were handed down. Michael Mitchell's intervention had made my cause into a news story, but any mention of it always had to include the words, 'We are unable to go into the details of the case for legal reasons'. It was difficult to maintain the public's interest when the facts were so nebulous and nothing new was happening. It had caused some people to question Act Now!'s integrity, including a few of the more idealistic members from within their own party, but not enough to build a groundswell of opinion to keep up any pressure to demand my release.

I never did find out the first name of my flatulent cellmate in Belmarsh, so I decided to be a bit more sociable in my new surroundings. I found the newspaper orderly, the inmate who dealt with all the newspaper and magazine orders, and asked him who the *Chronicle* readers were in the jail. That found me a few like-minded souls I could converse with, and I spent the rest of my time writing letters. Lots of friends came out of the woodwork, but not Tanya. I still wasn't keen on personal visitors. A few of my London friends came to see me, but the pain of catching a glimpse of my outside life left me more upset than the chance to chat with familiar faces. I was glad I had asked Bobbie not to come. After the first couple of weeks, I let everyone know it was best to write.

The thing that had the most significant impact on making life bearable was my decision to stop feeling sorry for myself. The prison was a modern one; every inmate had a cell to themselves. It had a farm, a market garden, even a gym. I had plenty of time to think, to contemplate where my life would go on my release. I learned to navigate my way around the byzantine labyrinth of petty and sometimes contradictory regulations that governed everyday life, and even managed to discipline myself to stop overthinking every soundbite and media comment I could find about what was said about me on the outside.

Then Act Now! lost a by-election. The pundits said the polls had underplayed the significance of the scandal on people's voting intentions: the people who were opposed to Act Now! were much more likely to vote as a result and some of their supporters had become lukewarm to the party and had stayed at home on polling day. I had been bigger trouble to them than they thought.

I had a small crumb of comfort seeing Damien Zane trying to put a positive spin on it. Every government has a few mid-term losses, he said, voters enjoy keeping us on our toes, and so on. But the real bombshell happened a few days later. There was a small group of Act Now! MPs who seemed to have genuine principles and libertarian beliefs. They must have become selected as candidates when Act Now! was getting started – they would never have been allowed to stand now.

The group's leader stepped up and said that they were growing more and more concerned by the authoritarian and repressive behaviour of their party leaders, that this was the very opposite of why they had come into politics during the first wave of euphoria of Act Now!'s ascendancy. The rebels' demands were straightforward: they would resign the whip and force a vote of no confidence in the government unless the Dissemination of Terrorism Act was amended to have pre-existing laws decide what could and could not be said, and have judges decide who went to jail. And unless anyone imprisoned by those parts of the Act being considered for repeal were released immediately. That meant me.

The irony of the situation made me smile for the first time in weeks. My first glimpse of freedom had come about because of the good intentions of the man I feared and hated more than anyone else in the world, Michael Mitchell. Now I was getting a second lifeline from renegade members of Act Now! itself. The group was big enough to overcome the government's majority if it came to a vote of no confidence and they voted with the opposition. I waited to see how the political calculations of the leadership would play out this time.

The rebel group surprised everyone by refusing to be cowed by the Act Now! leadership's attempt to get them to toe the party line. The *Chronicle* gleefully reported that the party only had itself to blame. It had been founded on the philosophy that no one should have to accept what the political elite tell them they have to do. Now that they were the political elite, some of their own MPs were giving the leadership a taste of their own medicine.

I tried not to get my hopes up; then I heard the breaking news that the Attorney General would be making a statement in the House of Commons that afternoon. I watched it live on the TV in the communal day room, winning the battle to have the channel changed to news instead of the usual diet of daytime soaps.

It was everything that I could have hoped for. A review of the Dissemination of Terrorism Act was announced, recognising that the legislation had been drafted at speed in response to a series of terrorist outrages.

And then came the words that I couldn't believe I was hearing.

'The measure of a government's tolerance and forgiveness is how it treats those out to undermine the values that got them elected,' said the Attorney General. He described me as a harmless but stubborn fantasist, and if I'd agreed with the terms of my supression order to stop libelling the government, I would have never have been put in jail.

'Mr Jones seems to genuinely believe that the workings of his imagination are real. A psychiatric report, however, has confirmed that his delusions don't present a danger to himself or society at large. He will be released without delay. Nevertheless, I should warn him that a court case against him is still outstanding, and no matter what his mental state, if he repeats the accusations upon his release that got him incarcerated in the first place, he will be taken into custody again.'

The words were greeted with a cheer by the few inmates who were watching with me. I shook everyone's hand, feeling like the celebrity of the hour.

In the end, it took two days for me to be released – the wheels of bureaucracy turned slowly, especially when bureaucracy wanted them to turn that way. The discharge was surprisingly underwhelming. My name was called and a van took me to the nearest train station, carrying my possessions in an anonymous canvas bag I'd had packed ever since I was told I'd be released. I was given eighty pounds and a train ticket home.

I bought myself a Pret sandwich when I got to London; the best-tasting sandwich of my life. I savoured the crunch of sourdough bread and fresh salad after weeks of bland prison food. Once at my flat, I took a long, long shower and then started getting in touch with the outside world again.

I phoned Sam and Alex to thank them. Alex told me she would be quietly returning to an editor's job in a few weeks once the kerfuffle died down, the station's bosses having been secretly delighted by her stance but forced to put on a show of reprimanding her for the benefit of the authorities. She described with relish the attempt by Barbara, the station's legal counsel, to halt the interview as it was going out live. Irate phone calls to the control room to get Mitchell to change the subject, then to silence him, then to take the programme off air: all ignored. Sam told me he had worked on the *News Today* story himself, insisting it stay off the paper's website until the first print editions were on the street to make sure the story couldn't be stopped. But they both told me they couldn't take a risk like that again, unless and until the Act was changed substantially.

The next call was to Bobbie. After we had toasted my release, I brought up the role that Michael Mitchell had played. Even after all these years, his name still conjured up horrors.

'I don't think it was anything sinister,' I said to her. 'I think he genuinely wanted to help me.'

Bobbie gave a disgusted snort. 'Michael doesn't help anyone but himself. No one knows that better than me. I'm over the moon you've been released, Duncan, of course I am. But I can't bring myself to be grateful to Michael for helping you.'

'You're being unfair, Bobbie.' I had to be careful not to stoke her resentment. 'He may have had ulterior motives, but the bottom line is I've been released, and he started the ball rolling. Don't get me wrong, I totally get that mentioning his name is distressing for you. But let's concentrate on celebrating that I'm a free man again.'

'And I hope you're not going to do anything to jeopardise that. I mean it, Duncan. You've done your bit to try to bring down Act Now!. Leave it to others from now on.'

'I don't have any choice,' I reassured her. 'Act Now! has made it very clear that one more peep out of me without any new evidence and I'll be heading straight back to jail, with a conviction for good old-fashioned contempt of court – not under the Dissemination of Terrorism Act. I will not be saying another word until this Act gets sorted out.'

'It's good to see you're thinking straight. Look, I know there's going to be lots of people wanting to talk to you tonight. I'll let you get on with that. We can talk later.'

I thought about mentioning Mitchell again, but decided against it. We had finished on a positive note.

I called Nigel next. He said it was a Good Thing that I got out of jail, and I shouldn't go to jail again as that would be a Bad Thing.

Midday, the story broke that I had been released, and a few paparazzi turned up at my front door. I let them take some pictures, but replied to every question with the same words: 'I'm glad to be released, and won't be saying any more.'

They eventually got bored and went away. I looked at the traffic on my Richard Foxe website: over two hundred thousand hits that morning alone, and many hundreds of supportive comments. It looked like I didn't have to say anything new. What was out there was proving enough to draw attention to what I'd already said.

I then set about devouring all the news stories that had been written about me that I hadn't been able to see or read before. We didn't have catch-up in prison, and it was the Michael Mitchell interview that had me gasping for breath. There he was: older, grey hair, but still with the controlled menace that had struck terror into my heart all those years ago. Fear, guilt, gratitude ... a cocktail of emotions ran through me as I listened to him talk. He was eloquent, charismatic and intense as he reminded the interviewer that I had been responsible for his wrongful incarceration for twelve years; that I was someone he should hate and never want anything to do with again. But that there was a higher principle at stake than his personal feelings towards me. He had spent years campaigning against wrongful imprisonment, and so he couldn't bring himself to ignore a case that wasn't due to a miscarriage of justice, but was a deliberate attempt to incarcerate and silence a member of the press who wouldn't be cowed by the government's demands to stay silent. It was powerful stuff.

I spent the rest of the evening acknowledging the well-wishers on my Richard Foxe blog, and reassuring family and friends that I was perfectly okay after my ordeal and had learned my lesson. I must have interacted with fifty people, maybe more, but there was one name that kept coming back into my mind; one person to whom I knew I should reach out and offer thanks. Michael Mitchell.

I went to his website and opened the Contact tab. I stared at the comments box, wondering what on earth to write. In the end, I kept it simple.

Dear Mr Mitchell, I was deeply touched by your intervention. It was a kind and courageous thing for you to do, all the more so because of our shared past. If there is anything I can ever do to repay your help, please let me know.

Regards

Duncan Jones

I gave him my personal email address.

I agonised long and hard about that last part. Did I really want to open the door, even a little, to possible interaction with him again? In the end, I left it in. He wasn't a monster, no matter what Bobbie thought. That was her trauma speaking. For a second, I wondered if I should do even more, offer to meet him to thank him in person. I decided that was a step too far, and was probably something neither of us wanted. I pressed Send and watched my words head off to someone I had hoped and prayed I would never have to deal with again.

It's a funny old world.

chapter eighteen

I was woken by my second phone ringing in the middle of the night. I picked it up, groggily cursing while I peered to make out who was calling. Nigel. He never makes social calls. I pressed the green button and groaned a hello.

'Duncan, it's Nigel. I've found Tanya.'

I sat upright, shaking the sleep from my addled brain. 'That's great, Nigel. What time is it? Oh, 3:15.'

I switched on the light and went over to the desk in the corner of my bedroom and sat down at my computer.

'Tell me what you found.'

'I was looking at all the people who had left nice comments on your Richard Foxe Facebook page. And some nasty ones too.' I could hear the disapproval in Nigel's voice. 'I was going to tell them to eff off, but then I remember you said it was best to ignore the nasty comments. So, I did. But some of them were very rude. I don't like it when people are rude.'

Nigel had sounded excited from the moment he called and I could imagine him swinging away in his chair. I waited patiently for him to continue, but there was only silence.

'Yes, people can be rude,' I said eventually. 'But how did they help you find Tanya?'

'I wanted to see how many rude people there were, compared to how many nice people. I read all the comments for the last year, and you had 7,847 nice comments and 712 rude ones. I went to your Mark Jackson author page, and there you had 312 nice comments and 178 rude ones. A higher percentage of people are rude to you as Mark Jackson than they are to Richard Foxe. He-he-he-he. There's an 87.93% chance that this is statistically significant; I worked it out. Interesting, isn't it?'

'Very.' I gave an inward sigh. This was going to take a while. 'But I still don't see how this helps us find Tanya.'

'Seventy-two people were on both the Richard Foxe page and the Mark Jackson one, even though you keep them completely separate. They were all after 22nd November, when Damian Zane told everyone about your two identities. All of them except one.'

'And who was that?' Suddenly I could see where this was going.

'Victoria Kovalenko. From Kiev. She visited both your sites on the same day, 17th September, and liked a post on each of them. The probability of someone doing that by chance is a zillion zillion to one. She knew Richard Foxe and Mark Jackson were the same person before Damian Zane told everyone.'

I pulled up my computer diary. 17th September was ten days after I'd admitted to Tanya I'd used her as the source for the Anton Shub stories and told her my two identities.

'Tanya mentioned a few times she had a friend from her schooldays living in Ukraine,' I told Nigel, 'but she never mentioned her name. All part of being careful, I suppose.'

The reminder of her duplicity seared through me again, rekindling the pain of betrayal. I pushed the thoughts away, to stay focused on what Nigel was telling me.

'And what do we know about Victoria Kovalenko?'

'Everything. He-he-he-he. She has all her Facebook settings to public. That's a Bad Thing. You know that, don't you, Duncan?'

'Yes,' I said, a little too abruptly. 'So, Tanya's on her Facebook profile? Is that what you found out?'

'No, she's not. It would have been a Good Thing if she was though, wouldn't it?'

I was crushed after the moment's hope. Even if this person was Tanya's friend, and knew where Tanya was now, she'd almost certainly check before passing on any details. Then Tanya would know I was looking for her, making her even more difficult to trace. The best I could hope was to get a message to her, asking her to get in touch. But as she'd made no effort to contact me while I was in prison, chances were that would be a fruitless exercise.

In my despair, I'd treated Nigel's last remark as a rhetorical question. But he doesn't do rhetorical questions, doesn't understand the concept.

'Are you still there, Duncan?' I heard him say. 'I said it would have been a Good Thing if Tanya was on Victoria Kovalenko's Facebook profile. It would have been, wouldn't it?'

'Yes, it would, Nigel. But she isn't. Can you send me a

link to this woman's page so I can have a look for myself?'

'But I said I'd found Tanya. You told me if I did, it would be a Good Thing. Even if you keep your promise not to write another word about the Russians, because then you'll go to jail again. Don't you want to know how I found her?'

I gasped. 'Of course, Nigel. I thought you'd said there was no sign of her.'

'There's not – on Victoria Kovalenko's Facebook page. But Victoria visited the town of Chernihiv just after Tanya disappeared. Historic town, 143 kilometres north of Kiev. There are photos of Victoria outside monasteries and a cathedral, laughing at who was taking the pictures. Then there's a photo of her last week, having a coffee in Krasna Square, but again no mention of who she was meeting. I checked the teachers' database, and a Tanya Petrenko is working in a primary school in Chernihiv. Given the town's population, the chances of one of the seventy-one Tanyas being there randomly is 794 to 1. That means there is a 90.2% probability that the Tanya in Chernihiv is the real Tanya. I worked it out.'

'That sounds good enough for me.' I punched the air. 'I don't suppose you know how many primary schools there are in the town, do you?'

'Eight. Do you want their addresses and phone numbers?' I could tell Nigel was pleased with himself.

'This is fantastic news, Nigel. It really is a Good Thing. You should be proud of yourself.'

I tossed and turned for most of the night, unable to sleep. What Nigel had discovered was only the first step. I had to find out what school Tanya was working in, without raising her suspicions. Then I had to get to Chernihiv, without alerting Act Now!. And finally, I had to make my case to Tanya why she should come back to England to help me, tell her story about working for MI5. Risk her freedom as a result. And after all the horrible things I had said to her. It was going to be tough to pull off.

By the time morning came, I had made a decision. This was too important for me to go it alone; I needed help. I texted Alex to tell her I'd had a breakthrough on the Act Now! story and we needed to talk later that morning.

When I arrived, the news department was in chaos.

'We'll need to keep this brief,' Alex told me. 'Act Now! has called a snap general election and the opposition parties have agreed. Two years early. The first opinion polls since your release have come out, and they've more than survived the rebellion within the party. If anything, their scores for "caring" and "compassionate" have gone up because it looks to most people that they've behaved magnanimously in letting you out of jail.'

'I don't know if that's good or bad news,' I replied. 'I would have had to go to trial eventually. I was hoping my trial and acquittal would help destroy their chances of re-election. If the polls say they're still ahead, I can see why they've done this now.'

'And the party hierarchy have deselected all the rebels and chosen new candidates to stand in their seats. Some of the rebels say they are going to contest the election as independents, but without a party machine behind them? No chance. The new candidates all toe the party line. Even if they don't increase their majority, the Act Now! leadership will be in an even stronger position now they're grabbing the opportunity to purge any dissidents.'

I took Alex through what Nigel had found out.

'I'm nervous I could screw this up,' I confessed. 'I need a Russian speaker to contact the schools in a way that doesn't arouse suspicion. And I'm pretty sure there will be a flag on my passport. If I get on a plane to Kiev, there will be somebody waiting for me at the other end, ready to follow me to wherever I go.'

Alex insisted I speak to Simon Green, the programme's top investigative reporter, and called him in. I eyed him warily. I'd refused to work with him before in case he stole the story, but he was charm personified, pretending that our inauspicious beginning had never happened.

'After your spell in prison, they probably think you've been put off investigating anything ever again, and you should keep giving that impression as long as possible,' he said. 'It's going to be no problem tracking down the school your friend is teaching at. How we get you to Ukraine might be trickier.'

He called me on my spare phone the next day.

'Okay, we've found the school. And I'm pretty sure it's her. My detective confirmed she started working there a few months ago.'

I was impressed that he was able to find a reliable private detective in Ukraine at the drop of a hat, but I supposed that was bread and butter stuff for someone in his line of work.

'I've sent him a photo of Tanya, and he'll stake out the school, find out where she lives. We should have a photo of her back from him in the next twenty-four hours to make sure it's the right person. Then he can pick you up at the airport and take you to her. That just leaves the issue of getting you into Ukraine without anyone noticing.'

'And how are you planning to do that?'

'It's going to require you taking a little risk, I'm afraid. I have a contact – who I'll deny ever knowing if anyone asks me – in the business of supplying false passports. All my dealings with him are off the books. *News Today* can't be seen to be involved in something illegal. With a week's notice, he can get one for you that will get you in and out of Ukraine. But if you're caught, it's go to jail time, there or in the UK. Act Now! would love to send you down for a genuine crime, so we'd need to make sure that no one knows when you are heading to the airport, or picks up that you're out of the country while you're in Ukraine. If you're happy to take that risk, I can vouch for the fact that the passport itself won't let you down. What do you say?'

I thought long and hard about it. It was a risk, that was for sure. But it was nothing compared to the risk I would be asking Tanya to take. I said yes.

Alex sent me the photo to confirm it was Tanya; a picture of her snatched in the street in her familiar balled-up sweater. I flew out of London City as soon as I got my fake passport; I reckoned it might be easier to spot someone following me in a small airport. I flew into Geneva, where I picked up a new ticket to Kiev and spent the next few hours dotting about the airport, checking every so often to see if anyone looked familiar.

Finally, I boarded the plane to Kiev. The detective,

Vitaly, would meet me at the airport and drive straight to the flat on the outskirts of Chernihiv where he had discovered Tanya to be living. Then all I had to do was persuade her to help.

Vitaly was not what I expected. I wanted a detective to be craggy and middle-aged, wearing a raincoat and battered fedora. I got a skinny kid in ripped jeans and a Metallica T-shirt. He was standing on the other side of the barrier, peering at a photograph he was holding, glancing up every few seconds to look at the hordes of people pouring into the arrivals area. He spotted me almost immediately.

'Malcolm!' he yelled. 'Over here.'

For a second I ignored him, then I remembered. Malcolm Donaldson, Richard Foxe, Mark Jackson, Duncan Jones. Soon I'd be able to field a football team with my various identities.

'You must be Vitaly,' I said. 'Pleased to meet you.'

'So, we are off to doorstep this Tanya babe? Heavy. But no rough stuff, okay? That's not my scene.'

I had no idea what this guy had been told he was investigating. I reassured him that I only wanted to have a chat with her, on our own.

'She has no idea that you tracked her down?' I asked. 'My visit will be a complete surprise?'

'Totally. I do this stuff all the time, wives wanting to track down their husband's mistresses, either to warn them off or get evidence for the divorce settlement. That's what this is all about, isn't it? I can always tell.'

'You're very perceptive, Vitaly. Yes, I've been sent from England to track her down. Just to warn you, she'll recognise me as soon as she sees me, and will probably tell me to go away, but I'm going to try to persuade her to talk to me on my own. I promise you, no rough stuff.'

We drove the rest of the way in silence. I was desperate to find out if Vitaly knew anything of Tanya's new life here, but the risk of raising suspicions that there was more to this than a wronged wife dealing with her husband's affair was too great. We arrived in Chernihiv around six in the evening. It looked a nice enough place. A tight cluster of Medieval churches on a green bluff overlooked the city's historic core. I was pleased that Tanya had ended up somewhere as pleasant as this.

We parked on a tree-lined street, the houses a mixture of dilapidated wooden buildings and some anonymous-looking new builds. Vitaly pointed to one of the newer houses, its broken iron gate giving onto a small path, the paint on the front door peeling away. A bag of compost lay split open on a bench next to the door, a row of potato plants in full flower. Gone back to planting potatoes, I thought, fighting back a sudden wave of tears. I pulled myself together and knocked on the door.

I saw a face flash at the window, the shadows too dark to make out who it was. The door remained closed. I looked around. Vitaly had driven off as agreed. I walked over to the window and peered inside. Nothing.

'Tanya, I know you're in there. Can we talk? I've come all the way from London to speak to you, so I'm not going to go away until you open the door. It will only take five minutes.'

The door opened, and there she was.

'Duncan, nice to see you.' The weary sadness in her tone belied her words. 'I'm impressed. Impressed but not surprised.'

Her flat was simply furnished; I recognised a suitcase-worth of knick-knacks from her place in London. She sat down and beckoned me to do likewise.

'So, what are you doing here?'

'I was in the neighbourhood and thought I'd drop by.'

My remark landed with a thud on the carpet.

'Okay, you probably know what happened to me after you left. Act Now! had me put in prison and were attempting to throw away the key. They got put under a lot of political pressure and eventually had me released, but if anything, that's made them more popular with the voters, not less. They've survived the scandal and called a general election. If the polls are to be believed, they are heading for an even bigger majority. If they get that, and five more years in power, I don't know what sort of country we'll be then.'

'A shitty mess. And you end up in jail for this. I cry when I hear.'

I saw a photograph of a young man on the mantelpiece, one I'd not seen before. The resemblance to Tanya was striking.

'Your brother?'

Tanya smiled. '*Da*. Now I am in Ukraine, he can come out of hiding in box under bed. Handsome, wasn't he?' She started to choke up a little. 'You were good to me, Duncan,' she said in a flat, monotone voice. 'You did not tell the world my name or that I told you my spy story

260

was true. MI5 say to me, my job is done; they let me come back to Ukraine to lead simple life, to be a teacher. I need to thank you for that.'

'I was going to tell. The first version of the story I wrote was very angry. But I knew once I wrote it, it would leave you horribly exposed. Then I thought about what you said, how I wasn't complaining about being made into a famous blogger. How you promised yourself you'd tell no more lies if I ever confronted you, and confirmed everything was true, knowing you'd then have to trust me to be discreet. That showed me that our time together was not a total sham, that there were genuine feelings. I wrote a second version, one that told the truth but also protected you.'

Tanya offered a pained smile. 'You've got to believe me, it wasn't all an act. It wasn't just me doing my job.'

'That's okay. But it will all have been for nothing if Act Now! wins this election. And it looks like they will, unless something changes.'

'Like what?' She paused for a second, then gave a gasp of comprehension. 'That's why you've come here, isn't it? You need to tell my story, to get people to see who Act Now! really are. You think it's the only way the story will have enough impact to damage them.'

'Yes. I'm sorry. But that's not all. I still have a court order hanging over me; I can't risk writing another inflammatory article about Act Now! and the Russians. If I did, I'd be straight back to jail for contempt of court and my story would be silenced again. It needs someone else to tell the story. And the person the story would have the most impact coming from … is you, Tanya.'

'I'm big yellow coward. I can't face thought of jail.'

'I couldn't face the thought of it either. But you've got the power to make a difference. If you speak out, it could be the turning point for people to start seeing Act Now! for what they really are.'

Tanya remained silent. I walked over to the mantelpiece and picked up the photo of her brother.

'How old was he when he died?'

'Nineteen. Only kid.'

'Tragic. I'm sorry, I've forgotten. What was his name again?' I knew the answer but wanted her to say it.

'Taras.' Now it was Tanya's turn to stare at the photo.

'Tell me about him.'

'All my best memories of him are from out in the country,' Tanya said. Her eyes had a dreamy glaze of recollection. 'He loved to go fishing, but our parents would not let him go to the little lakes near our house on his own when he was young. He would wake me very early, six, sometimes five in the morning, and we would cycle to the lakes with home-made fishing rods and try to catch fish in early morning, that was best time. Then we would take the fish to Grandma; she would dry them, make *taranaka*. Typical Ukrainian snack, which we would eat on our next adventure.'

'So, you were close in age?'

'Two years. *Da*, I was his best friend, no other kids around. He made me tomboy; we were always playing boys' games together. Guns made from sticks, we played capture the Germans. I always had to be German; he was patriotic Ukrainian. Always defending homeland. One day he played game for real.'

'I'm sorry, Tanya. I really am. You still played fighting the Germans in the 1990s? That's a long time after the war.'

'Homeland War is still big deal in Ukraine. You call it World War II, for us it was all about protecting our country. Terrible things happened then. Ukrainian people never forget.'

I thought it best to lighten the mood.

'But it sounds like you had an idyllic childhood, growing up in the countryside.'

'*Da*, it was. We would climb trees for cherries, collect wild strawberries in forest for Grandma to make jam. Taras was super-competitive, he always made me count how many we had found, so he could be the winner. If he had less, he would not come home till he had bigger number.' She laughed. 'He never realised I always let him win.'

Finally, I brought the conversation back to what we both knew we had to talk about.

'Do you remember I told you the story of my childhood friend, Bobbie, and how she ran away from that gangster? Because she feared for her life in a blackmail plot she got mixed up in?'

Tanya nodded.

'She spent the next four years of her life running away from what happened, instead of going to the police. Took the risk that she could be implicated in the money laundering crimes she had become involved in, that the guy would track her down and silence her. Finally, she did the right thing, the brave thing, went to the police and told them everything, and after that, she was finally able to be at peace with herself. She could look herself in the mirror and get on with the rest of her life.'

'Very brave. And I remember you tell me that now she has good life, in Scotland?'

Then the sudden realisation of what I was driving at sparked a flash of anger in her. 'And that is what you think I am doing? Running away from what is happening?'

I saw her face redden. She stood up and paced around the room.

'Do you know what happens to someone who works for MI5 and breaks the Official Secrets Act? They go to jail and it's a real sentence, not game they played with you, using crazy law to keep you behind bars. I don't have courage to do that, Duncan. I would like to help. But I can't.'

'Then Act Now! will win the next election. They will kick out the dissidents in their party, making themselves even more powerful. I will have gone to jail for nothing and all of the media people who have risked their careers, their livelihood, even their freedom, will all have done so in vain. I wouldn't ask you to do this if there was any other choice, Tanya. I protected you even when I felt angry and betrayed. Come back to Britain, tell your story, prove what I've been saying is true. I know it's a risk, but if we don't do something, all that we've both been through will have been for nothing.'

Tanya clenched both fists and waved them at the ceiling.

'Duncan, Duncan, why do you have to ask me this?'

She calmed down and glanced around the room, as her mind searched for what to say next. Her eyes alighted on the photo of Taras, and she walked over and picked it up. She stared at it for a long moment and then gently, lovingly, placed it back on the mantelpiece.

'I still have British visa,' she said, her voice barely audible. 'What time is flight?'

I felt ashamed at the thrill of victory running through my body.

chapter nineteen

I was woken in the morning by the sound of Tanya bustling away in the kitchen, preparing breakfast. I forced myself to sit up on the sofa. Pins and needles shot down my leg. A muscle tightened as a spasm of pain shot through my body.

'Ay-ay-ay! Bloody cramp!'

I stretched the leg for a few seconds until the pain went away. Tanya was standing in the doorway holding two mugs of coffee, watching my discomfort with unsympathetic glee.

'And you can wipe that grin off your face,' I said. 'I haven't spent the night sleeping on a sofa for about twenty years. This is no laughing matter.'

Tanya took this as her cue to burst out laughing. 'I'm sorry, Duncan, I shouldn't laugh. But you do look ridiculous. Here, I make coffee. You want I leave you five minutes to get ready?'

I took the coffee, and Tanya disappeared into her bedroom.

The phone call to Vitaly informing him of this change of plan had left him thoroughly bemused.

'You are spending the night with Tanya babe?' he had said, incredulity dripping from his voice.

'Yes. Surveillance requirement, I'm sure you can see why. She's agreed to go back to England with me; that's what I came here to do. I don't want to give her a chance to disappear again. Can you pick us up at ten and drive us to Kiev?'

'And you are spending the night there?' he said again. 'Just the two of you?'

'Yep. All in the line of duty. Goodnight, Vitaly. See you in the morning.'

The conversation had brought a smile to my face. Vitaly would have to be a bloody good detective to figure this out. I looked at my watch. Half an hour until he turned up.

'I'm decent,' I shouted through to Tanya.

She lugged a huge Louis Vuitton suitcase into the living room.

'Travelling light, are we?' I said. 'I brought a toothbrush and a change of underwear.'

'More information than I needed, Duncan.'

We were both working hard to keep the banter light-hearted, anything to avoid having to think about the trauma looming ahead when we got back to London.

'By the way, do you think we need to say anything to the detective I used to find you? He'll be here in a few minutes, and I think he's totally confused by what's going on. He thought I was hired by some wronged wife wanting to confront her husband's Ukrainian mistress. Me spending the night here has left him pretty perplexed.'

'Let him think what he wants. No problem for you, I think?'

There was a knock at the door and Tanya looked out the window. 'Is that him?'

I looked out and nodded. Vitaly spotted us and waved a greeting. Tanya waved back and drew the curtain.

She laughed. 'His eyes are on stalks. Very funny.'

Tanya called in sick to her school and we drove the two hours to Kiev in complete silence. I was tempted to try to wind Vitaly up a bit more, but decided it would be unprofessional. At the airport, I thanked him for his help. Off he went, still in a stupor of bemusement.

'Well, that was fun,' I said. 'Let's get your plane ticket and I'll check with my contacts in London.'

Tanya stood in line at the ticket desk, while I called Alex to find out the arrangements for when we got to London.

'You're booked into a hotel near the airport,' I told Tanya when I joined her. 'The show's editor, Alex Richards, and Simon Green, the guy who will be interviewing you – they'll meet you for dinner this evening, to run through everything. The plan is that first you'll be interviewed by my old editor at the *Chronicle*, and afterwards you go to the studio to film your TV interview. Then you disappear back to Ukraine, and the story will run in the paper the day after the interview, with the TV programme that evening.'

'And we hope that no one in Chernihiv watches British news stories. But if Act Now! win election, what then?'

The laughter of the morning was forgotten now. There was a tremor in her voice.

'Then you may be in trouble,' I replied. 'There's no sugar-coating this, Tanya. If Act Now! win the election,

I'm not sure what will happen. And don't forget, they are still the party of government until the election. There have been extradition arrangements between the UK and Ukraine since 1999.'

'At least you are honest,' Tanya said. 'But I have already decided, this is what I must do. You don't do things because you are sure you will win. You do things because you know them to be right.'

Her courage made me blink back some tears.

'It's not too late to say no, Tanya. If you don't feel okay after talking to Alex and Simon, you can still change your mind. Think about it.'

It was a full flight, and we were sitting in different parts of the plane so didn't get a chance to talk again until we arrived at Heathrow.

'I'll see you on the other side of passport control,' I said. I looked at the long queue for foreigners' passports. 'You might be some time. I'll get your bag off the carousel and you can meet me there.'

I was through passport control in less than five minutes, and after breathing a sigh of relief that my false passport passed scrutiny again, I headed off to baggage reclaim. Tanya's suitcase appeared a few minutes later. I stood there waiting for her, agonising again whether this really was a smart thing for her to be doing. I had gone to Ukraine to try to convince her to come forward. Now that she'd agreed to do so, I would never forgive myself if things went wrong. I thought back to my few weeks in prison. What would it be like to spend months, even years, like that?

Before Tanya went past the point of no return, I

would insist we go, one last time, through the potential implications of her actions.

I glanced at my watch. It had been twenty minutes since I left her to get the luggage. It was a long queue, but the wait was getting ridiculous. A call to her mobile went straight to voicemail. I wandered over to a bench to sit down, all the while keeping a lookout for her. After another ten minutes, I knew something was definitely wrong. I went back upstairs to passport control and scanned the queues for Tanya. She was nowhere to be seen.

Some security people sat in a booth behind one of the desks, and I started to walk over to ask if they knew what had happened to her. Then I remembered the false passport I was carrying. I was still air-side. They might ask to see it and I didn't know how well it would stand up to extra scrutiny. The risk was too high. My heart thumping, I went back and examined the queuing passengers again, carefully, slowly. She was definitely not there.

I phoned again; once more straight to voicemail. I was panicking now. Nothing else for it, I had to leave. If something had happened to Tanya, I needed to get away from the airport and ditch my false passport before I could take any action. I headed out and spotted the taxi driver holding his name board. I went over and introduced myself and apologised for the delay. I asked him to take me to Tanya's hotel, said that she was not joining us. I would drop off her luggage there, then think about what to do next. I was still valiantly hoping that, whatever the issue was, it would get resolved and she could head to the hotel and continue as planned.

Once I got rid of the bag, I called Alex from the hotel lobby.

'I think there's a problem.' I tried to keep the fear out of my voice. 'Tanya and I split up to go through passport control and I haven't seen her since. That was an hour ago. She must have been detained coming through immigration. I couldn't ask anyone at the airport because I had my false passport with me. I've dropped her bag off at the hotel, in case she is released, but I don't know what else to do. Any suggestions?'

'Act Now! must have put a flag on her passport. Shit. We were so concerned about getting you in and out of Ukraine without being noticed, we didn't think about her.' There was a short silence. 'Well, there's nothing we can do about that now. You need to get rid of that passport and get here to the studio so we can work out what to do. In the meantime, we'll start asking about Tanya.'

I went into the hotel toilet, ripped out the passport pages one by one and flushed them away. I borrowed some scissors from reception and went back to the loo and cut the back page into small pieces, making sure anything that could identify me was at least split in two. I flushed the remains of the passport down three different toilets, to be on the safe side. A false passport might have been useful again one day, but it was far too risky to hang on to. Then I headed back to Heathrow.

It took a while, but I eventually got some news from one of the immigration officers. A Ukrainian woman was detained by the immigration authorities, I was told, and she'd been transferred to the Sahara Unit at Colnbrook Detention Centre, near Heathrow. If I wanted to arrange to visit her, I had to fill out a form and wait to be contacted. No, I couldn't wait around until permission was granted. I filled out the form and headed off to see Alex.

I told her the latest. She looked concerned.

'If they've got Tanya locked up, Duncan, I'm not sure how we get her released.'

'Publicity. That's the only way. Run the story that she was an MI5 spy, travelling to the UK to speak out about her role in the Act Now! Russia scandal. Shout it from the rooftops. The longer Act Now! keeps her locked up, the bigger the story becomes.'

'I'll try,' she replied, looking doubtful. 'It's going to be hellishly difficult, right in the middle of the election campaign when we have a legal duty not to do tendentious reporting. But this is a special case. I'll push to go ahead with the programme tomorrow, even without Tanya. But we're going to have to give Act Now! the right of reply. Can you go on air to be interviewed instead of her?'

'If your lawyers will let me,' I replied. 'One of my release conditions was that I was to make no statements to the media until my case comes to court or the charges are dropped. After what's happened to Tanya I'm happy to do it, even if it means going back to jail. But I'm not sure your Barbara will let me.'

I was right. Barbara dug her heels in, said that running such an unsubstantiated story during the election, especially since the previous debacle, was a risk – the TV station could not be seen to be aiding and abetting the breach of a court order. A truncated version of the story would run, Damian Zane from Act Now! would be invited on the programme to give his response, but someone else would have to tell Tanya's story.

'Can't your IT guy do it?' suggested Alex. 'He's the most obvious replacement. He found where Tanya was in Ukraine and knows all the detail of the investigation. Why don't you ask him?'

I thought of Nigel in the TV studio with Damian Zane and shuddered.

'That would be an unmitigated disaster,' I told her. 'Zane would make mincemeat of him.'

'Well, who then? Think of someone, Duncan, and think fast. We need to get Tanya out of detention and on air before the election, and we're running out of time. I can line up a hack pundit to go up against Zane, but it would be better if it's someone involved in the story.'

I returned to my flat, demoralised and beaten. I'd talked Tanya into this, and before she'd even had a chance to say a word, she'd been thrown in prison. I cursed my arrogance and selfishness, but self-flagellation would do nothing to help her now. I needed to stay focused.

I went through my computer for everything on the story since my arrest and the subsequent outing of Tanya as an MI5 spy, looking for ideas. Trawling my emails, I realised suddenly who it needed to be to speak out for Tanya. The same person who had spoken out for me. A person whose involvement again would be sure to cause headlines. Michael Mitchell.

I recoiled at the thought of contacting him again, but the more I thought about it, the more it made sense. Mitchell's involvement in my case hadn't just been on a whim; his TV interview showed he had done his research.

He'd continued to comment on the issues raised by my imprisonment after I was released, so he was obviously following the story closely. But how could I reach out to him, ask for his help a second time? Michael Mitchell of all people?

If it meant that Tanya's chances of being released were increased even by one iota, I owed it to her to try. I sat down at the computer and penned my request, going through the background to her detention and asking if he would like to meet to discuss speaking out again.

He replied an hour later, a simple, terse response, suggesting we meet for breakfast. I fired off a thankful acceptance and slumped back in my chair as what I had agreed to sunk in. After more than forty years, I was going to be face-to-face with Michael Mitchell again.

chapter twenty

Mitchell agreed to meet me in the wood-panelled basement of Joe Allen, a retro steak and cheesecake joint on the edge of Covent Garden that doubles up as an assignation spot for morning-after breakfasts. There were only a few other diners, so I nabbed a corner table and waited for him to arrive. I sipped my coffee nervously, although the last thing I needed was a caffeine buzz. Two croissants lay untouched in the basket on the table.

He arrived twenty minutes late, looking around the restaurant until he spotted me. As he walked over, I stood, waiting to shake his hand. The hand of the man who once threatened to kill me. Now, over forty years later, I was going to ask for his help.

Mitchell shook my hand with all the enthusiasm of a losing football manager thanking a rival at the end of a grudge match. He sat down, squinting a little as his eyes got used to the gloom of the basement, and he said nothing.

'The porridge's good here,' I said, as he wordlessly picked up the menu.

'I've had more than enough porridge because of you.'

As jokes go, it was a good one.

'Sorry. Bit tactless. I'm a journalist, so I'll stick with waffles.'

Not as funny, but it got a smile of acknowledgement.

'I can't thank you enough for what you did to get me released from prison, Michael,' I said. 'But time is of the essence here, so I won't go on declaring my appreciation over and over again. The same injustice that had me behind bars has been meted out again, to a Ukrainian woman who came to the UK to speak out about Act Now!. MI5 used me to get the story out about the party. Act Now!'s leaders, their manifesto, their political machine – they were all set up by the Russians. So, I want to ask, will you do the same for her as you did for me?'

The waitress came over and took our order. As soon as she left, Mitchell clasped his hands together on the table, as if deep in contemplation.

'You will forgive me if I don't want to put myself at your disposal to further your career as a journalist,' he said, 'but I've devoted my life since my release to campaigning for the rights of prisoners and fighting miscarriages of justice. This Dissemination of Terrorism Act has to be repealed. Whether or not your stories about Act Now! are true, I'll leave others to judge. What do you want me to do?'

'Go on television, talk about Tanya's case, demand her release.'

'For that, I need to know more about her. What can you tell me?'

I spent the next hour taking Mitchell through the events leading up to today, finishing on Tanya's return to the UK and her detention at the airport. He listened intently, occasionally asking a question to clarify some point or other. I became more and more impressed by his quiet intelligence, the steeliness of his determination. I was coming to like Michael Mitchell. It was surreal.

In the end, he said yes. I'd already primed Alex, and I arranged for them to meet to discuss the story. Mitchell would be included as a panellist on a political discussion programme the day after tomorrow; Damien Zane would be invited to comment on behalf of Act Now!. Two other panellists were being rustled up, one for each side. Debating a topic like this during an election campaign had to be done with scrupulous fairness.

Sam had also been busy. The *Chronicle* had put up a lawyer to defend Tanya and he'd been told that she was still being detained under immigration legislation – not the Dissemination of Terrorism Act. There was a chance that she might not be charged, released or deported until after the election.

Which was why I was astonished when my phone rang and I saw Tanya's name on my screen.

'Duncan, I am standing outside police station,' she said. 'I have had very scary last twenty-four hours. But now I am let go, no further questions.'

'Tanya, that's wonderful! I'm so pleased! Surprised, though, I must admit. I've got the media all set to tell your story. There was to be a TV debate about you tonight, and being so close to the election I thought it would be even more difficult to get you released than it was with me. Look, this changes everything. Are you still okay with doing your TV interview?'

'*Da.* Even more so. Let's get the bastards.'

'Great. I'll get on the phone to Alex and get everything put back in place. It'll probably be tomorrow given the time. Why don't you head over to my place and stay here tonight? I can endure the sacrifice of another night on the sofa for the sake of my country.'

'You are true patriot. Okay, sounds good idea. You can give me tips on best English phrases to tell my story, so we can have big impact. I leave now.'

When I called Alex she had already heard the news about Tanya.

'Act Now! has told us that a Tanya Petrenko was detained by immigration officials due to some visa irregularities. When I asked them if it was part of the campaign against your Russia revelations, they said that any story that she might have been subject to a Dissemination of Terrorism Act order was pure speculation on your part. Another one of your ongoing fantasies, to which they've said they don't want to give any credence by commenting further.'

'It must have been the TV debate. They must have decided that dismissing her as a conspiracy theory nutcase friend of mine was the best strategy to minimise the impact. Well, they've scored an own goal. Tanya will stand up to any scrutiny you can put her under. When do you want her in the studio?'

'You'll need to give us twenty-four hours. We've got to ensure we present this as even-handedly as possible, given that we are in the middle of an election campaign. I'll get Simon Green set up again to meet Tanya, and then we'll record the interview with her tomorrow afternoon. We'll get Michael Mitchell and someone from Act Now! to come into the studio in the evening. They'll see the interview and Simon will then interview them. After that, let's see where the story goes.'

Tanya came straight over to my flat after her release.

'Very scary experience,' she told me. 'I felt I was criminal, just for being me. I ask, what have I done, why do you keep me here? No one has any answers, cannot tell me how long I stay in jail. Then, poof, in one second they let me go, say I can stay in UK.'

'I'm sorry you had to go through that. I was so stupid. I should have realised that Act Now! would have known you were coming back into the country. All this could have been avoided, if we'd thought it through – you could have told your story in Ukraine, had the interviewer come to see you.' I shook my head in disgust. 'Well, at least now you've been through the worst. Soon, it'll be behind you.'

'I used to think it would never be possible in Britain to lock people up for wanting to tell truth. If I can do even a little to stop them, I have proud story to tell my grandchildren.'

There was a knock at the door, and Tanya jumped a little.

'Are you expecting someone?'

'No.'

I looked around the room for something to protect myself with. Nothing. I went into the kitchen. I baulked at holding a carving knife, so the best I could come up with was a rolling pin. I held it behind me and went to the door.

'Who's there?'

'Amazon delivery,' said a voice in a thick Russian accent.

I put on the door chain and open the door an inch.

'Sorry, I'm not expecting a delivery,' I said through the gap. 'It's not a good time, please come back later.'

I stood back from the door, rolling pin at the ready. Tanya had joined me now. She saw the rolling pin and rolled her eyes.

'I get knife,' she said.

As she went to the kitchen, there was a hollow bang and the door shuddered from a blow to the other side. The wood around the chain cracked from the impact. It wouldn't survive another strike.

I grabbed my mobile phone and was fumbling to type in my passcode when there was an almighty crash and the door flew open. The screen came to life just as the phone was thrown from my grasp. A thickset man twisted my arm behind my back as a second man stepped in through the door behind him. As I was pushed to my knees, I saw Tanya appear, a carving knife held in front of her in both hands, pointed at the men. Her eyes blazed and she screamed something in Russian as the second man moved towards her. He feigned a move to her left, and as she twisted to avoid him and flailed at him with the knife, he grabbed her arm. With a single fluid movement, he had the arm holding the knife twisted behind her back.

'*Bros noj!*' he shouted, twisting Tanya's arm up between her shoulder blades. She screamed with pain, but wouldn't let go of the knife. '*Bros noj!*' he repeated, his other hand now around her throat.

The knife clattered on the wooden floor; the man kicked it away. A plastic cable tie was slipped around my wrists, pulled tight until the plastic dug into my flesh. I could smell cigarette smoke on my assailant's breath. Die of cancer, you bastard, I thought to myself. I watched helplessly as Tanya's hands were also bound. The effortless ease with which the two men had overpowered us was chilling. It wasn't just their strength, there was an economy of effort in their actions which suggested they were well practised.

I was pulled to my feet and pushed next to Tanya. One guy produced a gun and waved it in our faces. 'There's a car downstairs, you are both going to get in it,' he said. 'If either of you tries anything, I won't hesitate to use this.'

Tanya's assailant stepped outside, looked up and down the street, turned and nodded. The other man stood behind us and spoke in an ingratiating whisper. 'We are going to walk out to the car very slowly. There is nothing to worry about. We are going for a short drive, you have to answer some questions. Once you answer the questions, you will be free. In ten minutes, this will all be over. Now go.'

I was still struggling to make sense of what was happening. What questions? Who were these people? They must be heavies hired by Act Now!, nothing else made sense. That was why Tanya was released so suddenly. Let her out and wait until she met me so they could solve all their problems at once. There were not going to be any questions. They just wanted us in that car.

We were dragged to the front door. I felt an arm slip through mine, pulling me tight against a body hard with solid muscle. I heard Tanya whimper as the same happened to her behind me. In a few seconds, we'd be in the back of the car, powerless and driven off to our fate. My mind raced.

I struggled and wriggled as I was led down the short path to the street, trying to break free. Impossible. I was in the car in an instant, Tanya thrown in on top of me. The door was shut, and I heard the click of the locks. This was it. We were going to die.

'Lie down! Both of you! Not a fucking word!'

The two of us cowered down as the car drove off. I tried to think straight. They hadn't done anything in the flat, they must be taking us somewhere remote to dispose of us, so that Act Now! could argue there was no evidence that anything sinister had happened. I cursed myself for not yelling at the top of my voice before I had been pushed into the car – anything, everything to get someone to notice. But it had all been so fast. I had to do something when they stopped the car. But what?

I strained ineffectually against the cable tie. Even if I was brave enough to try something, there was nothing I could do. I had the bizarre thought that I had always wanted to go to Antarctica, and now I never would. I could hear Tanya talking in Russian to herself, muttering under her breath in a resigned monotone. I tried to force myself to focus.

Suddenly the car screeched to a halt and the windscreen exploded, sending fragments of glass everywhere. Tanya screamed, and we both dropped lower in the back seat. There was the sound of the front passenger door opening, someone getting out of the car. Shouts, sounds of a scuffle, then silence.

Fragments of glass were covering my body, but I didn't dare move to shake them off. The driver of the car had started groaning, which turned into a rasping sound after a few seconds. Had we crashed? Whatever had happened, we needed to react.

I stuck my head up. The driver was slumped forward against the steering wheel, his head twisted to one side. Outside, two men were handcuffing the other man.

'Get up,' I said to Tanya. 'I think it's safe.'

In the distance I heard a police siren. Dazed and confused, I squirmed around in the back seat and tried the car door, but it was still locked. I clambered over into the passenger seat, struggling because my hands were still tied behind me. Pellets of glass were everywhere, and I winced as they dug into me. Blood was seeping through the driver's shirt. I managed to open the door and stumbled and rolled out of the car. Tanya started to climb out of the back seat to follow me. She fell out of the passenger door onto her back, and I helped her to her feet as best I could. We staggered away, still trying to take in the scene around us.

When the police car arrived, two cops got out and went over to the men standing over the handcuffed assailant. Then one of them came over.

'Are you okay?' she asked.

'Yes,' Tanya said.

'Do you know what's happening here?' I asked.

'Sorry, I don't. We were responding to a 999 call, someone who witnessed the shooting of the driver of this car. I need to check on his condition and then I'll get back to you.'

Two more police cars arrived a few minutes later. Someone finally cut the cable ties binding our wrists and Tanya and I embraced, our bodies shuddering in the release of tension.

One of the two men who had been handcuffing the Russian came over, just as an ambulance arrived.

He addressed Tanya.

'Tanya Petrenko?'

She nodded.

'I'm an authorised firearms officer with the Metropolitan Police. My colleague and I were assigned to covert surveillance and protection of you following your release from detention earlier this morning. We observed your two assailants enter the property of Mr Jones here and when we determined their intentions were hostile, we moved in to apprehend them.'

He turned to include me in the conversation.

'I'm sorry we couldn't act sooner, but the best way to ensure your safety was to intercept them as they attempted to drive off. When we blocked the car on the road, the driver reached for his gun, so I had no choice but to shoot. He's receiving medical attention, his passenger attempted to escape but surrendered when confronted. Another ambulance is on its way so paramedics can assess your condition, and then I'd like to collect a statement from you both about the incident here.'

'We could have been killed,' I blurted out. 'Who are these people and who told you to follow Tanya?'

'Your questions will be answered in good time, sir. Best if you get checked over, and we'll take things from there.'

A second ambulance arrived, and Tanya and I were ushered inside. As the door closed, it felt like we'd found sanctuary from the horrors of a few moments ago. The paramedics went to work, and my body started shuddering from the release of tension. Tears flooded my eyes as I thought about what had just happened.

A few minutes later, there was a knock and a policeman put his head round the door.

'Best if you drive off with these two,' he said to the ambulance driver. 'It's turning into a bit of a circus here. Media arriving in droves.'

Over the next couple of hours, I started to find out the details of the afternoon's events. When MI5 picked up news of Tanya's sudden release, they had made a direct request to the Metropolitan Police for armed surveillance, making sure that only the operational officers involved knew what was going on. They must have suspected something was going to happen and were ready and waiting when it did. That's what saved us.

★ ★ ★

Their plan having backfired spectacularly, Act Now! put their cover story into operation, no doubt the one they had planned to explain the disappearance of Tanya and myself.

Tanya and I were lovers, their supporters in the media claimed, and the two of us had dreamt up the whole Russian conspiracy theory during our relationship. After being discredited, Tanya had left me and returned to Ukraine, where she had started a new life with an unnamed Ukrainian gangster. Then she regretted splitting up with me and finished with the Ukrainian gangster, coming back to London to restart our relationship. Ukrainian gangsters don't take kindly to being dumped, and evidently this was a particularly psychotic one. In a jealous rage, he arranged for the two of us to be disposed of, hence the shoot-out on the streets of London.

It would be a stretch to make the story stick, but that wouldn't matter. All Act Now! had to do was hold on to their lead in the opinion polls a few more days. Then, with a general election victory behind them and a mandate for even more radical policies, they could do what they wanted.

There was only one last chance to stop them. Tanya's interview.

★ ★ ★

I sat down to watch *News Today* that night, full of trepidation. The plan for a pre-recorded interview with Tanya had been scrapped. Instead Simon Green was going to talk to her live on air, with Michael Mitchell there to provide further comment. As Act Now! had refused to participate, no opposition politicians would be allowed on the show to comment. I could hardly breathe with the tension.

The opening credits faded away and Tanya was sitting in the studio, an empty chair next to her. That must be for Michael Mitchell. Simon Green sat across from her.

'There's a change to the topic of tonight's programme,' he announced. 'Instead of the discussion about immigration, given the dramatic and violent events that played out on the streets of London today, we are going to air exclusive accusations from our studio guest about the scandal involving Russian support for Act Now! in the general election.'

He turned to Tanya.

'Tanya Petrenko, can you describe the events of this afternoon?'

Tanya gave a little nod and started to speak in a steady, low-pitched voice.

'I was at flat of Richard Foxe, political blogger. He came to Ukraine to ask me to return to London, to tell my story to you on this programme. I was stopped at Heathrow, kept at jail near airport, I thought I was to be sent back to Ukraine. But instead your government release me, so I go to see Richard, we prepare to come here for interview. Two armed men break into flat, kidnap us, try to take us away to be killed. But they are stopped by police, one is shot, the other caught. So, I am still alive to tell my story.' Tanya gave a weak smile and took a deep breath to compose herself.

Pictures of the scene of the arrest appeared on the screen, and videos of the aftermath of the shooting, from two different angles, sent in by viewers. After they had been shown, Simon turned to Tanya.

'Can you describe your feelings after the police intervened?'

As he spoke, video of Tanya being led to the ambulance appeared on the screen, the car with shattered windscreen in the background.

'I should say grateful,' she replied. 'But the truth is, I was in big anger. The doctors tell me that I need to rest, take it easy for few days, need to recover from shock. But I can't wait. I need to tell what happened and tell it now. I cannot wait till doctors say okay.'

'And why is that?' Simon, of course, knew the answer.

'Because it was not some stupid story that jealous

lover was behind this. It was your government, and I need to tell my story before election.'

Simon nodded. 'There have been rumours flying around Westminster for months now, that the investigative blogger, Richard Foxe, has uncovered evidence linking the Russian government to the Act Now! political party. What has been your part in this?'

'I am Ukrainian national, previously living in London. I was recruited by MI5 last year as part of investigation into whether Act Now! was controlled by Russian government. My job was to get results of investigation into public.'

Simon feigned a look of astonishment.

'These are shocking claims, Ms Petrenko. Let's deal with them one by one. How exactly were you recruited by MI5?'

Tanya took Simon through the story of her job as an event manager at the British Council and how, after the death of her brother, she had been recruited to gather information on Russia's involvement with Act Now! from Russian oligarchs. Photos of her appeared on screen with Anton Shub and a few other high-powered Russian businessmen, even a mid-level Russian politician. I didn't like how it made her look, but she answered the questions about them with class and dignity.

'And now we come to the most sensational part of your story. You claim you were asked by MI5 to take on a new role, to help publicise the findings rather than collect information. Why would they ask you to do that?'

'Because they could not make news themselves, especially in early days when proof still coming in. My job was to help choose journalist, use him to tell story. Only when it was completely proved would MI5 be able to act. They chose Richard Foxe.'

Tanya smiled. 'But he was smart guy. He find out this plan, and my job was over. I go back to Ukraine to hide. He reveal my story and he get into big trouble. Then he come to Ukraine to find me, say to me it is time to tell my story. So here I am.'

My heart was bursting with pride at Tanya's performance. She answered every question directly, keeping her tone matter-of-fact, her simmering anger lending her words authority and credibility. She spent the next five minutes detailing and explaining exactly how the MI5 operation worked, and what her part in it was. Combined with the footage of the shooting, it left little doubt she was telling the truth.

They played the footage of Tanya being led to the ambulance again and when they returned to the studio, Michael Mitchell was sitting in the seat next to her. Simon started his questions.

'Michael Mitchell, you have long campaigned for penal reform and to address miscarriages of justice. I'm going to ask you in a few minutes to comment on this case, and the recent detention of the blogger Richard Foxe that seems to be at the heart of it. But first I want to ask you about your personal connection to these events. Can you tell us what that is?'

Mitchell paused before replying.

'Yes, it is no secret I have a connection to Richard Foxe. In the 1980s, he wrote a novel under another name that implicated me in a murder that I didn't commit. I spent fifteen years in jail as a result. I have no affection for him, or for anything he's trying to do. But what has happened to him, and no doubt to others, is so shocking that I find myself with no choice but to speak out in his support, and to condemn the actions against him.'

'And those are?' Simon leaned forward, caught up in the intensity of the moment. Sitting at home watching all this on TV, I found myself doing the same.

'Detention on the order of a politician, rather than an independent judiciary. Suspension of *habeas corpus*, a right that goes back to Magna Carta. And that's before you get to the other allegations about Act Now!, which I'm not qualified to talk about.'

This was a smart move by the programme-makers. By focusing on the legal principles of my detention, rather than the allegations behind them, they could debate the story at length, without falling foul of the same gagging order that I was still under.

The programme wrapped up with a statement from Act Now!, pointing out that despite his pardon for murder, Mitchell was still a convicted criminal, guilty of fraud and money laundering. They stuck to the story that the attack on Tanya was the work of a Ukrainian gangster and nothing to do with them, and warned that they would not hesitate to use the courts if they felt the programme had continued to spread slanderous comments about them.

Simon wrapped up the story, pointing out that Act Now! had been invited into the studio to debate the issues raised but had declined, and that I could not be interviewed because my gagging order was still in place. It was a powerful piece of television journalism. I hoped it was enough.

A follow-up story appeared on the *Chronicle*'s website just after midnight. It contained the news that *News Today* had been served with an injunction banning the programme from being shown on catch-up; and that a writ for slander had been served on the programme-makers personally.

I checked the websites of all the other major media outlets. Nothing. With everyone else, the legal deterrents were obviously working. I stayed up till two in the morning reading the comments and discussion on the story, then it disappeared from the paper's website. Almost immediately there was an email from Sam, saying that a court order had instructed it to be taken down, that he had also been charged with libel, but the newspaper was already on the streets before the injunction had been granted. However, his was the only newspaper brave enough to cover the story. No matter how powerful the impact was of Tanya's testimony, if people couldn't get to hear it, it could be too little too late to affect the election result.

I finally succumbed to tiredness, desperate to find what would happen next.

★ ★ ★

There was silence until the next day's six o'clock news.

'We have just had a statement from MI5, released in the last few minutes,' the newsreader announced. 'A spokesman has confirmed that Tanya Petrenko, the Ukrainian woman at the centre of the Act Now! Russian conspiracy story, was an employee of the security services from 2020 until March this year. The nature of her role cannot be revealed for reasons of national security, but sources close to the head of MI5 have indicated that her relationship with Duncan Jones, better known as Richard Foxe, the investigative blogger who originally broke the story, was part of her remit. After the attempt on her life on the streets of London yesterday, MI5 say they have had no choice but to confirm her identity. In the last few minutes, an Act Now! spokeswoman has said that MI5's announcement is a deliberate and despicable attempt to influence the general election, and has triggered a constitutional crisis of unprecedented proportions. We go over now live to Charlotte Peterson, our political correspondent who has more on this breaking story.'

A few seconds later my phone rang and it was Sam, breathless with excitement. 'Have you heard the MI5 announcement?' he asked.

'Just this second on the news. What's going on?'

'I've no idea. MI5 have never revealed anything like this before, so they've as good as said that it's true they've been investigating Act Now!, without saying it explicitly.'

'They must finally feel that we've reached the threshold where they can give the story legitimacy,' I replied. 'And the attempt to kill one of their agents was probably the last straw. What are you going to do now?'

'We're going to defy the injunction, lead with the MI5 quote on our front page tomorrow, and this time we're convinced we won't get the story barred. And we expect every other newspaper to pile in behind us. You can't be sued for libel for repeating what MI5 themselves are saying.'

The story did run the next day, but paradoxically it was the articles in the tabloids that made the biggest splash. Their reporters had been busy since Tanya had done her interview, but not on political secrets. Her whole modelling portfolio was on display, with a particular emphasis on the lingerie shots. It was a tabloid editor's dream, a juicy political scandal and more half-naked photographs than you could shake a stick at. The *Sun* promised they'd have a picture of Tanya modelling lingerie every day until polling day, to dispel any election blues. The *Mirror* had a cartoon of Tanya in a boxing ring, standing over an unconscious Damian Zane in the same pose as Cassius Clay standing over Sonny Liston, with the headline, 'UKRAINE GIRLS REALLY DO KNOCK YOU OUT'. This was not a story that was going to go away.

The first snap opinion poll came out the next day, a ten-point shift against Act Now! pushing them into third place behind the two main political parties. The assault on their credibility continued unabated right up until the day of the vote, more and more of their supporters distancing themselves from their increasingly toxic image. I spent election day in a trance, fruitlessly going from one website to another for any clue as to how the voting was going. Numbers going to the polls were down, interpreted as being due to the disillusionment of the Act Now! voter base.

The exit polls confirmed the party's collapse. The prime minister-to-be gave her acceptance speech at her constituency in the wee small hours, promising that the

Act Now! 'experiment', as she called it, would be a wake-up call for her party, and no doubt the others as well, never to take voters for granted ever again.

A new dawn of democracy was breaking in Britain. Act Now! would never threaten it again.

epilogue

I looked in the mirror, concentrating as I slid a collar stay into my crisp white dress-shirt, the unfolded cuffs draped around my wrists. I smiled to myself, remembering the photo of Peter Capaldi in the same pose, the day I met Tanya. I had been co-nominated for Best Investigative Reporting at the British Journalism Awards. There was a taxi waiting downstairs, sent by the organisers to make sure I was there on time. I managed to make a half-decent attempt to put on a tie for the first time in years, but the cufflinks defeated me. I turned to Bobbie and smiled.

'Can you help me with these?'

Bobbie popped them through the buttonholes and stood back to take a good look at me.

'You scrub up well for an old bloke,' she said. 'I'm going to feel a complete scruff at this do of yours.'

'Nonsense, you look great. Means a lot to me, you schlepping down from Scoraig for the ceremony. And I bet there will be a lot of West End producers wanting to grab a word with you at the party afterwards. I've told them all that they have to talk to you first before anyone gets to put *The Art of Deception* on the stage in London.'

'They'd have to do some pretty impressive persuading.

I thought long and hard about coming back to this life after my meltdown at the opening night, and honestly, I'm still not ready. I'm on the sleeper back to Scotland tonight, to get back to my quiet life as soon as possible.'

I tried to hide my disappointment. 'The offer's there if you want it, but not for much longer. It's hot property, that play of mine, and people are queuing up to be part of it. If you're so afraid of the bright lights, why did you decide to come down here?'

'Are you kidding? Miss the chance to finally meet Tanya? Couldn't pass that up. I want to give her the advice I would have given her if she'd ever asked me about speaking out about Act Now!. That whatever schemes you come up with, the best course of action is always to run a country mile from them.'

'Just as well for the country's sake that you never got that chance. Do me a favour: if anybody asks you, at least try to pretend that I'm a serious and sensible journalist who always thinks things through. I've got a reputation to try to hang on to now.'

Bobbie went to gather her things; she noticed piles of paper strewn over my writing desk.

'What's all this, Duncan? It looks like the beginnings of a novel to me. Have you started writing again?'

I blushed. 'I was going to tell you once I'd got the first draft done. Bloody useless at keeping a secret. Yes, I am. Being forced into writing that play under enormous time pressure seems to have got rid of my writer's block. And I know it sounds strange, but meeting Michael Mitchell, seeing how he could put his personal feelings about me aside to champion my cause, made me feel differently about him. The guilt I've always felt over what happened to him seems to have evaporated.'

Bobbie changed the subject. 'And Tanya, she's done well out of this, hasn't she?'

'Incredible. She's a dream come true for the media. Glamourous, sexy spy who brings down the government, and smart to boot. She's got an agent now. He's lining up all sorts of things for her on the telly. There's even a chance she'll be on the reboot of *Strictly*.'

I glanced at my watch. 'We'd better get going. Don't want to miss my date with destiny. If I win, that is.'

Bobbie refused to believe that I had no clue if I'd won Best Investigative Reporting, but it was the truth. Makes for more drama, apparently, if everyone's kept in the dark.

It was an hour-long taxi ride to the awards ceremony. I was glad someone else was paying. On the way, I told Bobbie the plot for my new book, a historical drama in which an Elizabethan courtier, Sir Henry Lee, gets his comeuppance for trying to overthrow the monarchy.

'His portrait hangs in the National Portrait Gallery. Scary-looking guy; I never liked him much, so I wanted to make him suffer. I was told once I should try my hand at historical fiction, so here I am.'

We chatted as we drove through the London streets, talking about the future, teasing and laughing at each other, as if it was half a century ago. Just what I needed to put me at ease for the big night ahead.

When we arrived at the awards venue, Tanya was waiting for us, resplendent in a figure-hugging designer dress. I made the introductions and watched as she and Bobbie chatted like long-lost friends.

'I think Duncan is trying to stop himself looking too much like cream-loving cat,' Tanya said to Bobbie. 'Centre of attention and a babe for each arm.'

We went into the glitzy ballroom. I felt a pang of regret that Nigel had decided not to come along. The plan had been for Tanya, me and him to go up on stage if we won the award. But he promised he'd be watching at home. I thought of him swinging in his chair, and that made me smile.

The three of us joined Simon Green, Alex and Sam at our table and the ceremony got underway. I was pleased our award was early in the proceedings. The words Best Investigative Reporting appeared on the screen behind the stage, and the compère went up to the microphone.

'This has been a tumultuous year for politics,' she said, 'and never has the freedom of the press been more important in holding politicians and political parties to account. To announce the winner of this category is a man who has spent fifteen years fighting injustices and righting wrongs in our prisons and courtrooms. Ladies and gentlemen, Michael Mitchell.'

I knew in that instant that we'd won, but my main concern was for Bobbie sitting next to me. Michael walked onto the stage, sprightly for his advanced years, and half the audience stood up as everyone applauded. I turned to Bobbie. A rictus grin was fixed on her face for the benefit of the cameras, her arms making a clapping motion, but her palms not touching each other.

'I don't fucking believe it,' she hissed at me through clenched teeth. 'Did you know about this?'

'Hadn't a clue,' I replied, also keeping a grin etched

on my face. 'Just as big a surprise to me. Honest, Bobbie.'
I stopped clapping and turned to hear what he was about
to say.

'Ladies and gentlemen, this has indeed been a year
when investigative reporting has shaped the political
agenda,' Michael Mitchell said. 'But it could have easily
been the last year that this would have been possible. We
have seen the dangers of becoming so obsessed with the
threats to our ways of life that we allow the government
to pass laws that restrict the very freedoms they tell us
they are trying to protect. I'm delighted that one of the
first actions of the new government was to repeal the
Dissemination of Terrorism Act, a law that very nearly
prevented tonight's winners from telling their story.'

There was a round of applause; I wasn't sure if I
should join in. In the end, I just grinned at Tanya.

Michael waited until it died down, then continued.

'Not only that, it also put them in danger of losing
their liberty and even their lives. It was a good day for
democracy and freedom when all charges against tonight's
winners were dropped.' His voice rose against the
applause. 'There can be no doubt as to who the winners of
tonight's award should be. Richard Foxe, Tanya Petrenko
and Nigel Stockton.'

Tanya and I went up on the stage, the standing ovation
ringing in our ears. I thanked Michael from the podium
for his help in the story; he gave a gracious nod. Then I
thanked Nigel in his absence, as well as Alex, Sam, Simon,
all the people who'd played a part.

'And finally,' I said, 'I'd like to thank Bobbie Sinclair.'
I looked straight at Michael Mitchell. 'When the legal

pressure was at its greatest to prevent us telling this story, she also took the personal risk of putting on a play that revealed the story behind Act Now!. She should also be on this stage tonight.'

'Then I think she should be,' said Michael. 'Roberta, would you like to come up on stage?'

I looked over at Bobbie, horrified by what I'd just done. Michael had deliberately used the formal version of her name, the one that only he used back in the 1970s, taking the three of us back to that time. Bobbie was shaking her head, affecting modesty. But Alex, Sam and Simon were having none of it. They pulled her from her seat as the clamour for her to come up to the stage continued unabated. With a reluctant shrug, she walked forward.

I got a look that would curdle milk as she passed me, when her back was to the audience. Michael stepped forward and shook her hand. She gave him a stare that had more than forty years of pain caught up inside it. Michael stood back, his arms stretched out wide, giving a distant, unfocused smile, then leant forward and whispered something in her ear. Bobbie gave the smallest of nods and she walked over and stood next to me, and we waited for the applause to die down.

'Remind me to take you outside and kill you when we get off this stage,' she whispered.

When we walked back to our seats, the adrenaline was still coursing through my veins. As Tanya sat down, Simon leaned over and squeezed her hand. She smiled at him and raised an eyebrow. No doubt I'd find out what that was all about later.

The show was over at ten thirty, giving Bobbie just over an hour to catch her train. We walked out to the hotel lobby for her to organise a taxi.

'So, go on then. What did he say to you?' I had been waiting for her to tell me, but couldn't contain myself any longer.

'He said always forgive your enemies; there's nothing that annoys them more. Oscar Wilde, I think.'

'He's got a point. Unless you let go, realise what's in the past can stay in the past, you can't forgive yourself, can't move forward. Forgive what he did to you, but don't forget it.'

Bobbie looked thoughtful. 'You're right, Duncan. We've both spent too long being imprisoned by our past. It's time to put it behind us. Time to forgive Michael Mitchell and stop spending our lives running from our demons. Maybe I should put on your play in the West End after all, and invite him to the opening. We'll see.'

And with that, she gave me a goodbye hug and headed back to Scoraig.

Thank you!

Thanks for reading *A Friend in Deed*. I hope you enjoyed it. If you did, it would be great if you could post a review. Every review, no matter how short, helps authors find new readers. You might also be interested to know about my other books. *Love's Long Road* is set in the 1970s and tells the story of Duncan's friend, Bobbie and the reason for the enmity between her and Michael Mitchell. *Silent Money* tells Michael's story and how he became a crime lord in 1970s Britain.

If you would like to contact me directly to let me have any comments on any of my books, you can email me at gdharper@gdharper.com. If you belong to a book club and would like to discuss one of them, I would be happy to join you via Skype or the like for a Q&A at the end of your discussion.

Best wishes.

GD Harper

Acknowledgements

Thanks to Elena Kravchenko for her inspiration and writing advice. And to Liz Allen, Sue Dawson, Jill Fricker and Trevor Hadley for their detailed and perceptive feedback on the story. Grateful appreciation to Seith Ireland for his input on the legal scenes, and the numerous bloggers and websites who provided me with snippets of information here and there, especially Wikipedia. However, any errors or omissions are mine alone.

I'm also deeply indebted to Debi Alper, Helen Baggot, Sheena Billett and Michael Faulkner for their editing and proofreading, and to Matador and Spiffing Covers for their help with book production.

And finally, thanks to Agnes for her love and support. I wouldn't have been able to write this book without you.